Readers love the Lifting the Veil
series by SUSAN LAINE

Hunter's Moon

"I found *Hunter's Moon* particularly enjoyable. The impressive saga illustrates honorable main characters, betrayal, delusional characters along with deadly conflicts."

—Literary Nymphs Reviews

"*Hunter's Moon* is, I think, the best installment thus far in the series. It had a bit of action, tense moments, and a beautiful love story that kept you guessing till the end."

—Joyfully Jay

Monsters Under the Bed

"…I was impressed by the depth of emotion shown by the characters of a short novel with an ensemble cast and a relatively un-mysterious mystery."

—Live Your Life, Buy the Book

Love of the Wild

"I was intrigued from the first page and couldn't wait to find out what was going on."

—Shameless Book Club

"*Love of the Wild* is a well written and engaging love story that takes the quest to find a mate off the usual path and introduces a unique twist."

—The Romance Reviews

By SUSAN LAINE

Falling for Rain
Flushed
Haunted Heart
Sage Advice
Sauna Lover
The Sensualist & the Untouched
Two Tickets to Paradise (Dreamspinner Anthology)
The Witching Hour

HEROES AT HEART
Yellowbelly Hero
Yellow Streak

ISLESHIRE CHRONICLES
Lofty Dreams of Earthbound Men
Wishing Wings

LIFTING THE VEIL
The Wolfing Way
Genie's Wish
Hunter's Moon
Love of the Wild
Monsters Under the Bed
Stealing Dragon's Heart

SECOND CHANCES
Accidental Chemistry
Twice by Chance

SENSES AND SENSATIONS
Love in Plain Sight
A Luminous Touch
Sensible Commitments
Sounds of Love
The Sweetest Scent

THE WHEEL MYSTERIES
Sparks & Drops
Devil's Own
Fireworks & Wild Cards
The Wheel Mysteries: Books 1 & 2 (Author Anthology)

Published by DREAMSPINNER PRESS
www.dreamspinnerpress.com

STEALING
DRAGON'S
HEART
SUSAN LAINE

Published by
DREAMSPINNER PRESS

5032 Capital Circle SW, Suite 2, PMB# 279, Tallahassee, FL 32305-7886 USA
www.dreamspinnerpress.com

Stealing Dragon's Heart
© 2016 Susan Laine.

Cover Art
© 2016 Anne Cain.
annecain.art@gmail.com
Cover content is for illustrative purposes only and any person depicted on the cover is a model.

ISBN: 978-1-63476-971-6
Digital ISBN: 978-1-63476-972-3
Library of Congress Control Number: 2015918964
Published March 2016
v. 1.0

Printed in the United States of America
♾
This paper meets the requirements of
ANSI/NISO Z39.48-1992 (Permanence of Paper).

As a devoted admirer of ancient Chinese culture, I dedicate this book to everyone with a similar infatuation—and to all those who adore dragons.

I would also like to thank my editor, Andi, for all the amazing work she's done for me. Hugs!

Prologue

"FINN, I'VE got a great job for you. One that will allow you to retire in style and wealth as the undisputed champion of your roguish class."

I resisted the powerful urge to roll my eyes at Griffin's overblown phrasing. I was in Griffin's office in Sydney, Australia, because the criminal facilitator had a task in mind for me, but the fact that he was selling it so hard made me wary.

"Oh?" I kept my tone flat. Appearing uninterested during criminal negotiations was the proper and expected protocol. Whatever Griffin wanted from me, it would undoubtedly be risky and dangerous. To me, to be precise, not to him, Griffin being a mediator only. I briefly wondered who his client was.

"There's a valuable item I'd like you to commandeer. It's held in the penthouse of a bigwig collector in New Shanghai."

I bit back a grimace. "After my last caper, you know I'm not exactly welcome in New Shanghai." In fact, I was persona non grata for a variety of reasons, not the least of which was my habit of acquiring unique and priceless artifacts—that happened to belong to other people.

The Orient wasn't one of my favorite hangouts, not since all the shit following the Great Unveiling thirteen years ago. The world had changed. No place more so than the areas around the Pacific Ocean, which now teemed with strange, frightening creatures of the deep seas that could devour whales and smash passenger liners, for fuck's sake.

But the major transformation affecting me and my trade was the walled fortifications that now protected all major coastal cities. Be the barrier constructed from stone, steel, energy, or magic, it was bad for my profession. Hard being a world-class thief—the notorious Finn Grayson—when escape routes were all but nonexistent.

Breaking into fortified cities was suicide unless you had a foolproof getaway plan. And that usually required a team of experienced operators and well-greased wheels of contacts. There was a time I could have pulled it off on my own. Maybe I still could. But the risks these days were much greater.

"You know, Griffin, those so-called Fire Ring cities are not only virtually impenetrable, but nowadays they house large criminal populaces and private armies too, none of whom I'm rubbing elbows with. I'll pass."

I started to rise from my seat. Griffin snorted and waved a dismissive hand. "Bah. That is nothing to a consummate professional such as yourself. You are the best... aren't you?"

Oh, great. A definite appeal to my ego. I hated that it worked. "Give me the specifics and an extrication plan, and maybe I'll reconsider." I crossed my arms and lifted my chin in defiance. "Otherwise I'm walking out the door."

Griffin chuckled, resting his hands on top of his protruding belly. He was a man who appreciated the finer things, especially fine wines and five-star cuisine. He didn't walk; he waddled.

"You always strike such a hard bargain," he chided playfully. At least he didn't wag a finger at me. That would have been excessive even for him.

I shrugged. "Just looking after my own interests. I place a high value on my life since no one else will do it for me."

"True enough." Griffin grabbed a file folder sitting on the desk between us and handed it to me. "Here's all the pertinent information on the item. I have nothing more to give you. Your choice, of course." He leaned back to wait for my decision.

I read the dossier closely, beginning to end. The target was a large suite in a newly built crystal spire on the fortified waterfront in a five-story penthouse owned by one Cameron Feilong. Not much public information existed on this reclusive and wealthy artist, poet, and author, whose mother was a British dignitary of the peerage and father a Chinese antiques dealer.

A single photo showcased a tall, muscular man clad in body-hugging yellow silk robes decorated with black swirly patterns. He had long black hair, an intelligent high brow, a notably hawkish nose, and slightly slanted blue-green eyes. Had he not been my potential adversary, I wouldn't have minded spending a night or two in his bed.

As for the object to be appropriated…. "The Shard?" Why didn't that name mean anything to me? I usually had the lowdown on every big-ticket item in the world. Of course, the Unveiled planet had gone and changed on me when I wasn't looking.

Griffin nodded, his expression blank. "Yes. A fabulous, priceless, and ancient artifact of great notoriety in underground circles. How Mr. Feilong obtained the item is a matter of some conjecture. Nonetheless, he will not part with it for any sum of money, not even an obscene amount."

That worried me. "You made him an offer? If he refused he might see me coming."

"So you will accept the task?" Ignoring my legitimate concern, Griffin leaned forward, elbows on his desk, his fat fingers intertwined as if in prayer. He appeared calm and collected, but I sensed his underlying eagerness. His hands, even crossed, trembled a bit. For whatever reason, he was intent on procuring this rare artifact. By any means necessary? *Hmm.*

"How much?" No fee had been mentioned in the dossier.

Griffin's mercurial smile should have made me nervous. Unfortunately I was already blinded by dollar signs. "Fifty million dollars sounds like a nice round sum, wouldn't you say?"

I quirked an eyebrow. For that indecent sum I would have sold him my father. Had the bastard been alive, that is.

"Agreed."

Chapter One

"WELCOME TO New Shanghai, the jewel of the Great Chinese Empire."

The message repeated from the screeching speakers in Chinese, English, and a dozen other languages in an endlessly repeating loop. I sighed. I'd avoided the Empire for years—since the Day of the Dragon.

Of all the countries in the world, China had endured the biggest transformation: The communist government had been overthrown in a single night of fire, blood, and chaos as swift punishment for their destruction of China's cultural heritage and nature. A new Draconian Empire—built by the dragons of the Yellow River, the Gobi Desert, and the skies above Mount Tài— now dominated all of China from the mountains and the plains to the forested shores and the sea, and a Yellow Dragon Emperor now occupied the throne.

Despite the fallout of the Day of the Dragon, one thing hadn't changed in the Orient: the Great Chinese Empire was still at once welcoming and closed off to outsiders. Perhaps it was something in the water.

A young Chinese businessman next to me was listening to entertainment news on his iPhone with one earbud on and the other dangling against his expensive silk tie. He was so close I could hear everything with one ear, barely focusing.

"...actress Lola Linton was arrested yesterday in Woodland Hills, Los Angeles, for an RUI. Both Linton and the Dionysian centaur she was riding were heavily intoxicated. The police took both into custody. Linton's attorney had no comment. In lighter news, early this morning technology billionaire Anthony Hathaway's publicist announced Hathaway's engagement to Lady Kamala, an Icelandic elvish princess. The news came as something of a shock as Hathaway was recently named one of the top five most eligible bachelors in the United States and was rumored to be involved with blonde bombshell supermodel Kit Downton. In other news, three nights ago a male student at Oxford, England, was the victim of an attempted murder by a doppelganger. Eyewitness accounts confirm the apparition lashing out at the student. The attack was thwarted by campus security. This assault is the ninth reported crime by a doppelganger in the past year in the EU area alone. Elsewhere, the town of Miyazaki, Japan, experienced a ferocious attack by a *Bake-kujira*, a ghost whale. Local rice farmers have reported their crops dying or disappearing as the skeletal ghost whale, impervious to all known weaponry, is reputed to be an ill omen with a penchant for...."

I tuned out then, focusing on the view before me.

Sunlight reflected from the elvish crystal shield around the port of New Shanghai. The field glimmered like a dancing swarm of billions of fireflies in all the colors of the rainbow. It was really quite beautiful. However, the colorful prisms ensured my nearly complete, painful blindness as the reinforced junk made its final approach to the harbor. But I put my industrial-strength sunglasses on and watched New Shanghai loom larger and taller before me.

The walls made it impossible for the coastal cities to spread outward. So like others of its kind, New Shanghai had grown higher and deeper. What once had been a teeming city of fifteen million was now a packed and stacked hell of twenty-five million and counting. Hundreds or thousands of stories were piled on top of each other. Space was a luxury, as was privacy.

To give the city some much needed light and fresh air, the continuous structure now covering the entire city of Shanghai—though not covering the Yangtze River, which was controlled by river dragons—had been constructed of graphene, carbon nanotubes, and transparent aerogel. Shafts of air and light that had no definable beginning or end cut through the architecture.

The most majestic sight, however, was the greenery. Like the Hanging Gardens of myth, flowering vines and branches dotted the glass marvel. Parks, copses, orchards, and whole forests grew on the rooftops, though only accessible to a select few.

Shanghai of old had been hard to navigate if you didn't know your way around; New Shanghai was a multilayered maze that sent its travelers into spontaneous fits of despair and loss. The only thing missing was a Minotaur.

Although I'd heard several bands of Taurs did hunt farther inland.

NOW THERE'S something you should know about me. I'm not an adrenaline junkie. The crazy stunts I pull to steal what I want are something I consider a job requirement, the necessary evil associated with being the best thief in the big bad world. But do I intentionally seek out thrills that could end with my demise? No.

That said, I've never been afraid of heights. Good thing, too, as I stood by the railing on the roof of one of the tallest skyscrapers in New Shanghai.

Dressed in black, also a job requirement, I held myself in check as I studied another skyscraper staring back at me across a chasm—visible in little glimmers of colorful lights like stars in the night sky. The distance between the buildings was 476 feet. And the drop? Well, all I'll say is that it was over a thousand feet. Should I fall, I'd die on impact.

I'd shot a stainless-steel cable to the roof of the other building using a sniper scope. A pulley was attached to the cable, and my harness attached to the pulley. I was ready to go. In my backpack I had all the necessary tools of the trade, plus a few extras.

I stepped off the edge, resisting the urge to scream with excitement.

Gliding by the force of gravity, I slid down the inclining wire. The two buildings weren't identical in height, a fact that had provided this relatively easy entry into an otherwise secure building.

As I approached I shot an EMP grenade to the other roof, knocking out any surveillance cameras that might be deployed there. The range of the grenade was quite limited, so it wouldn't affect anything else, such as a penthouse security alarm that would summon the guards.

The brakes of the zip wire worked perfectly, and my journey through the air came to a swift but smooth halt above the gravelly rooftop. I released my harness and readied myself to proceed.

There are three ways to break into a building: under, over, or through. As I'd chosen my version of a flying trapeze act, I had several options available. One, I could descend down the side of the building to the desired floor with the aid of angel abseiling, as I liked to call it. Two, I could use the roof access hatch or maintenance door, since there pretty much always was one or more of each. Or three, I could use the ventilation shafts connecting every floor all the way to the roof.

But I hadn't brought angel abseiling equipment with me. And access to the stairwell would undoubtedly be connected to the security feed in the lobby or surveillance office.

So my only viable option was the ventilation system. I've never liked them. They tend to be cramped, dirty, and full of fans swirling at maximum speed that can scalp or flay, depending on what part of the anatomy comes into contact with them first. Plus, they smell. Dust mixed with foods, alcohol, dirty laundry, cigarettes, and perfumes. No one ever mentions that in action flicks as the hero uses them to make his escape.

But on the plus side, some mega-tall structures have air and electrical shafts running through their centers, with ladders, vents, and best of all, space. I could always dream.

Less than ten minutes later, I unscrewed the vent bolts with an awesome silent power tool I'd constructed myself for just such scenarios. I left one intact so the vent swung gently out of my way, and I had an unobstructed view into the penthouse suite.

Through the ventilation shafts, I'd observed one patrolling guard on the first level of the penthouse but none on the four levels above. Also, I'd detected no security offices or surveillance rooms. That seemed odd to me. Especially considering the number of priceless art objects and historical artifacts on display at each level.

I put on my night-vision goggles. On the primary setting, the monochrome view gave me a clear picture of the second floor of the penthouse suite. Even the tiniest amount of light grew easily detectable, so I usually didn't need to use the secondary setting, which was thermal imaging. This time, however, I wanted to cover all my bases.

Despite the absence of guards or the elusive and mysterious Mr. Feilong, paper lanterns and candles on a variety of pedestals were lit. The glow sharpened as I focused on them, almost to the point of blinding me.

With thermal imaging, though, I saw no shining, blurry blobs moving anywhere. Only the one guard below me, and he had stopped patrolling and now sat in front of what appeared to be a TV set. I couldn't hear any sounds from him (or her) as they were on another floor.

The second weird thing that caught my attention was the distinct lack of infrared or laser beams safeguarding this massive, multilayered treasure hoard. I'd never seen a place that housed piles of unspeakable riches, or a single rare item, that didn't come with a thief-proof security system. Sure, every system had a flaw; you just needed time to figure it out.

But this lack of guards and a security system? Got me on edge.

Apart from the candles, nothing and no one else emitted a thermal image. I stashed the goggles away and, despite my alerted instincts, inched my way down from the vent shaft. I landed on a rich Oriental rug with a soft thump.

Perhaps at this point a brief physical description might be in order. I'm twenty-eight years old, relatively tiny at five six, small framed at 139 pounds, lean, agile, and swift, with short brown hair and hazel eyes, more greenish than brown.

My features are not exactly striking. I'm unremarkable. While that means I don't attract a fuckton of men at clubs, it also means I leave no lasting impressions in the memory of potential eyewitnesses. Not that I've had any of those since I was seventeen and got caught with my pants down. Long story. I'll tell you later.

In any case, my small stature makes me nimble to the point of acrobatic. My landing was so soft that I only heard it because, well, it was me. No one else would hear me. That is why I gave you my stats, so you'd know why I was so good at my disreputable job. So there.

I was extremely impressed by the penthouse, particularly the museum-style layout. No rooms cordoned off, merely wide, open hallways exhibiting treasures. And these items? Wow. If I stole as few as five individual pieces, I could buy myself a tropical island and be set for life. Paintings by Gauguin, Cézanne, Picasso, Rubens, van Gogh, Klimt, Pollock, Monet, and so forth. Any one of them could make me a very rich man.

But the other pieces were far more along my line. These were, of course, cultural and historical artifacts, rare and irreplaceable, such as an ancient Persian cuneiform clay tablet or an equally ancient Incan jeweled headdress, an intact sexual stone relief from Banteay Srei or an ancient Egyptian sarcophagus with the mummy still inside. These objects were nigh impossible to obtain and absolutely impossible by legitimate means.

Unless they were a diplomatic gift from a regime.

The funny thing was, I saw one of each in the various dimly lit halls of the penthouse. In addition, numerous other treasures lay in plain sight. On one pedestal stood a Jordanian copper codex in excellent condition;

on another, intact fossilized skeletal remains of a prehistoric animal from the Gobi Desert; and on a third, a fabled crystal skull, lit within by a jade-green glow.

My head was spinning. I'd never seen so many rare, priceless artifacts in one place so shamelessly on display before. Except in a museum or gallery. Private collectors tended to specialize in one or two categories of items over everything else, based on personal interests.

As I walked around, forgetting all about inspecting my environment for booby traps or security measures, I saw sealed wine rooms, open libraries with regulated temperatures behind walls of safety glass, and locked cases of medieval manuscripts and Dead Sea scrolls. I saw stone pieces with cave paintings on them, bronze objects from Knossos, a complete Antikytheran mechanism that was totally unknown to me, half a dozen Terracotta Warriors that I was certain were authentic, unique, half-assembled Viking boats, a table packed with perfectly preserved spearheads, and endless fabulous relics from cities all across the history of the Chinese Empire.

I walked along the candlelit hallways, utterly mesmerized by the sights before me. In all the years I'd been in this shady business, I'd not seen such a cornucopia of priceless artifacts. It was a dream come true.

At one point I passed by a dragon-shaped clay piece, painted gold, with a warm glowing belly and smoke coming out of its nostrils, so it undoubtedly had a burning candle within. It didn't look valuable. However, situated along a wall with numerous other amazing artifacts from the Chinese Empire, it appeared perfectly fitting. I stumbled along in a daze. Wonders surrounded me at every turn, no matter where I looked. This place was insane.

"I'm in heaven," I murmured, enthralled by the sweet visions unfolding before my very eyes. Everything I'd ever craved in my professional career was present in these halls, taunting me from glass and crystal cases, mocking me with their delightful promises of what we could mean to each other.

Yes, I admit it. I have an extraordinary relationship with the items I covet and steal.

But, despite all the magnificence and beauty around me, I did not see the Shard.

Where the hell was the one item I actually needed to find?

A passing thought of forgetting the Shard and taking any or all of these other rarest of the rare artifacts instead flew through my mind. This was a client job, after all, not one of my own interests or challenges.

But whether I liked it or not, this *was* a client job, and in good conscience, I couldn't abandon it. That would cause way more problems for me in the future. In the criminal world, it was best not to alienate or antagonize anyone, especially bigwigs with vast resources and armies of thugs.

That was the moment when everything went crazy.

My body jerked of its own volition, and I was suddenly a mere puppet, controlled by the strings of an unseen puppet master.

I lurched forward, unable to stop myself. I stumbled to the wall, snatched two Viking broadswords from their brackets, and crossed them on the dark red rug on the floor. My hands lifted above my head as I rose up on my tiptoes. An Irish jig filled the air, the bagpipes and drums beating a rhythm my feet followed on their own.

Before I knew it, I was dancing a jig over the crossed swords, leaping and bouncing over the sharp blades, my rising steps graceful and my feet exact—while my upper body swung about precariously, like a windmill in a tornado, tilting this way and that.

I could barely keep up with my apparently possessed feet.

Whatever this was, I was in way over my head, and I started to curse out loud. "What the—'He that first cries out stop thief, is often he that has stolen the treasure.'"

The phrase fell from my lips in my own voice but not by my own intent. Unfortunately for me, I couldn't even slap a hand over my mouth as it spilled out quotes by people who weren't me. I vaguely recognized the phrase from some British poet, but I honestly didn't have time to do deep research into my memory banks.

New hops and skips and the pace of the jig was intensifying. Soon I'd skyrocket right off my feet, dammit. Here I'd been worried about technology—when I should have been alarmed about magic.

"Hey, listen," I half pleaded, half shouted. "Stop this, okay? I'll leave, forget all about this place, and I promise never to come back. This was just a prank, you know, a dare? Funny ha-ha and all that jazz. A mere whim, just a—'A hunting we will go, a hunting we will go. Heigh ho, the tower-o, a hunting we will go! A hunting we will go, a hunting we will go. We'll catch a thief and give him grief. An' we won't let him go!'"

What the fucking hell was *that*? A nursery rhyme? One that had words changed in it? Oh, dear God, could this situation get any more ridiculous?

Someone was definitely screwing with me. And whoever it was, he had a wicked sense of humor.

Chapter Two

I HADN'T guessed my feet were capable of such feats of grace and nimbleness. But I was straining, my muscles protesting motions I didn't create. Though my pose apparently was controlled, I could lower my chin enough to observe how I managed to avoid the blades on the floor the entire time. That was good, even though I had on soft shoes with thick heels.

"Hey," I called out again, louder this time. I had a sneaking suspicion my bane wasn't an automated magic spell intended to capture thieves but someone or something that was a having a laugh at my expense. "I'm sorry I trespassed and offended you. I love beautiful things. I can't resist them. I just wanted to see your collection and bask in its glory. I never meant any harm. I swear if you give me a chance, I'll leave and never come back. With all my heart, I wish—I wish to wish the wish you wish to wish, but if you wish the wish the witch wishes, I won't wish the wish you wish me to wish."

Dammit. Guess whoever my host was, he wasn't buying my sincere act.

And my feet were starting to hurt as the pace of the jig picked up.

I leaped over the swords, keeping my balance while dancing on the balls of my feet. I'd always been agile, but my body was no longer my own, so I soon grew weary and was in pain.

The swords flew up from the floor and back to their brackets on the wall. As the magic abandoned me, I plopped down on the rug on my butt, panting. Lights flashed before my eyes as I regained my equilibrium and breath and was eventually able to stand on wobbly legs.

The dragon-shaped clay statue on the pedestal that had appeared to be sleeping, glowed more intently as its long, stout snakelike body uncoiled and grew obscure. Then it simply grew. And grew some more.

Wide-eyed in pure instinctive fear, I scrambled backward on the floor in a rush until I hit a corner and couldn't retreat farther. When the golden dragon filled the entire hallway, I knew I was in serious trouble.

"Oh shit. I'm in a dragon's lair."

A low rumbling echoed in the penthouse, vibrating along walls that shook from the thunderous sound. "Clever boy," the dragon said.

Its golden scales shone and reflected a thousand lights around it like an aura or a full-body halo as it snaked forward on its four legs. Curved horns rose from its forehead, feelers from the sides of his mouth resembling a long midnight-black mustache, straight spikes along its spine, and the tip of its tail, hidden in a tuft nest, had a five-pronged thorn. I could only pray they weren't poisonous.

Since I was already caught, but not quite red-handed, I decided to plead my case. "I'm sorry. I only wanted to see your collection, so beautiful and rare and—"

The dragon snorted, its nose all but touching mine as it leaned forward. Its round golden eyes narrowed in suspicion as it cocked its head. Oddly, its breath smelled of smoke but also of apples. "When the thief is seen stealing, he says he is joking; but when the thief is not seen, he steals."

Another proverb? Christ, was I in trouble if I needed to prove I was a civilized man and an educated gentleman. But I had to play the cards I was dealt. "'We hang the petty thieves and appoint the great ones to public office.' Aesop, I believe." I wasn't a treasure trove of sayings, quotes, and proverbs. I had to end this quickly. "Lesser evil receives the harsher punishment when the big thieves rule the world, don't you agree?"

Smoke puffed out of the dragon's mouth as it chuckled. If nothing else, I did seem to amuse it a little. "The thief admits he's a thief. Justice shall be swift." It reared back, its horns all but touching the ceiling. Flames emerged from its mouth.

I saw my death reflected in those golden globes that were his eyes.

"WAIT!" I called out, my hands out in a futile effort to stop the dragon from attacking. "Everyone knows dragons are hoarders of everything valuable and rare. Considering the amount of priceless artifacts in your collection, would you even notice if one went missing?"

When it came to arguments, that wasn't one of my shining moments.

"Yes." The dragon's huge paws crashed by my sides, pinning me between them. As a result, the walls and floor shook, flakes of mortar raining down on me in a cloud of dust. "And I would care too." A growl huffed out, as did vapors of smoke that had me coughing in a fit as they clouded around my head.

But even in the midst of my discomfort, a thrill shot through me at the melodic voice of the dragon as it purred and caressed my senses. A sure sign I was losing my mind, or perhaps this was a case of instant Stockholm syndrome.

"I haven't stolen anything," I declared in my defense, water running from my eyes.

"Not yet," the dragon replied smoothly. Guess it had me there. No, *he* had me there.

I tried one last time before I'd resort to prostration and downright begging. "The item I was going to, um, borrow is of little monetary value. It's not even a drop in the ocean compared to all these other artifacts that could fill entire water planets."

The dragon stopped. I watched him from under my brow, worried but also seeing an opportunity. The mythical creature seemed pensive, almost lost in thought. I considered sprinting back to the vent or to a door or a window. Then the dragon said slowly, its low voice chilling me to the bone, "What did you come here to steal tonight, thief?"

I could have lied. I probably should have because that'd mean I could theoretically try and steal the object again at some later date. But my sense of self-preservation warned me that ship had sailed. "I haven't seen it yet. I was still looking." A growl gave my answers some urgency. "It's called the Shard. I don't know what it is, but I was hired—"

For such a majestically sizable animal, the golden dragon turned around so fast it was like watching a column of fluid water moving sideways. In an instant the dragon was gone.

I hesitated. My instincts told me to run, that I wouldn't likely get another chance.

And yet I didn't. In fact, by the time my head caught up with my better nature, my feet were already on the move, on the trail of the quickly vanishing dragon. I ran down the hallways and corridors in search of the elusive magical being that had made me sing nursery rhymes and do an Irish sword dance.

I rounded a corner and stopped dead in my tracks.

In the center of a bright candlelit room rose a pedestal made of yellow marble. The strangest thing surmounted it, though. Tiny heaps of black soil dotted the base of the pedestal, having fallen from the top where a barren bonsai tree rose, its branches empty of needles. Nothing but a dead husk remained.

But whatever else had been there, it was obviously missing, judging by how the big golden dragon coiled around the pedestal. The air thickened, an electric tension crept in, and then the creature roared in anger, shaking the walls around us.

"A Shadowalker? In my home?" He shouted so deafeningly loud I had to cover my ears. I think they still bled.

His bellows forced the whole tower to tremor and quake. The windows, though made of security glass, vibrated, cracked, and finally shattered into a billion pieces, blowing outward to the sky. I sure hoped no one was taking a midnight stroll below this building.

Wind thundered from the dragon's mouth, throwing me off balance until I was clinging to walls to stay upright.

For the second time in one night, I foresaw my death.

I stumbled back on my feet, whirled around, and dashed toward the closest window.

One step over the threshold and I jumped.

IN HINDSIGHT, my choice for a quick escape wasn't my smartest plan ever.

I had a base-jumping parachute tucked under my gear; the golden dragon had wings.

Fuck.

I pulled the cord, and the parachute opened, a flapping sound sharp in my ears. For a second I thought I might have actually succeeded in my rapid-exit strategy.

Then huge claws ripped the fabric of my parachute and sent me plummeting down to the fast-approaching ground. I'm not ashamed to admit I screamed my head off.

The golden dragon swooped beneath me—its delicate-looking wings were oddly prismatic and rainbow-colored, like the wings of a butterfly—grabbed me in its massive paws and pulled me close to its surprisingly warm and soft chest. I had several knives hidden in my clothes. But the thought of injuring a mythical being, especially one that had just saved me from a collision with the street below, upset my already churning stomach.

Back in the penthouse, the dragon unceremoniously dumped me on the floor. I rolled around until my forward momentum halted as I hit a wall. Grunting in pain, I went to work on my base-jumping harness with shaky fingers.

I just managed to get the tangled cords and straps off when a human hand gripped my throat and lifted me against the wall so high my feet no longer touched the ground. While the pain wasn't initially excruciating, the strain on my muscles was great.

"Give it back to me, thief, or I will end your miserable existence," the man growled. I had zero doubts he'd carry out his threat.

With a loose hold on his arm, I struggled against him, trying to get enough air in my lungs to speak. "I didn't… do it… I swear… to God." My words were nothing but a garbled mess. But I hoped he got the gist of it.

The tall man bared his teeth—including a pair of animalistic or vampiric fangs. My blood chilled in dread. "You lie," he accused me.

As his grip tightened, I was deafened by the roar of my blood in my ears, my muscles grew hot and achy, and my vision blurred into a haze. But I'd still recognized the man from his picture in the case folder.

Cameron Feilong. The mysterious and secretive collector—who also happened to be an ancient, gigantic golden dragon.

As in his picture, the impressively muscular man wore yellow silk—a formfitting long-sleeved shirt, pants, and a short robe over them—but he was barefoot. The sides of his long hair were braided but the rest flowed free at his back like a shadowy waterfall. His slightly slanted cyan-colored eyes stared back at me with such fury.

"But I'm not lying," I gasped out, fighting the fierce grasp he had on me. "I don't know what the thing looks like. I hadn't even made it to the part of this floor where the pedestal is. I'll swear on anything you wish me to, Cameron."

Perhaps it wasn't smart to call him by his first name. Chinese culture didn't approve of overfamiliarity. But if he was intent on killing me anyway, I didn't see a reason not to. Besides, he had a strange quality about him, a magical mesmerism that enchanted me to the point I couldn't look away. He was so transcendentally beautiful. I'd never met a dragon before.

Cameron let go of me so suddenly I fell to the floor like a sorry sack of potatoes, all in a heap, struggling to breathe. "I didn't take the Shard," I murmured in a hoarse whisper, rubbing my pained throat. "I'm sorry it's gone, but it wasn't me."

He loomed above me, a mere black silhouette now, without details. "If that is indeed the case… thief… surely you now understand your role in all of this?"

I nodded slowly, seeing red as righteous indignation built inside me. "Yeah. The thief who'd get caught and subsequently killed by a dragon— while the artifact was secretly stolen by someone else. I was used. I'm the scapegoat."

I hadn't been hired because I was a master thief; I'd been hired solely to get set up as a distraction and as a patsy to be murdered.

And that wasn't merely a smear on my good name as a world-class master thief. That was a personal attack on me. On my blood I vowed then and there to find whoever was responsible and seek revenge for such a slight.

At the moment, though, my life and death depended on the goodwill of an angry and violated dragon.

Chapter Three

"WHEN ANGER rises, think of the consequences," Cameron Feilong said slowly. Then he stepped back, giving me room to breathe and stand up. "Confucius is a worthy guide in life." He studied me severely. "I will grant you a chance to explain."

I nodded, swallowing hard. "Um, my throat's a bit bruised. Might I trouble you for a glass of water, please?" I'd learned a long time ago that to gain someone's trust, the best course of action was to ask for help. Their response would tell you much about them.

He sighed. "Follow me."

Cameron led me through several exhibit halls toward a spiral staircase leading down. This new floor had more household amenities, so I assumed this was his living space. Like above in the exhibit areas, fabulous pieces of art, culture, and history were placed to appeal to appreciative eyes. Mine sure adored what I saw.

I was a thief for many reasons. Economics and survival were right up there. But they weren't the main reasons. I loved the beauty that came from the minds and hands of creative people. If I ever had enough money, my future palace would feature priceless historical objects and artifacts similar to those in Cameron's abode. But unlike my current stolen items, they'd all be acquired legally, with proper documentation and provenances. I'd admire them morning, noon, and night.

Despite the traditional moon doors, paper partitions, and silk banners, the furnishings were smart and modern, sleek and expensive. Cameron had fine taste in interior design and decor.

While I was still looking around, Cameron walked up to me and offered me a glass of water. I drank it down greedily.

"Thanks," I muttered, offering a lopsided grin in return.

But Cameron's sculpted features remained blank, like those of a stone statue. "You're welcome. Please, sit." He gestured toward the white leather couch in front of the floor-to-ceiling windows with a remarkable view over a nighttime New Shanghai, colorful lights blinking on and off in the distance like stars.

A curious mix of meditation and fury reigned in my inner world. I'd been betrayed and left to die at the hands—well, claws—of a furious, slighted dragon. And only one name popped up in my mind.

"Leo Griffin." I faced Cameron, who sat on the other end of the couch, watching me. "I confess I am a thief. The best in the world, actually. On occasion I do client jobs. The middleman I tend to use in this part of the world is named Leo Griffin. A week ago in Sydney, he hired me to steal the Shard. I don't know who the actual client is, and he doesn't know who I am. That's how client jobs work and how I prefer to operate."

"Given that another thief managed to steal the object out from under you, that is pure conjecture," Cameron said coolly. And he wasn't wrong. I couldn't assume any more.

I sighed, worrying my bottom lip. I'd worked with Griffin for seven years and made both of us a shitload of money. I trusted him. Well, I trusted him as much as a criminal could trust another of the same profession.

"My name's Finn Grayson," I said, surprising myself with the admission. That definitely ruled out any chance of me retrying to steal the Shard in the future. Then again, the damn thing had been stolen already, so it was a moot point.

Cameron snorted, quirking an eyebrow. "How gracious of you."

I frowned, getting angrier. "Look, pal. I'm just as pissed off as you. I was duped by a guy I thought I could trust, at least enough to assume he wouldn't try to kill me. I want to get back at the people responsible just as much as you do. The way I see it, we're in this together."

Cameron said nothing. But his gaze never left mine. I knew jack shit about dragons. Could they read minds? Could they detect intentions? Could they smell lies? I had no idea. Since the Great Unveiling, I'd avoided contact with the mythical and supernatural worlds like the plague.

I decided to take a mental chill pill. "May I ask, what kind of dragon are you?"

A crooked smile gave Cameron a predatory look, but I could tell he was amused. "I'm the Yellow Dragon Emperor's nephew."

Holy. Fucking. Shit. I'd almost robbed the dragon royalty of the Chinese Empire.

Dammit. I swore when I got my hands on Griffin's fat neck, I'd squeeze the life out of that swindling swine.

"I will never ascend to the throne, however," Cameron supplied further information seemingly of his own free will. "I'm not pure dragon. I'm a fairy dragon. My ancestry stems from both the dragon and the elven worlds."

I swear I heard a click as my jaw dropped. I'd never thought there could be more than one kind of dragon in existence. This post-Unveiling world was so damn complicated. "Uh-huh," I muttered in confusion.

Then again, now that I thought about it, it made sense. At first Cameron had showered me with practical jokes, like making me dance an Irish jig while reciting poetry. Fairies, the small ones, were playful, mischievous pranksters who loved a good jest. Quite unlike the elves, who were snooty and aristocratic, aloof and supersmart. Two races of the same species, but oh so different.

But now that I observed Cameron's stony expression, I couldn't help but wonder how much of him came from the dragons. The seriousness, surely?

"I don't wanna, uh, sound impatient or anything," I said hesitantly, "but have you got a plan of action?"

My first step would have been to track down Griffin and hang him by the nose hairs till he coughed up the name of his client. But I deferred to Cameron's expertise in tracking down the lost Shard since, judging from Cameron's reaction, the object was irreplaceable.

At that moment the guard I'd observed from above by thermal vision ran in, honest-to-God saluted, and said in a rush, "A swarm of police officers are in the lobby to see you, sir."

I had a hunch what that meant. If the media and law enforcement got their hands on a mythical creature hurting or killing a human, that would be bad news all around. Someone had set me up to be killed by a dragon—who'd been set up in turn to take a fall.

That's when realization hit me. I wasn't the only one who'd been betrayed. And that implied the existence of a conspiracy by my acquaintances *and* Cameron's.

I'D NEVER so much as dreamed of flying on a dragon, not even as a child. And let me tell you, it's not as sweet and cool as you might believe.

Well, cool was definitely a good word. The altitude Cameron flew at was chilly at best and freezing at worst. The harsh winds made it impossible to appreciate or admire the scenery as my eyes watered like rivers. My fingers were numb and barely able to hold on to the rough scales beside the spine spikes, and the rough, swift turns and up-and-down wavy motion made me seasick till all I could think about was vomiting.

Undoubtedly I was green in the face—or blue from the cold.

In any case, I couldn't wait for the trip to be over. And by trip I mean our escape. Now we were potential fugitives. Or at least we would have been had there been any evidence of a crime back at the penthouse suite, which there wasn't. So perhaps we weren't really on the run from the law after all.

I dared to hope. But the setup had been quite skillful. I could only hope our adversaries hadn't thought far enough ahead to anticipate Cameron and me surviving and working together.

By the time we landed, I was exhausted and numb to the bone. Even my brain seemed to have frozen over.

Cameron was remarkably gentle as he lifted me from his back and hugged me close to his warm chest. If I could have purred in pleasure, I would have. Cameron was a fairy dragon. Was that the same as a fire-breathing dragon? I had no clue. I promised myself to do some in-depth dragon research online at my earliest convenience.

After I'd thawed to my satisfaction, with my eyes closed, I asked, "Where are we?" I had to ask since despite our landing, the air remained chilly, and snow scrunched beneath Cameron's feet.

That's when I realized in a rush that Cameron had morphed back into a man—who was carrying me like a baby.

I floundered out of his embrace, straightened my clothes, and scurried off to the side, pretending to smooth my hair and act all cool. "So, uh, where are we again?"

Around us, as far as the eye could see, lay nothing but frozen tundra and snow-topped peaks, with a scattering of firs and pines dotting the otherwise white landscape. Places like this could give a man snow blindness, I thought, squinting in the morning sun.

I shivered as the cold seeped into my very bones, and I noticed neither one of us was exactly dressed for these natural conditions, me in my black thieving clothes and Cameron in his yellow silks.

No way were we in New Shanghai, or even the Chinese Empire anymore.

"Alaska," Cameron said, his voice devoid of any emotion. He kept much of himself hidden, evidently. I would have killed for a more comprehensive explanation.

I settled for a simple question. "Why?"

Cameron glanced warily at me. I saw doubt and mistrust in his eyes. I couldn't blame him, me being a thief and all, and something of his gone with the wind. "There are five Shards. The one entrusted to me is only one of them. Together… they are dangerous."

My mind overflowed and bubbled with questions. But I kept a tight rein on them and tried to make sense of all his words suggested. Obviously Cameron wasn't telling the whole story. That was to be expected. I had yet to even gain a glimpse of this elusive Shard. Cameron's comment seemed to imply that the five Shards could be brought together somehow, perhaps as five separate pieces of a larger artifact?

Whatever these Shards did, together or separately, was apparently grave enough for Griffin to sell me out and hint at a larger conspiracy. Griffin knew me; someone else knew the thief who had stolen the Shard; and a third knew Cameron. Any more than two people were enough to form a conspiracy in my book.

If a powerful fairy dragon had been placed as the Guardian of a single Shard, who or what would be guarding the other four? And was there a plan to steal all of them? Had one or all of them already been taken?

Ah. I had an epiphany. That's why we were in Alaska. To see another Guardian of yet another Shard.

"What's so special about these Shards?" I asked, though I wasn't really expecting an answer.

Cameron leveled me with a cold stare that brooked no argument. Yet he said, "They're the most important things in the world. If we can't find my Earth Shard—if the others are stolen as well—the world as you know it will end."

END OF the world. The Apocalypse. Armageddon. Ragnarök. Whatever the name, I was certain reality would top fine phrasing in all its gory detail.

"How the hell can these Shards be so powerful?" I asked, howling into the wind.

"Individually, they're not," Cameron replied calmly, as though he were reading from a menu at a cheap roadside diner instead of explaining the catastrophe that might result in the demise of humanity and the planet we both happened to live on. "That is why they must never be brought together."

"Can they be destroyed?" I asked, concerned. The Shards were obviously remarkable, but surely their obliteration was better than Earth's annihilation, I reasoned.

Cameron shook his head. "No. That would result in a cataclysm, a terrifying chain of events potent and all-encompassing enough to ensure the destruction of this world."

I rolled my eyes. It's not that I thought Cameron was prone to hyperbole. But come on. Could he be any more of a doom-and-gloomist? "Okay. Where are we going now?"

"To inform the Lupine Progenitors of what has happened."

I scratched my head in bafflement. "Who?"

"They're the first werewolves in existence."

Huh. I hadn't known that. Then again, there was tons of stuff I didn't know about the Unveiled world. "How'd they become that?"

Cameron gave me an odd look. "Is that really a priority now?"

I blushed. "Um, no?"

Cameron rolled his eyes and snorted. "Good guess."

I suppressed a growl. "You know, at times you can be quite the bitch."

"I'm a male. And female dragons aren't called bitches," Cameron replied coolly.

I frowned, confused as to why he'd offer up such an odd remark. "Oh? What are they called, then?"

Cameron grinned and winked at me. "Dragons."

Despite the cold, I laughed, warm and fuzzy on the inside. "Funny guy."

So his humorous fairy side did come out to play at times after all. I liked the sound of that—considering we were headed into a direct confrontation with people who either didn't know what they were doing with the Shards or wanted the world to end. I honestly couldn't tell which was the worse, more frightening, option.

Chapter Four

"WHERE *EXACTLY* are we?" I asked, hugging myself to ward off the freezing weather. My gaze swept the white vista, but I saw nothing man-made, certainly no towns or cities, not even a tiny village. On the horizon the white landscape melded together with the gray, cloudy skies until the very edge of the world seemed to blur.

"Unnamed mountain range," Cameron replied as he trotted through the snow banks like nothing could get to him. "There's a national park to the east and another to the south. Where we are, however, is uninhabited."

"Swell," I muttered under my breath, my teeth clattering. "Are we gonna be plodding along here for long? 'Cause, dude, I can't feel my toes."

"Soon." Cameron added no more. Damn, but he could be annoyingly cryptic at times. Were all dragons this mystical and aggravating? If so, I sure hoped whoever we'd come up here to the ass-end of the world to meet wasn't a dragon.

I hated to admit this, but I missed Cameron's warmth when he'd held me close to his chest. That was the problem with a night job. Not only did I lose days and sunlight, but I ended up missing all the wonderful one-night stands at clubs and bars. It was harder to pick guys up during the day.

As a result of my current sex-deprived state, I was horny. Usually the excitement and challenge of a theft kept me in a constant groove with a hint of sex thrown in. Now, with the mission a bust, I had nothing to stave off the arousal created by the hot masculine dragon.

I lost track of time as I labored forward in the snow, with nothing but sparkling white in my field of vision and my legs sinking into the drift above my knees. I was having a hard time moving at all, every step a monumental accomplishment. Why the hell couldn't we have landed a bit closer to our destination, dammit?

"We're here."

It took me a second to make sense of Cameron's words. The breeze had deafened me, and the freezing probably nicked off a chip or two from my earlobes.

Raising my gaze and blinking to gain some focus, I saw nothing but more mounds of snow. "Where?"

One of the mounds began to rise up. Snow giants? Yetis? Polar bears? Dire wolves? I had no idea what to expect, so surreptitiously I inched behind Cameron's broad back.

"Hail, Guardian," Cameron called out, raising his hand in an open greeting.

What I'd assumed to be a monstrous snow and ice creature turned out to be an opening hatch. Warm mellow light emanated from inside, not to mention delicious odors that made my belly growl hungrily.

No one appeared in sight. Cameron led me to the thick metal hatch. A rickety-looking ladder dropped down into a cavern of some kind. It was hard to detect any details from our vantage point. Cameron descended first, with me right on his heels. I grabbed the handle of the hatch, pulled it back down, and then turned the wheel to lock it.

I don't know what worried me more: what might lurk outside in the snow banks after our trip underground or what awaited us below, in the shadows.

BREAKFAST. THAT was what waited for us.

The cavern was larger than I'd surmised, cozy and comfortable, with a bed tucked into a corner, bearskin rugs on the stone floor, wooden chairs with wool coverlets, and a huge fireplace with a lively fire burning within. A pot hung above the flames, and it seemed to be the origin of the mouth-watering aromas.

Lounging in a plump chair was a man unlike any I'd ever seen.

Bigger than Cameron, the man had to be at least six nine. Clad in a simple cotton shirt and pants and a massive dire wolf skin, he had long disheveled blond hair, a scruffy fair beard, and one gleaming blue eye like the purest sapphire. His right eye seemed blind; it was milky white, with a jagged scar running over it. The hairs on his body had silver strands in them, but telling his age was impossible. An earthy, musky odor clung to him, perhaps from his attire. Then again, the raw, animalistic smells could have come from the man himself—if he was a man at all.

Taking a big gulp from a metal goblet, the man growled, his stare fixed on the fire. "It has been ages. What brings you by my humble abode, Cam?"

Cameron sat in a chair opposite the wild man and smiled softly. "I come bearing news, Sigmund. Not fair tidings, I fear."

The man grunted, glancing briefly at me. "Who's the pet?"

Had the man not been a giant compared to me, I might have objected in words. Instead I backed off into the shadows, though I anticipated him seeing me even in the dark, if his reflecting eye was any indication. Definitely not human, then.

"He is Finn," Cameron supplied, without a single glance. "He is helping me retrieve the Earth Shard. It has been stolen."

Straightening up, Sigmund growled low. I swore his hackles rose. That fur couldn't have been a part of him, could it? His one blue eye was as sharp and narrow as a bright diamond. He scared me.

"A Shard is missing? How? Tell me everything," Sigmund commanded, his voice at once soothing and ominous, the duality even more mystifying.

Cameron left nothing out from his account of the previous night, including my involvement.

The only bit of news to me was Cameron's awareness of the culprit at the scene of the theft, although I vaguely remembered his using the word before. "I sensed a presence. A Shadowalker."

Sigmund frowned, his bushy eyebrows knitting together in vexation. "That is ill news indeed. I was under the impression we'd dealt with that threat long ago."

Cameron sighed. "The past rarely stays as buried as we'd all like."

Once Cameron grew quiet, Sigmund too fell into silence. Neither man spoke for a long time. I had a feeling I was observing two mythical beasts, both so ancient that their thoughts would have been utterly alien to me even if I'd been privy to them. A sense of agelessness and timelessness encompassed the underground sanctuary, and I felt out of place, a trespasser on hallowed ground. I'd always thought of myself as an outsider, but never to this extent.

Finally Sigmund sighed and took another drink. Fumes rose from his goblet. Perhaps he was having a hot beverage, like wine. It sure didn't smell like coffee.

Sigmund waved a hand at me. "Come, mortal. Sit and dine with us old codgers."

After wavering for a moment, I took a seat on a wooden chair with a soft pillow on it. The chamber was warm, and I would have fallen asleep had I not been so famished.

"Take a bowl, and sate your belly," Sigmund advised, gesturing to an empty bowl and a spoon on a side table.

I did as instructed and fetched some stew from the pot above the fire. No salt needed. The food was divine, hot and rich with aromas. If I had to guess, I'd say it was rabbit, but I didn't care all that much. I was hungry, and it was hot food, so I ate greedily.

Sigmund chuckled. "I'd forgotten how mortals dine, as if time itself runs out if they're not fast enough in their gobbling."

I spoke without realizing it because most of my focus was on scrumptious smells, a hot meal, and my ravenous stomach. "Your words imply you're not mortal. You're immortal?" Had I slapped my mouth shut, it wouldn't have been soon enough.

But Sigmund didn't seem upset by my question. "I am immortal, yes. I am the first of the lycanthropes. The Prime of the Lupine Progenitors. Before me, there was none."

Wow, how cool was that? "And you're one of the Guardians of these Shards?"

Quirking an eyebrow, Sigmund gave Cameron a curious, surprised look.

Cameron shrugged. "He was sent to his death by those who stole the Shard from me. I figured his presence might prove an asset. We have been Guardians for ages, long before the dawn of man. His perspective is... fresher."

Nodding, Sigmund appeared to accept Cameron's explanation. He turned his mirrorlike gaze upon me. I wondered what he saw in me, the lowly thief or the man who could be good if need be. "I am the Guardian of the Watchtower of Metal."

I grinned to myself. I was starting to get on top of things. "Ah. So you're responsible for the Metal Shard."

Sigmund grinned, seemingly pleased with me. I tried not to beam or toot my own horn too much. "There are five Shards that correspond to the natural elements. Earth, Metal, Water, Wood, and Fire. Each has a Guardian from a mythical race."

I glanced at Cameron. "Dragons guard the Earth Shard."

"Yes," Sigmund affirmed succinctly. "The lycans, by which I mean myself, guard the Metal Shard."

"Is your ward secure, old friend?" Cameron asked, poised on the edge of his seat. He radiated tension, and I could totally relate. I didn't want the world to end; that would make it really hard to rob anyone.

"My vigil remains uninterrupted," Sigmund confirmed. "The Metal Shard is shielded by ice and steel and magic, untouched by villainous hands."

"Have any of the others been in contact with you?" Cameron asked, his head cocked as if to listen to a voice far away. I had no idea what was going through his mythical, ancient mind.

I bristled. "We had to travel all the way up here to the frozen wasteland to speak with a Guardian you could have spoken to with your cell phones, or whatever you've got?"

Cameron launched a heavy stare at me, admonishing me without words. I shrunk a little. "Normally Guardians can communicate with each other through the special bond we share in our sacred roles. But now a veil of black magic conceals that link. We have no choice but to meet with the rest of the Guardians face-to-face." He turned back to Sigmund. "So you haven't spoken to any of them lately in person about their Shards being in jeopardy?"

Sigmund snorted, shaking his head, and snowflakes flew from his mane. "You are the first visitors in centuries who aren't my own kin. And I rarely travel."

"Doesn't it get lonely for you out here?" I asked with a sudden flood of sympathy. I had no idea where it came from.

Sigmund laughed, a deep-belly rumble that reminded me of rolling thunder. His whole body shook. "You are kind, mortal, and amusing. Would that I could enjoy your company longer."

Confused, I said, "We're not in that much of a hurry."

Cameron rested his hand on my arm, and my skin tingled, his touch sending frissons of pleasure through my body, shooting right to my groin. But he appeared unaffected by the current running between us. "Alas, we cannot stay, Finn. Sigmund's curse puts you in grave danger."

This time I shivered in fear, an instinctive and primordial dread born from predators in your sight, closing in on you, the prey. "O-oh...?"

Sigmund's smile was rueful, and his eyes glistened, perhaps with unshed tears. "A long time ago I did... a horrible, unspeakable act. As a result, I was cursed to become a werewolf at each three nights of the full moon. And nothing sated my hunger like human flesh. I hunted in the dark and turned a hundred early humanoids into Progenitors. They in turn transmitted their bite and my curse to other humans, spreading my affliction to the innocent and the unwary. That fate is one I have to pay for, and if that means eternal solitude, so be it." He leaned forward, the goblet screeching and dimpling in his grasp as his hands morphed into wolf paws and claws. "Even now, though under the enchanted protection of a dragon, you smell tasty to me."

I swallowed hard. There'd been plenty of ways I'd imagined dying. Being ripped apart by the fangs and claws of a werewolf wasn't one of them. "Okay." I stood in a hurry, nervous and fidgety, and placed my empty bowl on the wooden table, leaving it clattering unsteadily. "We'll be on our way, then. Cam?"

As I backed off, smiling like a loon because I didn't want to turn my back on the First Wolf, I saw Sigmund lock amused gazes with Cameron. Was this a joke? But when he spoke, I got that his smile wasn't really about faking cannibalistic ferocity with a jest. "He calls you by your first name? How... intimate."

Cameron chuckled. "Humans live short lives. They tend to shorten everything, even their names."

Sigmund laughed in his rumbling manner, gathering his gigantic gray wolf skin tighter around his broad shoulders. If he stood, I believed his head would have reached the ceiling. "I admit, I'm curious if they do the same when it comes to the act of love." He grinned at Cameron. "Maybe you can report back to me on that."

Cameron gave Sigmund a chiding look, but his friend merely laughed again. Cameron said, "Be on the lookout, old friend. I worry those who stole the Earth Shard are far from done in their perilous quest. I fear for the safety of us all."

Sigmund rose from his seat. He filled the room like a giant, the fire behind him casting him into shadow. The wolf skin on his back seemed like fur on a live beast now, and I puzzled anxiously about what he would look like as a wolf. My morbid curiosity was likely to get me killed one of these days, I suspected.

"I have been alone for thousands of years," Sigmund declared as he poured himself a new drink. He sounded weary but also yearning, and the thought of him being alone forever didn't sit well with me. Sigmund gulped down his mulled wine. "No one knows where I reside except my Progenitors. And those children of mine would never betray me or the blood we share. No one will find me or the Metal Shard here."

A horrible thought occurred to me—at the exact moment when the ground began to shake and rumble.

"Unless... the bad guys followed us here," I whispered tremulously.

This time we'd all been duped.

Chapter Five

THE HATCH shielding us blew away in a deafening blast, the shockwave shoving me on my ass. I jumped to my feet, breathing in a cloud of smoke and snow, with my knives in hand, prepared to fight in close quarters.

But I should have known I'd not only be the underdog, I'd be the invisible boy too.

The cavern echoed emptily. No villains had yet descended upon us. Or to be precise, upon me. Cameron and Sigmund were gone.

Then I heard the roar from above. Cameron and Sigmund must have already reached the surface and wreaked havoc on their enemies. A clambering crash sounded, and the earth shook beneath my feet as I ran toward the ladder. Heaps of snow and puffs of smoke landed about my head and shoulders as I climbed up, the bitter smell of fire in my nostrils.

As I scaled the last rung, the mayhem appeared around me.

I realized the golden dragon I'd seen back at Cameron's penthouse hadn't been as big as he could get because the dragon I now watched shadowed the sky above me. Glimmering colorful wings flapped fast, creating snowstorms and icy gusts as Cameron swung his long pronged tail and with it took one of the three military helicopters circling above us down from the sky.

I ducked as the broken, battered, and burning fuselage bounced over the hatch opening. My breath lodged in my throat. I'd never been in a battlefield, be it a human war or a fight between mythical beasts. I knew when I was neither wanted nor needed.

From my cover I stared wide-eyed at the destruction around me.

A slew of military storm-trooper types swung down from the other two helicopters, dangling on ropes with full-automatic weapons on their backs and fronts. A huge machine gun fired from one of the helos targeting Cameron, who thankfully flew far too fast for the bullets to hit him.

Then a gigantic mass of fur and claws leaped against the helo, crashing into its front and shattering the glass. The dire wolf Sigmund had turned into was bigger than a house, definitely bigger than the helicopter it encompassed. Its silvery hackles rose in fury, and razor-like claws sprang forth from its paws with deadly accuracy. The rotors stopped moving, and smoke came from the engine in thick plumes. Then Sigmund leaped off, and the entire craft began to spin out of control. It dropped from the sky like a dead bug.

Screams, shouts, and gunfire deafened me. But I remained convinced an ancient dragon and the first werewolf in existence could hold their own and then some. I doubted they—meaning the bad guys—could breed or invent an army that could take down a dragon and a dire wolf. In fact, I expected quick and utter surrender from our foes in no time.

But at the back of my mind, an elusive insight niggled and gnawed at me. There was something I was missing.

At that moment I caught movement in my peripheral vision. A figure clad in white moved quickly away from the battlefield. The clandestine shape proceeded so surreptitiously I was instantly on alert.

I snuck out of my hidey-hole and dashed after him.

Since there was so much snow in heaps and piles and mounds, it was relatively easy to stay out of sight, despite my dark clothing. Keeping my secretive prey in sight was another matter. Whoever it was seemed to glide over the frozen tundra like a figure skater or a pixie.

And then the mysterious figure vanished like he'd dropped off the face of the world.

I ran faster toward the last point where I'd spotted him. Well, running was obviously an exaggeration. Trudging along, blind and weary to the bone, was a far more accurate description of my progress.

Then I fell.

The ground disappeared beneath me, and with a tiny shriek, I fell along a steep slope covered in snow and ice, slithering helplessly on a natural winter slide. Time lost all meaning.

I landed painfully on my ass in what appeared to be the bottom of an underground ice grotto.

Huge ice stalactites hung from the roughhewn, cavernous roof, and equally massive stalagmites shot up from the rocky ground like crystal claws reaching for me. Everything glimmered blue and white and black. Innumerable precious gems stuck out, embedded in the ice, adding to the shimmering effect, like the night sky full of stars. A stark beam of light from the rift in the earth illuminated the vaulting space stretching far above and around us.

Only, it wasn't a rift above me. I'd dropped a good long way, but I saw it for what it was: a metallic hatch like the one back at Sigmund's place, only different, sleeker and, dare I say it, more futuristic in design. That realization matched with the sight of the cavernous walls, all hewn and having once known the touch of a human's, or a monster's, hand.

In the glow of the morning sun, I saw ancient ruins buried beneath the ice and snow. Massive stone and ice reliefs covered the glacier walls, frozen columns, and also the new arched cave openings that descended deeper underground. The reliefs depicted giant wolves and other mythical, monstrous creatures unlike any I'd seen or heard of. They were out of this world. Only, since the Unveiling, they were as real as you or I, but far less known.

What shocked me most was the debris scattered about the grotto ruins. Rusty pieces of machines the likes of which I didn't understand, vaguely reminiscent of fantasy art or steampunk creations. Broken, ripped, or splintered, none of them were usable as anything more than scrap metal.

I couldn't help but puzzle over what kind of ingenious devices they'd been. This destroyed ramshackle was coated by centuries of snow and ice, so they had to have been created long before humanity's industrial age.

Had there once been a civilization of werewolves living underground? What heights had they attained before rising to the surface to start their packs? Were there entire lost glacier cities deep in the earth, forgotten by time? My head spun as my imagination ran wild.

In the center of the cavern rose a white ornamental stone altar, entirely covered in ice and rimmed by rows of ice stalagmites, like monstrous teeth ready to devour an intruder. And on top of the altar, trapped behind a huge block of ice and a twisted cage of metal spikes sticking in all directions....

"The Metal Shard," I whispered in awe.

Now I understood why they were called Shards. The object glinted in rainbow colors as though it were an amalgam of dozens, maybe hundreds, of different metals. The mysterious Metal Shard resembled a rugged crystalline spike, jagged as though it were merely a raw sliver ripped or shattered from a larger object.

I felt monumentally stupid. Of course they were pieces of a larger artifact. That's what Cameron had meant about bringing them together, forging the slivers into a whole. It had to be a magical artifact, I guessed, an enchanted doomsday device, judging from Cameron and Sigmund's high level of concern.

Though I was no mythical being or Guardian, I had to protect the Shard. I got up unsteadily, my head dizzy and buzzing. The cage locking the Metal Shard within was made up of a staggering number of various metals—from platinum and silver to steel and iron. Whether these spikes were indicative of the Shard's significance, composition, or nature, I had no clue.

Then I saw the strange white-clad figure approaching the altar.

"Stop!" I shouted, my mouth working before my mind reminded me I was sorely lacking in weapons. I had my knives, and I was pretty good at throwing them, but I suspected my faceless foe wore armor plating.

My assumption was confirmed when the figure whirled around, revealing white skintight body armor. He was a *she*, if her noticeable bosom was any indication. Her head and the lower half of her face were hidden behind a white mask and cowl, but I did see her eyes, pale and bright like diamonds, akin to the ice surrounding us. Beyond that I had no clue who or what she was.

Being a reasonable man, I opted for logic. Surely even world-class villains had a modicum of common sense, right? "Don't take the Metal Shard. You don't understand what you're doing. You'll kill us all and destroy the world."

The woman cocked her head as if assessing me. I slowly stepped forward, holding my hands up in a sign of peace, or at least nonaggression. She had to see my point of view, I argued with myself, and realize her role would bring the world one step closer to oblivion.

Something red and brilliant flashed in her hand as it shot up.

Fire burned through my upper chest as the shot I hadn't seen coming fried my body. Laser pistols? Weren't those impossible to create with either modern or futuristic technology, let alone with magic? I stumbled to the side, trying to avoid further shots aimed at me.

But the woman ignored me. She turned toward her target.

Before she'd taken so much as a step, the air filled with metal blades, aimed at the intruder. Whether flung forth in straight lines or in rotating blade storms, the metal weapons emerged from the walls of the cavern, from the altar, and seemingly from the cage surrounding the Metal Shard.

With a yelp, I flattened myself against the chilly ground, covering my face and upper body, curling into the fetal position. The zing and clatter of metal rang around me, a symphony of chaos, deafening me even though I covered my ears.

What shocked me most, however, was the sight I beheld through my slitted eyes. The woman dodged the metal projectiles with a swift lightness that surely wasn't imbedded in the human genome. She jumped over them or glided beneath them, her body twisting and twirling like that of a gymnast from hell. I'd never seen anything like it. Once I actually saw her use a thrown blade as a stepping-stone for another leap through the air. It was as though she were a feather, weightless and thus able to vault and bounce, evade and skirt each round of weapons aimed at her.

Finally she passed the metal storm raging around her and reached the altar. Flames shot from her hands, either by magic or from a gun I couldn't see. The ice, frost, and metals coating and covering the altar rippled and then dripped as they all turned to liquid. Drops became rivulets, and finally the shell shattered and broke apart with the sound of a tinkling sleet shower.

Yelling for some childish reason as good lost to bad, I stormed toward the woman in white and jumped on her back, despite the sharp pain splintering my shoulder. She grunted, and we both fell on the frosty ground, tumbling and fighting.

I had little experience in hand-to-hand combat, but I was reasonably certain I managed to deliver some effective blows and smarting kicks. I didn't see any identifying markers on her, but I did feel the skin of her cheek as I grazed it with my knuckles.

She was cold as ice.

She punched me in the stomach, quite hard actually. All the air left my lungs, and my vision blurred. She rolled out from under me and then cracked me on the back of my neck with her elbow. Then she kicked me in the burn wound she'd inflicted upon me. I rolled away from further attacks, but I think she no longer saw me as a threat.

Down for the count, I swam in an ocean of agony. I expected to die then and there, and a swarm of painful and pleasurable memories clashed within me, struggling to be the one I'd hold onto in the face of certain death.

"Stupid mortal," the woman muttered as she hurried to the altar, grabbed the Metal Shard, and ran off, vanishing into the shadows toward the hatch. But my vision blurred, and I couldn't see how she climbed back up to the surface.

I was unable to so much as lift a finger to stop her. My defeat was a definite blow to my ego. Shame washed over me in acidic waves, bruising me further. Then I no longer felt anything because I lost consciousness.

I GROANED as the pain returned, along with my awareness. Light splintered my vision.

"Shh, be careful, Finn. Be still, and let yourself acclimatize to the moment." Cameron's warm, strong hand gently pushed me back down. I lay on a bed—it had to be because it was soft and warm—and it called to me with its sweet siren song.

"Is he all right?" Sigmund asked. I couldn't see him. Then again, my eyes were closed, which probably accounted for my blindness.

"I'm sorry," I murmured, only half awake. "I lost the Shard. She took it. I fought her but…. Fire… and ice…."

Cameron smoothed my hair, his touch far more intimate than any he'd given before, and shushed me silent. "Rest now. We'll talk later. Sleep." He poured a spicy-flavored hot beverage down my throat. While it singed, it also relieved the ache and exhaustion I felt. Before I knew it, I was fast asleep again.

When next I awoke, I heard Cameron and Sigmund discussing something in low tones not too far away. Judging from their words, I hadn't been out for long.

"…ice and metals covering the Shard have magical properties. It's more elvish crystal than ice, and the metals stem directly from the Shard itself. That woman shouldn't have been able to penetrate the shield," Sigmund said, his roughened voice nothing but an angry growl.

"Agreed," Cameron said slowly, sounding pensive. "Only a blackfire spell by a skilled Shadowalker could have broken the seals so effectively. Unfortunately, those beasts can hide from our search enchantments. I fear we might not be able to unearth our foes as easily or as fast as we need."

"The Wood Elves won't listen to our gripes," Sigmund said, his tone brewing fury. Guess there was no love lost between the two mythical species. It piqued my curiosity, and I itched to hear that story. "They think they're safe and untouchable in their tree havens and sky cities, protected by their advanced technology. I doubt they'll grant you an audience in a year, let alone in a day. They are creatures of protocol and rigidity."

"We share blood, so they must and will acknowledge me," Cameron said rationally, and I agreed with him. "Two Shards have been taken. The elves have no choice but to take our case seriously."

The two men, Cameron and Sigmund, sat close to the fire, silence surrounding them once more. I couldn't see their expressions, but I saw their gestures, how Cameron touched Sigmund on the shoulder in a friendly manner, the kind only time and amiability could cultivate.

"I know you can't travel with us, old friend," Cameron spoke softly. "I will do right by you, find the Metal Shard, and return it once more to your vigil."

Sigmund chuckled warmly, an affectionate sound that I quite liked. "I need no vows from you, Cam. I know you will do all you can to retrieve what was lost. I have faith in you. And I have faith in your healed little human pet—who is even now misbehaving and eavesdropping on us."

I blushed so fiercely my cheeks burned, embarrassed at getting caught. Coughing to show I was awake, as unnecessary as that was, I murmured something akin to an apology. With a bit of difficulty, I staggered to my feet, relinquishing the welcoming warmth of the handcrafted bed I'd slept in. Surprisingly I felt almost back to my old self. Whatever concoction Cameron had given me, it sure did the trick.

I had something to prove after my failure at capturing our foe, so hoarsely I said, "Did I forget to mention in my delirium that when I fought with that woman in white, I slipped a GPS tracker inside her armor plating?"

Chapter Six

"DON'T YOU folks use cell phones or tablets or, dammit, smoke signals?" I grumbled as I was once again held by Cameron the dragon, close to his scaly, remarkably warm chest. His flight was jerky and the winds at our altitudes constantly chilly. I wanted to land and kiss the ground.

Cameron's laugh vibrated through me. "Communication signals can be intercepted, and those species with telepathic capabilities don't advertise or allow strangers to be privy to their inner mental sanctum. And I told you, black magic interferes with our forms of contact."

I admit my curiosity was piqued. The Unveiled world held many unknowns, and we were still stumbling about in the dark. The idea that some people with dire intentions might listen in on a conversation about the Shards was one thing; for these same foes to gather intel from Cameron's mind was far too terrible a possibility to disregard.

"Can you....? Um, are you...?" The civil part of me didn't want to pry; the childish part of me that wanted everything immediately kept my mouth moving.

As usual, Cameron didn't answer. He could be terribly secretive at times.

"Where are we going now?" I asked, as if talking could keep me warm. In truth, it was Cameron's warmth I craved. Whether in dragon or human form, a connection existed between us. I couldn't explain it. When he was a man, I desired him; when he was a dragon, curiosity held me in its grip.

I wondered what it would be like to make love to a dragon. Would he prefer to have sex in dragon form? That would be... challenging to the point of problematic. As a man, I had zero doubt we'd click in bed. I could see him now, hovering above me like a statue of a sex god, his imposing, muscular body claiming me, his scaly skin rough and silky at once against my skin, his fiery breath teasing my neck, maybe even singing ever so slightly....

"We're traveling to Charybdis," Cameron said in his level tone, shaking me out of my weird, though hot, fantasy life.

If memory served me, the name came from Greek mythology. "Isn't that, um like, some kind of giant vortex at sea?"

Cameron laughed. "Exactly right."

Now I felt nervous.

BENEATH US, the monstrous whirlpool churned and swirled in an endless spiral, gulping down everything and anything that dared to swim near its heaving and undulating waves. I felt dizzy just staring into it, mesmerized by the constant flow.

I was about to ask Cameron what now when he called out, "Close your eyes and hold your breath. Trust me."

The dragon Cameron circled high above the whirlpool that washed white with the fury of the ocean. With no land in sight, I felt the cold clutches of fear tear at my insides. I had no idea where we were, what ocean this was—though I think we were in the Pacific Ocean—and how far I would have to swim or float to survive, if that was even remotely possible.

Then Cameron went stiff and straight, like an arrow, and pointed himself directly at the swirling mass of water. He plunged down toward the center.

At first I screamed, but at the last second I remembered his instructions, so I closed my eyes and took a deep breath. My heart skipped a beat. I don't think I'd ever been so afraid in all my life, and I'd jumped from skyscrapers and airplanes, for fuck's sake.

Water surged over me, soaking me to the bone, gushing waves at me, the pressure high enough to compress me, forcing me to fold in on myself. Again in so short an amount of time, I felt death brush against me.

Then I heard Cameron's soothing voice. "You can open your eyes and breathe now."

Throwing caution to the wind, I did as he said.

Cameron must have gone down at extraordinary velocity because we were in sight of the ocean floor. And there in the pitch black, with no surface visible, I saw a plethora of lights and colors, rising from an underwater city. From the tallest towers and the largest domes to the smallest statues and the most minute radiant fish, the place was alive with coruscating rainbows of illumination I would never have expected at these depths.

And that thought gave me pause. "Why aren't I bursting apart?" I slapped a hand over my mouth, though it was far too late to stop myself from drowning. Then I realized I wasn't, in fact, dying. An air bubble, rippling with magical energies, surrounded us. "Cool." I no longer cared how Cameron did it. It was magic, and it was wondrous. "What is this place?"

"Welcome to the Grianan of the Undine." I was brimming with questions. Thankfully Cameron beat to me to the flood. "The Divine Order of the Undine has lived here, underwater, for eons. This is their Grianan, or palace. The Undine are considered holy and sacrosanct by most of the mythical beings. We revere them for their skills as mediators and their powers of healing."

"Wicked cool," I muttered in awe.

"We must seek audience with the Reverend Mother, Muirín," Cameron said.

I asked the first of the numerous questions plaguing me. "Who or what are these, um, Undines?"

"Mythical, elemental, and spiritual beings associated with water, oceans, lakes, and rivers, both fresh and saltwater." Cameron could be concise when he wished, but he still hadn't sated my ravenous curiosity. With gratitude I continued to listen as he granted me the boon of his knowledge, which seemed to be infinite. "You are aware of mermaids, yes?" I hummed in agreement. Cameron continued, "They are but one of many species dwelling here. Naiads, nereids, water nymphs, and so on. The list is long. It has been ages since I have visited the Deep, but I can assure you we are safe."

I snorted. "I got that the moment I figured out I wasn't drowning to death, gasping for air like a lunatic." Cameron sighed patiently. I think he found my mixed metaphors amusing, the same way he found a lot of human idiosyncrasies a wealth of personal and public amusement.

A full spectrum of light illuminated the dark ocean floor. Only it wasn't quite as pitch-black as I'd assumed. Whatever the source, lit-up algae or fish radiating colors beneath their transparent skins, the place sparkled. I didn't need to squint or point my tiny waterproof flashlight anywhere.

Seaweed and coral formed much of the ocean floor's flora, and fish, squid, and jellyfish, all translucent and brilliantly colored, formed the fauna. In a way I felt as though I were floating in space, cold darkness surrounding me but colorful starlight spinning around me too. It was magical. If it hadn't been for Cameron, I would never have seen a place like this. Heck, I wouldn't even have known of its existence.

Cameron veered past natural columns that smoked and others that bubbled, like all the majesty of hell was within them. I didn't dare reach out and touch them, be they cold or hot.

The tallest tower resembled an oval water bubble, with algae and seaweed growing on its translucent surface, blues and whites mixing with greens and reds. A swarm of yellow and red fish swam past me as Cameron set us down on the steps leading up to the tower.

I refused to let go of Cameron in fear of… well, at that point the list of things to worry about was extensive.

But I shouldn't have needed to be concerned at all. The bubble Cameron and I were in collided with another bubble by the entryway. That's when I realized it was a corridor of air, and it continued in various directions from the structure. *Huh.* It hadn't occurred to me that the dwellers of this underwater temple city might prefer to breathe oxygen too.

Two guards flanked the entrance arch. I wished I hadn't stared like a moron, but I did.

Though both were bipedal, their hands and feet were webbed to the point of appearing as flippers. Their skin was scaly, the hue a mix of green and blue, and they had no hair on their heads but instead what looked like long tentacles. Their round eyes glowed blue, sapphires in the underwater dimness. They stayed just outside the bubble, floating in the ocean, but I had a sneaking suspicion they would surge through the thin barrier if I did anything stupid.

Then a group of women emerged from the shadow of the structure. Only… their upper bodies were feminine; below their hips they were fish.

Oh. My. God. They're mermaids. I tried to breathe and look normal—unsuccessfully.

Their long hair waved about them, with delicate silver jewelry surrounding their faces in curious headdresses of fine detail and aesthetic design. They wore black-and-gold, equally intricate, gem-studded armor plating that resembled corsets above the waist, with pieces of black lace covering their arms, and they held spears and tridents in their hands and had knives and blades strapped to their hip belts.

"I thought you said they were nuns," I whispered to Cameron out of the corner of my mouth, confused.

"No. I said they were a holy order of warrior priestesses." Cameron's words suggested I hadn't been listening, a parental rebuke in his chiding voice. I grumbled inwardly. Had he said that, I'm positive I would have remembered.

One of the women came forward. She didn't glide through the water like a fish or a mermaid; she stepped forward on two graceful legs covered in greaves and boots. She pierced the bubble but without breaking its cohesion and integrity, to come and stand before us. These people were clearly ready for war or any contingency close to battle.

Her green eyes appeared human, but on the edges of her face, her skin glowed with green scales. "Master Feilong," she said, bowing with her hands clasped at her chest in a sign of devotion and reverence. "You honor us with your presence. How may we be of assistance, Your Grace?"

Damn, but that use of Cameron's title sent a thrill of excitement coursing through my veins. I wasn't a celebrity whore by any means, but Cameron's regal stature did awaken something hot and needy inside me. Perhaps it was pride at being chosen to be his companion, if only for a time.

"Thank you for receiving us so graciously without any prior notice of our arrival, Reverend Mother." Cameron bowed as well, now a man again, his hands hidden inside the long sleeves of his short yellow silk robe. "Our matter is an urgent one, Muirín, requiring your immediate attention."

Her gaze landed on me. I gulped. Staring into her eyes was like staring into the depths of a well, the waters serene and cool but the pit bottomless and fathomless. Dizziness overcame me again. It took every ounce of strength within me to hold her gaze, my instincts crying at me to hide away.

Muirín must have seen into my very soul—at least that's how naked and exposed I felt. Yet regardless of what she saw in me, a quirky smile lifted the corners of her mouth.

"Very well, then," Muirín finally acquiesced in a melodic voice that resonated through the waters around us. "Follow me, please."

THE LARGE domed space at the top of the tower that resembled a tube possessed an aura of holiness akin to a cathedral. Skeletal pieces of gargantuan sea monsters decorated the room, while paper-thin partitions and silk banners hanging from the ceiling on metal struts added to the airy ambience of the sacred space.

I was struck silent in awe as I inched forward, gawking around me wide-eyed.

Thankfully Cameron wasted no time in getting to the heart of the matter. "Two Shards have been stolen. Mine and Sigmund's. We fear the remaining three are in serious jeopardy."

Muirín's eyes widened in shock. Having a knack for reading people from the shadows unseen, I had no doubt she was innocent in all this. "There have been no incursions into our territory. No threats made on the Water Shard." She beckoned Cameron and me to sit on white armchairs that looked like plastic but probably weren't, considering how silky soft they felt against my fingertips. "Please, tell me everything."

Cameron repeated the same story he'd told Sigmund. Only this time he added news about the private army attack at Sigmund's cave and the lady in white. "My friend Finn here managed to plant a GPS tracker on his assailant. The signal points here, so they must already be here, or at least near the barriers."

Muirín glanced at me, her wise and ageless gaze stripping me of all falsehoods, vices, and excuses. I blushed and squirmed in place. She inclined her head to me. A sense of worthlessness washed over me, but I tried to smile.

"As a Guardian, I bow before you, Sir Finn Grayson." Funny. Cameron hadn't told her my surname. That, plus the knightly titular use, and my nerves were truly frayed. "It has been many a decade since a human last stepped inside these hallowed halls. But you are most welcome. And your aid in our darkest hour is most appreciated."

"No, no, thank *you*," I murmured in response like a fool, rubbing my heated neck.

Muirín smiled gently, as though she understood me and my awkwardness completely. "The Water Shard is kept safe behind a magic barrier under Black Turtle Hill. No creature, mortal or otherwise, has set foot on those tiles or gazed upon those waters for eons."

"How do you know it's still there, then?" I asked, speaking before my brain caught up.

But Muirín smiled at me kindly. "The Shards are bound to their Guardians. I would feel its absence as starkly as I'd feel my heart missing a beat."

"That's supercool," I said in admiration. "But the fact is that while the bad guys might have followed Cameron and me to Sigmund's cave, they didn't follow us here. The signal is clearly coming from close-by. That begs the question: who exactly knows about these Shards, where are they hidden, and who's guarding them? Seems to me that list couldn't be a long one."

Cameron shook his head, a glum expression marring his handsome features. His long hair breezed around him as he moved. "Unfortunately the Shards are kept secret from humanity, but in the mythical world, many species know about them, for there was no need for such secrecy before the Great Unveiling that joined our two worlds."

"Okay," I said, accepting his interpretation but adding a twist of my own. "But how many know for a fact what these Shards can do together? Those who know about a potential end of the world would surely avoid using them. I mean, that's basic common sense, right? So, who knows about their existence but not what they actually do if brought together?"

Muirín regarded me with a pleased expression. I simultaneously beamed and flushed red. "That is a good question." Her gaze shifted to Cameron—whose smoldering eyes watched me intently in a way that made my pants magically shrink and my blood boil. "Master Feilong, those who are aware of the true purpose of the Shards are composed almost entirely of the ruling bodies of each race and realm. However, the existence and magnitude of the Shards' magic is not common knowledge among the general populace."

Thoughtful, I suggested, "So the culprit is perhaps someone of enough significance to be in the know but maybe not in specific detail?"

Cameron frowned, lost in thought, his left hand rubbing his jaw where a tiny tuft of facial hair curled. How come I hadn't noticed that before? After all, it was such a… a dragony feature. "That still leaves far too large a group to investigate, trace, and interrogate. We wouldn't even know where to begin."

I snorted. "Sure we do. We've got a lead." Cameron stared at me with narrowed eyes. I liked that intense look a lot. "The bad guys may or may not be here, or ever will be, but my fence, Griffin, sent me on a fool's errand, to die as a distraction. I say we start with him."

A small twitch at the corner of Cameron's lips spoke of his amused satisfaction with me. Yet he addressed Muirín. "Reverend Mother, arrange for additional protection for the Water Shard immediately, while Finn and I see what we might learn from the humans."

The warrior priestess nodded regally in agreement. "I will do as you instruct, Master Feilong. But you are aware as well as I that there are only two ways for anyone to obtain the Water Shard from our bastion: by collapsing Black Turtle Hill and disrupting the flow of magic in the protective shield, or… or by destroying the Guardian of the Water Shard."

I gasped, but Cameron merely nodded, obviously having been aware of this possibility from the start. "Yes, I know. Be safe, old friend. Once we have found answers, we shall return and offer any assistance you may require in defending the Water Shard."

Seething at being kept in the dark, I followed Cameron out of the temple. As he created an air bubble around us, drew me close to his hot chest, and swiftly swam to the surface, I knew we'd duke it out soon enough.

That is, if we didn't die first.

Chapter Seven

"THIS ISN'T an equal partnership, I see," I commented casually as we waded through the throng in one of New Shanghai's countless marketplaces.

It was hot, and I mean tropical swelter. A moist heat that passed through all layers of clothes to wither the body and smother the will to move. The mass of people swirling about us in undulating waves didn't help matters.

Smells of raw and cooked foods mixed with body odors and trash, and the general background din was borderline deafening. But I knew Cameron had heard me.

"Oh?" He sounded disinterested and cool, same as always. I briefly wondered if he'd sound as composed in bed, or would he roar with passion, his features animated and his gorgeous body glistening with sweat from amorous exertions....

I shook my head, annoyed with my raging libido. We were in mortal danger. This was no time for seduction. "You're not telling me everything," I accused him point-blank.

Cameron shrugged. "There's a lot I'm not telling you."

I gritted my teeth, glaring at him. "Is that all you've got for me? Sorry but you're out of luck? I might get myself or both of us killed in ignorance, so I think it's time you start sharing."

Those teal-colored eyes assessed me. I held still, letting my blazing anger bolster my self-confidence. "I disagree," Cameron said. And that was apparently the end of our argument, since he turned his back on me and resumed his wade through the crowd.

I fisted my hands, ready to do serious damage. If he hadn't been an ancient dragon who could kill me with a breath, that is. "We're not done," I whispered toward his retreating back. "Not by a long shot." Then I ran after him.

I hadn't been to Asia in ages, but some people were fixtures who never went away. The same could be said about the slew of petty thieves who operated in every city in the world, whether they existed behind a wall or not. Through my contacts I'd learned that Leo Griffin had come to New Shanghai the same night I'd fumbled the robbery. I had no idea why, unless his presence had been a plan B to ensure I was dead and buried and the Earth Shard in his possession. Nonetheless, we'd heard a rumor about his whereabouts, and we were headed right to his location, assuming he hadn't moved on.

Though I wasn't well acquainted with the mythical world, even I had heard of Nine Dragons Tavern. A safe haven for otherworldly beings desiring to drown their sorrows in drink, same as any old ordinary humans. Only at this tavern, the policy was strictly *no humans allowed*. I was positive Cameron would order me to wait outside; but I was equally positive I'd find my own way in if that happened.

The facade surprised me, being quite unassuming, even boring. Granted, the dragon motif was common in this part of the world, and the tavern sign boasted one entwining around the letters. But were there nine dragons, somehow shown on the sides, base, or roof of the two-story building? Were there dragon depictions on the windowpanes or the red-painted door? No. Which was all kind of… bizarre.

Cameron, as unfazed as ever, knocked on the door. But no one answered; the door simply opened on its own. Since Cameron hadn't told me not to, I followed him in.

I was damn near blown away by the smoke that clogged the air in thick gray blankets, obscuring the view of the interior. Hushed voices came from all around me, the speakers unseen. Only the faint glow and crackling of fireplaces gave any indication of how large the space was, and the subtle clinking of glasses and bottles suggested there were folks all about the tavern.

I coughed to clear my lungs and throat. The fog thickened till my eyes watered, and I could only smell grilled or charred meat and the spicy noodles this town was famous for. "Cam?" I called out softly into the smoke because I could no longer see him.

Stumbling, I made my way, almost blind, until Cameron clutched my hand in his and tugged me along. "Watch your step, Finn," he advised me, quite needlessly in my humble opinion.

"Easy for you to say," I grumbled back, clearing my throat. "I can't see a thing."

"The smoke screen is for the benefit of humans who shouldn't be here," Cameron said.

I scoffed, tears running down my undoubtedly soot-covered cheeks. "Benefit? Don't you mean hindrance?" It did help, in a way, to know what surrounded me. *Magic.* Perhaps my lungs would survive today after all. "How the hell could Griffin see anything here either? He's human. I can vouch for that. Come to think of it, *why* would he be here?"

"I imagine we shall find out soon enough," Cameron replied, his tone soothing. I think he was trying to comfort me. Little did he know his words had the opposite effect.

THE DEEPER into the labyrinthine building we went, the denser the smoke—and the more lost I became. I couldn't describe how the place made me feel, as though up was down and down was up, as though corridors ran straight and spiraled at the same time, and as though the structure expanded to a far greater area that I'd surmised from observing the humble facade.

Which I now knew to be nothing but a camouflage, magically hidden in plain sight.

I heard the fast scraping of wooden chair feet the exact moment Cameron stopped, with me bumping into his back and stepping on his heels. "Sorry," I mumbled, unable to see more than an inch before me, if even that. I was utterly dependent on Cameron's assistance. Alone I'd have zero chance of leaving here in one piece. Cameron patted my arm gently, reassuring me despite our hazy surroundings. Well, to be clear, I suspected I alone walked in the gray.

A strange man snickered close to us. "Well, well, well. If it isn't Lifts-His-Tail."

The snarky comment oozed bitterness and hurt. I figured the ridiculing and provoking phrase might have been the dragon equivalent of hate speech about being gay and taking it up the ass, or at least that was how I interpreted it. Manly men and dragony dragons seemed to possess the same ability to be homophobic dickwads, intent on spewing their venomous hatred for no justifiable reason.

I wanted to jump to Cameron's defense, though I had no clue what, in fact, his sexual orientation might be. But I should have known the dragon could hold his own just fine without any interference from me.

"Well, well. If it isn't Snarky-Scales." Cameron's voice dripped sarcasm, but I heard the underlying soft, warm vibe. He knew the man who had insulted him—and cared for him. The rush of jealousy within me was irrational, but I grimaced despite myself, realizing now that the man was in fact a dragon like Cameron. Perhaps they were... old lovers? Current lovers? I didn't like one bit being here with someone who had known Cameron intimately.

A menacing growl from the other man warned me that these warm feelings might not be returned in the same spirit. "What are you doing here? And with a human pet? Or have you come bearing gifts, regardless of their cheap quality?" I was mildly insulted but knew better than to open my mouth when I couldn't see my enemy retaliate.

Cameron sighed, a regretful sound that made my stomach churn. I didn't like the idea of him cowering or apologizing to anyone, least of all someone who'd insulted him. "Finn is not mine to give. Please, Chi Wen, I don't wish to argue. My business is grave."

The man invisible in the mist snorted. "Your business is always life or death... dear friend." He must have kicked a chair forward because Cameron moved only a little and sat down, leaving me holding on to his shoulder, blind as a bat in a dust storm. "Want a drink?"

"No, thank you, Chi Wen." Cameron sounded calmer now, back to his old serene self. That pleased me even as I tamped down a new surge of jealousy and envy. "I have reason to believe your tavern is harboring a criminal. Leo Griffin. I have a score to settle with him. Is he here?"

That was a bit more direct than I would have liked. But I had to trust Cameron knew what he was doing. It sucked being in the dark, literally *and* metaphorically, but I chose to remain still and quiet and to listen for as much new information as I could.

"What is this one you seek?" Chi Wen asked, his tone neutral.

"Human," Cameron supplied. "A fence and a facilitator of crimes."

Chi Wen chuckled, his voice slightly confused. "You deal with the scum of the earth these days, eh…. Guardian?" Before Cameron or I were able to contradict, Chi Wen continued in a cold tone, "You've got a lot of nerve showing up here after everything you've done and demand my help."

"Don't talk to him like that," I hissed angrily, upset over his continuous berating.

Chi Wen chuckled, in surprise I could tell. "Ah, the pet speaks?"

"Finn has risked his life to help me," Cameron cut in, his voice dropping dangerously. Had I been Chi Wen, I would have worried then.

But Chi Wen appeared undeterred as he snorted in obvious disgust. "You never had trouble finding those willing to die for you or one of your precious causes. What I'd like to know is what game you've got going on right now?" His contempt repulsed me, but I kept my peace, trusting in Cameron's ability to reach his (hopefully) *ex*-friend.

"Griffin stole from me and tried to get me arrested for murder." Cameron could have knocked me down with a feather. Why the hell was he telling this odious man everything? It made no sense to be so forthcoming with our enemies so close to our heels—and with one unknown, to me at least, right in front of us.

When Chi Wen let out a surprised gasp, I understood perhaps Cameron's approach had been a wise one after all. "Whose murder?" The tension in his voice grew thick in the room.

"Mine," I supplied, wanting to contribute to the discussion even to a small degree and perhaps to show him I was better than him by rising above his snide remarks.

"The Earth Shard has been taken," Cameron said. His voice quivered ever so slightly with regret and self-recrimination. That annoyed me since there'd been nothing he could have done differently. We'd both been betrayed. It wasn't his fault. If anything, it was mine. I'd distracted him from his solemn duty and made it possible for the Shard to disappear. It was my turn to get wrapped up in remorse and guilt.

This time when Chi Wen growled, I recognized the sympathy and righteous fury there. "Griffin?" he asked for confirmation. I heard no response from Cameron, but he moved a bit, so I assumed he'd nodded in agreement. "My brothers and I would never harbor human criminals in our establishment. A theft from a dragon is bad enough; stealing an Elemental Shard is an unforgivable offense. No one here would be that stupid, reckless, or evil."

"Nonetheless my sources tell me he's here," Cameron said smoothly, casually hiding my role in all this. "You know as well as I that the Shard must be recovered. What harm is there in having a look around?"

I could sense Chi Wen's hesitation, his conflict within. Since I couldn't see anything in the tavern, I assumed this place did cater to the seedy underbelly of the mythical world. And the proprietors wanted to ensure their safety and anonymity.

Still, every second we wasted arguing was a second we wouldn't get back without a time machine, and I started to get antsy.

Someone, or something, sniffed behind me. I went stiff in a sudden burst of fear and adrenaline. I'd never realized how much I depended on my sight until now I had none.

"What's behind me?" I asked, swallowing hard, my voice no more than a whisper.

Cameron's soothing voice came to my rescue. "A *preta*."

"What the hell is a preta?"

See, this is why I avoid the Far East for all I'm worth. Unlike the Christian view of the world, with its single and predictable hell, the Chinese Empire and the other eastern religions and myths recognized thousands of hells, each worse than the one preceding it. Numerous creatures existed in those vile lairs, and apparently one of them was breathing down my neck as we spoke.

Cameron rose and placed a calming hand on my shoulder. "A hungry ghost. Their skill in tracing those who have committed sins, vices, and crimes is legendary. It will track our elusive Mr. Griffin through hell and high water."

Something slick brushed against my nape, causing me to shudder. "The, uh, the hunger part, that's like, um… metaphorical… right?" The thought that what had touched me was the tip of the creature's long snakelike tongue gave me goose bumps. I think I vomited in my mouth a bit.

Cameron pulled me closer to him, a warning in his tone. "You have committed crimes, Finn. The preta can smell and taste it on you. But fear not. For you are safe with me."

I suppose I could have defended my prior actions then. But the fierce panting behind me suggested I shouldn't add to the list of offenses by lying. Whatever that thing was, it sensed all my bad deeds. And I didn't even dare to consider what part of me the hungry ghost might consume had I been its prey this evening.

Something scaly and sharp nipped at the back of my head. Teeth? Claws? I yelped.

Chi Wen grunted something in Chinese, but I didn't understand most of it, which told me it wasn't Mandarin but Shanghainese, a local dialect I wasn't versed in. But the hungry ghost must have understood because a squelching sound—footsteps made by webbed feet?—suggested the creature was retreating away from me.

Cameron whispered in my ear, "Stay here, Finn, while we search the tavern." Close to protesting, I was struck silent when his lips brushed against my cheek. "Trust me."

Cameron, Chi Wen, and the hungry ghost left me alone amid the impenetrable gray haze. I figured I should have cared, disagreed, or argued. I'd never liked being the passive onlooker.

But the hot tingling on my skin from Cameron's touch distracted me long enough that by the time my erection waned, I was alone.

Chapter Eight

I FUMBLED for the chair Cameron had been sitting on and planted my butt on its reassuringly solid surface. Then I twiddled my thumbs, anxiously awaiting the return of the conquering heroes. Never before had I felt this useless. My fate was out of my hands, and I didn't like it one bit. I was a thief after all; I didn't believe in luck because it was a factor I couldn't control.

Vague mumbling ebbed and flowed from the direction of the tavern's main room, but no one entered and no one spoke to me. My clouded vision began to grate on me. I closed my eyes to make my blindness a matter of choice rather than the result of circumstances.

I couldn't tell how much time had passed. But when Cameron and Chi Wen stumbled back into the room, their rough panting and muffled curses alarmed me instantly.

"What's wrong?" I grilled, standing swiftly and aiming my sightless gaze toward what I hoped was their direction. "What's happened?"

But Cameron didn't address me. "Wen, I'm so sorry for your loss."

My blood ran cold. "Somebody talk to me."

"My brother Suan Ni… is dead," Chi Wen replied wanly. He was crying, I heard him. "Murdered. He didn't deserve it. He never did anything wrong. He never wronged another soul. He was a creature of comfort and quietude, the kindest soul among us, a friend to everyone."

I was so in the dark I was surprised my vision hadn't gone pitch-black. "I'm sorry," I said softly because that's what should be said when someone has died, whether you knew them or not.

I didn't notice Cameron until he rested a heavy hand on my shoulder and squeezed, in need of an anchor if I read him right. "Griffin is dead too." I drew in a sharp breath, in shock. Questions flew in my mind in utter disarray. "Suan Ni must have given Griffin sanctuary. We found them… dead together in one of the upstairs suites."

"How?" I asked, my voice cracking in terror. Griffin had been a fixture in the thieving underworld for decades. Before his recent betrayal, I would have called him colleague and friend. For him to be gone… my world, as I knew it, lost some of its sensibility. Dealing with Griffin hadn't always been smooth as silk, but he'd grounded me whenever avarice or recklessness tried to talk me out of common sense. Griffin had been an anchor of a kind.

Cameron's growl gave me a heads-up. "They'd been burned to a cinder. Blackfire."

"The woman in white," I whispered. I cursed out loud. This was my fault. If I'd taken her down when I had the chance, Griffin and Chi Wen's brother would still be alive. But something was amiss. "I don't get it. The GPS tracker indicated that the white-clad woman was at the Grianan of the Undine. How could she be here too?"

I knew the answer a heartbeat before Cameron uttered, "She must have discovered the tracker and used it lure us to the underwater temple under false pretenses. We thought she'd be close to the Grianan, but in truth she was here, committing a double murder. And now…."

How could she have noticed such a tiny GPS tracker inside her armor plating? It sounded like some kind of twisted version of the Princess and the Pea. Panic washed over me, making me shake and sweat. "The Undines…."

Cameron's rough voice wasn't so much a caress as a punch in the gut. "They're under attack. We must go at once."

HOW FUNNY life was. A few short hours ago, I'd troubled over how on earth to convince Cameron none of this situation was his fault. He'd been a dedicated Guardian. That he couldn't have foreseen my arrival or our simultaneous betrayal only showed he was flawed like humans.

Now I struggled to convince myself not to blame myself for two deaths that were the direct result of my meddling. The woman in white had used my own trick against me, and now Griffin and a completely innocent dragon, Suan Ni, were dead, burned to a crisp by sinister magic.

How was this anything but my doing? I was so angry with myself I seethed, seeing red and fidgeting even while tucked against dragon Cameron's hot, scaly chest.

Before we saw Charybdis, we knew something was wrong.

The vortex remained unchanged, a whirlpool portal down to an underwater realm.

But massive bubbles rose to the restless surface from the deep, bursting apart as they came into contact with the air. The smell of smoke tainted the otherwise clear, fresh atmosphere. A battle waged beneath the waves, and my heart skipped a beat as the roar from below echoed in my ears.

"God, Cameron, hurry," I urged him in desperation.

Cameron dove into the churning watery mass, the magic air bubble appearing around us instantly. A few thousand meters rushed past us as Cameron sped through the ocean, an arrow of vengeance aimed at our unseen enemies.

At first the deafening silence of the soundless sea weighed heavily on me, a tightening pressure pushing against me. The deeper we went, the more starkly I realized that if the air bubble vanished from around us, I wouldn't have time to drown. Instead, I'd implode, crushed by the weight of the ice-cold waters in the depths.

By the time the Grianan came into view, hell, havoc, and ruin had been unleashed on the unsuspecting hallowed ground.

Sleek underwater crafts rocketed all around the once beautiful realm, now bombarded to smithereens. Explosions swept through the holy city, washing it away with the tides. Towers tilted, blew up, and fell; domes cracked and disintegrated; and the oxygen corridors imploded, sending concussion waves through the water and gigantic air bubbles rising to the surface. Storms of silt and sand from the bottom of the sea obscured our sight, but it was clear we were witnesses to the downfall of the Grianan of the Undines.

In shock I stared at dozens, perhaps hundreds, of floating corpses of mermen I'd seen guarding the main tower. Their milky-white eyes stared ahead, lifeless and cold. Though I'd been wary of them, now I found myself weeping for them, lamenting the loss of so many unique beings, sentient and intelligent, as precious to the world as any species.

The warrior priestesses fought in the distance, their battle cries barely reaching us no matter how fast Cameron moved. But he acted in rage unlike any I'd seen. He scared even me, his ally.

The dragon's roar had me covering my ears, the pain sharp until I felt moisture against my fingers, sticky blood coating them. Whatever magical force Cameron held within, he used it, his fiery breath, his huge scythe-like claws, the mass of his scaly bulk, and his pronged tail lashed out, his strikes hitting on target each time.

The underwater vehicles firing on the Grianan tore apart, blew up, or sunk deeper to the ocean floor, unable to rise again when Cameron charged at them. Cameron dove from one to another, taking each out with swift efficiency, his rage a palpable power resonating within me.

I wanted to participate in the struggle, but once again I was useless.

Cameron's claws tore through metal, his teeth bit into weapons, the impact of his body sent shockwaves about us. The sea stormed around us, and I clutched Cameron in fear. If I fell, I'd die. But I couldn't close my eyes to the slaughter and mayhem. I bore witness to a mythical war that might end us all.

When the few remaining underwater crafts began firing on Cameron, I felt it likely I'd die at the bottom of the sea, a crushed husk decaying away on some ocean floor.

But Cameron proved an elusive target. He dashed, twirled, dove, and plunged, never too long in one place. He was nimble while the enemy crafts weren't as maneuverable. His punches hit true. His enemies kept missing.

Until the bubble wobbled around us, and flames burst around Cameron.

He'd been hit. Fiery droplets of golden blood floated weightless in our bubble. The magical sphere had held fast, but the ammunition had pierced Cameron's body. I couldn't see where. I tried to climb his body like a jungle gym, but he writhed and groaned, and there was fire everywhere.

I smelled my hair burning, and my skin ached horribly where his fiery blood dripped on me. The bubble didn't burst, but we were no longer swimming or diving purposefully; we were sinking, dropping down in a heap.

Wherever Cameron had taken the hit, it was serious.

We hit the sandy seabed with a heavy thud. He groaned in pain, his eyes closed. I tried to avoid being crushed by him as he rolled onto his back, me turning with him, clutching his scales in abject terror.

If Cameron succumbed to his unseen injuries, be it unconsciousness or death, would the fragile air bubble burst? I wouldn't survive a second.

"Cam?" I shoved his wide barreled chest. His eyelids fluttered, and he let out a soft tiny whimper. "Cam, don't you dare leave me here to handle this shit on my own. Cameron! Don't sleep. I need you."

Around us, the bubble rippled and shrank. My nerves were frayed, but I kept my cool. If Cameron lost consciousness, I only had myself to turn to. Not a great prospect, I admit it.

His dragon image distorted briefly, and then he was a man again. His eyes rolled to the back of his head, and a guttural groan escaped his throat. A torn opening in his yellow silk shirt revealed a burned gash from which blood trickled down his hairless, muscular chest.

The wound pooled above his heart, scaring me to death.

"You're a dragon, I know, but I'm praying your heart's in the same place it is in humans," I whispered. If his heart was above where it was in humans… well, I guess we were shit out of luck.

In my many pockets, I had a few basic emergency supplies. I reached for a pressure bandage and rolled it around Cameron's chest, over his shoulder, and under his armpit. That covered the hole well enough. Not much else I could do without an actual doctor or better medical supplies. Blood slowly seeped into the bandage, and it changed from bright white to dark amber. But at least the rate seemed to slow, so there was hope yet.

"Cam?" I shook his uninjured shoulder gently, trying to rouse him. The wound itself didn't seem that bad, so I figured the ammunition used had some kind of dark magical properties or perhaps some biochemical agent intent on poisoning or inflaming the target. I wasn't an expert on either of those possibilities, so my meager ministrations and debatable explanations as to why Cameron wasn't waking up were the best I could come up with on short notice.

An explosion nearby sent a shockwave toward us. The bubble shook with the force of the concussion. Then it began to roll down the minor slope toward a dark blue chasm.

I think I screamed. I mean, I must have since my ears rang from the sound. Both Cameron and I spun inside the sphere of air, like laundry in a machine, as the ball rotated and bounced on its way down. Every rock, coral, or pebble was a threat that could pierce the delicate barrier separating us from the chilly deep.

And though I was gyrating inside the energy ball, I could see the rainbow prism of the bubble shift from sharp colors to grayish hues. If this magical sphere was anything like a regular soap bubble, when the colors bled to black, the bubble would be thin enough to burst at the slightest touch. Add to that the fact the damn thing was shrinking? We were definitely in trouble.

As we continued to roll uncontrollably, I did my best to hold on to Cameron, shielding his head from collision and pressing the bandage tighter against the wound. As a result he was fine while I was bruised and battered.

I did the only thing I could under the circumstances. I shouted my head off. "Help!"

Chapter Nine

"CAM, IF we live through this… I'm either gonna kill you or kiss you," I vowed as we reeled downhill toward the bottom of the ocean. "Or both."

I hit my head, don't know on what. Dizzy to begin with, I distinctly felt the inevitable rise of nausea in my equally roiling belly. I tried to see what was ahead, but the speed of the air bubble had increased as the incline steepened, and the bright lights of the Grianan faded behind us. Soon everything became nothing but a gray blur.

I fully expected to die. A familiar feeling after the last couple of days.

Two pairs of strong arms grabbed me. I kicked and screamed, afraid to die, but they pulled me through the air bubble—into another bubble.

I drew hungry drafts of fresh air into my lungs. Only then did I see my rescuers. The warrior priestesses, several of them, swam beyond the sphere, with me as the sole occupant.

But they left Cameron lying where he was, inside a crumbling air bubble, threatening to burst at any second.

"No, Cam!" I yelled, pounding the bubble's malleable spherical wall with my fists, but to no avail. The mermaids began to glide the air bubble through the waters, back the way we came, toward the Grianan.

In horror, I watched as the soft, partly coral-covered seabed gave way until Cameron sank slowly into it, vanishing from sight. The air bubble evaporated. And all the while, I drifted farther and farther away from the dragon's final resting place, tears flowing down my cheeks.

Without Cameron, what chance did I have of stopping our enemies?

Anxious about the carnage and perdition I'd eventually see, I plopped down on my ass and hugged my knees, waiting with bated breath for what was to come.

The holy city lay in smoldering ruins. Beautiful towers crumbled onto the seabed, air corridors blown away, domed roofs collapsed. Amid the devastation I caught glimpses of enemy watercraft, all destroyed and scattered in pieces on the rugged ocean floor or floating with undersea currents.

Everywhere I looked I saw a sea of dead, be they mermen or just men. I hadn't known them, these miraculous creatures of the deep seas. Yet I felt hot tears on my cheeks, running like leaky faucets.

"Oh, Cam...," I whispered, sadness and despair overwhelming me.

This was my fault. I'd had the chance to stop the woman in white, and I'd failed. As a result, a whole city wiped from the face of the earth. I trembled with guilt, unable to quench the horrible twist in my gut.

How much worse could the situation get?

I got my answer definitively as the mermaids stopped in front of the air corridor of the main temple, apparently the only one left. Mentally I did my best to regroup and dragged myself out of the bubble and into the temple.

After I trudged up the stairs, I saw her. *Muirín.* She lay on the cold, wet stone floor amid the rubble, blood pooling out of a chest wound, two handmaidens weeping at her side.

"No," I murmured. The despair was fading, replaced by fire-hot anger and the desire for revenge.

I ran to Muirín and knelt next to her. Her chest heaved but slowly and lightly, and her green eyes were mere slits.

"Reverend Mother," I called out to her, taking her hand.

Her long brown hair spread around her head like a dark halo. Her green scales had lost their luster and were now wrinkled and dry, falling like withered autumn leaves. Her skin had grown paler and grayer. Her eyelids fluttered as she focused on me.

Recognition sparked in her green depths. "Finn...."

I shook so hard I couldn't tell if her hand shook too. "Muirín, I'm sorry. I'm so sorry. This is all my fault. I'll get help."

Muirín smiled softly, shaking her head. Droplets of blood clung to her lips. "Please, don't. There's no need. The wound is deep. I am near death."

My jaw quivered, my throat clogged up, and my vision blurred with unshed tears. "No, please, wait. Don't die. I can get help, I swear."

Muirín squeezed my hand. "You must go." She coughed achingly, and her face dotted with blood spatter. "Finn, go to Black Turtle Hill. The path there is clear. Save the Water Shard. I feel it is in grave danger. Go now. Hurry."

I was about to argue that I couldn't swim through the ocean like mermaids could when a gentle hand on my shoulder stopped me. The handmaiden from before leaned over me, extending what appeared to be a metal bracelet.

"Take this, human," she said firmly. "It will shield you from the ravages of the ocean."

What else could I do? I locked the bracelet around my wrist. The caress of its warm, fluid surface resembled water, the way it felt on a hot summer's day to immerse myself in a cool pool.

Blue and green lights flicked on. Something surrounded me, invisible but tangible. A kind of second skin, made up of unknown energy or mystical magic. I didn't know and didn't care.

I faced Muirín. I sensed it was the last time. "I'll save the Shard. I promise."

Her smile, sweet and kind, was there one moment, gone the next. Her green eyes went glossy, and I knew she was gone.

I couldn't bear to look, ashamed of my cowardice. I stood and ran to the edge of the air corridor and walked through it, expecting to be crushed under the merciless weight of the ocean.

But I continued to breathe normally, the water whirling around me never touching me. The energy shield encased me so close to the skin that it seemed more like a futuristic diving suit than an invisible bubble. I found I felt lighter and faster now, so I nodded to myself and sprinted into action.

Muirín had been right. The winding path from the temple to the hill was marked with white stone slabs, decorated marble archways, and banners twisting in the current.

I never stopped to consider this would likely be my last day and last act on this earth. All I could see was Muirín's sweet smile and her eyes losing their light of life. Then I saw the image of Cameron, slowly submerging into the ocean floor, and I wished I had kissed his forehead as a sign of good-bye, just once before the end.

Anger boiled within me. I sought revenge. How could I not?

BLACK TURTLE Hill described my destination quite accurately. A round hill, like a turtle's shell, rose from the ocean floor in desolate solitude. The stone it was made of, and even all the plants and corals covering it, appeared black as midnight.

The path approached the mound from downhill. And there, at the foot of the knoll, a lone arched doorway bid entry. As I got nearer, I saw the energy barrier blocking the doorway. But I recognized it for what it was. An air corridor.

Or in this case… a monumental air bubble.

Apparently the corridor contained the entire underwater cavern beneath Black Turtle Hill, expanding along its inner walls. Instinctively holding my breath, I stepped through the yielding energy barrier, and my normal weight and speed returned to me.

A wondrous sight spread around me. The hill's black obsidian stone surrounded me.

Everywhere pools, columns, and fountains of water—some cascading down, others rising upward against gravity and normality—rose, churned, and bubbled. These waters all appeared to be different: teal-hued tropical lagoon waters arose in one column, icy-gray polar ocean waters pooled heavily in another, crystal-clear river waters surged in a third, and calm sky-blue lake waters rippled in a fourth. I couldn't have counted all of them had I tried.

In the center of the domed hall stood an altar on a raised dais. Unlike the one I'd seen in the north, the one that had housed the Metal Shard behind metal blades and frost and ice, this altar trickled and cried, sweated and beaded moisture. All the water columns in the cavern's expanse weaved around the altar, like a gigantic ball of twine or a surreal maze of waterspouts, completely made up of liquid and magic.

I stared, eyes wide in shock, my mind reeling from one new, brain-boggling discovery after another. How could I ever return to my old ordinary life after all these mythical miracles and dangerous adventures?

Of course that question was predicated on the possibility of surviving said adventures. Which was by no means guaranteed.

Especially when I saw the white-armored woman approaching the altar with the Water Shard atop it, encased in a swirl of liquid.

She'd slipped through my fingers once, and dozens, perhaps hundreds, had died. There was no way I was letting her get away a second time.

I sprinted toward her, plucked two throw knives from their holsters, and hurled them across the narrowing gap between her and me. I knew better than to aim for her midsection with its armor plating. I went for her leg and her arm.

The knife aimed at her arm pinged a sharp melodious sound as it hit a brassard and did no damage. But the other blade sliced her leg above the knee, between the cuisse and the greave.

She grunted in pain, lost her balance, and fell to the ground. She rolled down the steps leading up to the altar dais until she came into contact with one of the closest water columns.

Only… it wasn't water.

A sharp hiss broke through the sloshing din as acid burned a hole through the armor on the woman's right arm. She screamed and yanked her hand away, panting roughly.

As though she were immune or indifferent to pain, she did a forward roll and was back on her feet in the five seconds during which I almost got to her.

"You," she hissed as fiercely as the acid pool had singed her. "I should have killed you when I had the chance."

"Right back at you," I declared, praying to every god and goddess in the omniverse to help me fight and win against this dreadful enemy.

I decided not to wait for her to draw out whatever weapon she had fired at me on our last encounter. With vengeance on my mind, I charged her, at least remembering not to yell out any theatrical battle cries—only to be met with surprisingly steely hands that gripped me and, with embarrassing ease, tossed me over her shoulder. Add to that a stiff kick in the gut, and I was down for the count.

"Bitch…," I remembered to insult her, although I could have done without the wheezing in my voice. Not particularly manly, that.

The woman scuttled away from me, not that I was in any position to attack her again. She sneered at me. "Stupid human. What did you imagine you'd accomplish with that crazy stunt? I've fought monsters and demigods. You're no match for me."

With that, without waiting for a cute quip or a smart retort from me, she kicked me in the side, sending me down the steps toward the acid column.

I had a mere half second to come up with a plan before I'd be scorched to death like the victims in those Alien movies. Better than getting eaten or used as a host for nasty critters, I thought sarcastically, even daring a small chuckle.

In a flash before my eyes came an unbidden image of Cameron, his smirk as a dragon and his kind touch as a man. Regret pissed me off. The woman in white brought it out of me.

My face and shoulder caught fire as I touched the acid pool, the burn worse than any experience in my past. But even as I stopped rolling and managed to steer clear, I still had my weapons.

I snatched one of my knives and brushed it at the swirling pillar of acid. The spray was well aimed, if I say so myself, as a sharp, arrow-like jet splashed against the woman in white.

She cried out in pain, her whole upper body drenched in acid. Not even covering her face helped. Her snow-white armor appeared to be made up of dozens of smaller pieces, several of them now seared through and smoking. Shrieking, she ripped each smoldering piece off and threw them aside. Her speed was remarkable.

I managed to stagger back to my feet, though the pain consumed me and I had no vision in my right eye. Using my uninjured shoulder as a battering ram, I lunged for her. She let out an *oomph* as I barreled into her midsection. My forward momentum pushed her back until her body disappeared into another water pylon.

Her voice disappeared, cut off as the current in the water pillar yanked her along to rise higher, floating helplessly in the coiled stream and unable to break free. Hell, she should count herself lucky that particular flow had turned out to be plain old water.

Though the acid burned holes through my skin and flesh, I felt victorious. The Water Shard was safe, my enemy defeated, and my only wish was that a healing magic spell would restore me to my former self. A man could dream.

I laughed despite the torture that had been inflicted upon me. I hoped Cameron liked his men with a few scars. Or a missing eyeball.

That is… had he been alive. A joyless thought served as a precursor to a fresh wave of anger and desire for retribution. I hated that Cameron was forever lost to us. But… I had saved the Water Shard. That mattered. And in situations like this, even small victories counted.

I faced the altar, loving the sight of the Water Shard safe in its liquid enclosure.

Then I turned around to find the exit and report my success to Muirín's handmaidens.

But the cavern filled with men and women, all clad in white armor, holding swords and futuristic weapons that gleamed red and yellow, green, and blue. And they all advanced toward me with death in their icy blue eyes.

I knew I'd be no match for them even as I stumbled blindly backward to get away from these coldhearted, white-clad ninjas, or whatever the hell they were.

Since I had no eyes in the back of my head, I floundered right into one of the pillars of water, falling into a swift, rising tide of warm tropical waters exactly as a razor-sharp katana cut through the stream, splicing the current, missing my head by a mere inch.

Which was nice. Now instead of burning to death in a vat of acid, I could look forward to death by drowning.

Chapter Ten

YOU KNOW how sometimes you awake from a deep sleep and the headspace between the dream world and the waking world is hazy, and for a time you can't tell which is real? To me, that spells bliss.

And it spelled it again—until my poor body started sending alarming messages of how badly I'd been hurt in the struggle with the woman in white. I groaned in pain, twisting and turning on a soft bunk. First floating like a cloud, then dropping to the ground like a heavy stone.

"Easy, Finn. Be calm." The soothing sotto voce voice was instantly familiar.

Cameron. He's alive.

The weight of the world lifted from my shoulders, and relief washed over me. "Oh, thank God," I murmured, my voice garbled even to my own ears. I think I might have barked out an hysterical laugh. "Fuck, Cam. We've gotta stop meeting like this."

To my surprise, Cameron chuckled. A warm hand gently swept through my hair. Not a goddamn thing in my whole life had ever felt so good. "Agreed."

"How on earth did you manage to...? I saw you get swallowed up by the seabed." My head spun as I felt dizzy and giddy at the knowledge of him alive and well.

"The healing grace of the sisterhood of the Undines is not confined to stone buildings or the sisters themselves. It's inside us and all around us in nature, no matter how deep under the sea we might be." Cameron spoke as one might mention facts so self-evident everyone should know them. But I was still playing catch-up.

"How'd I survive that water… maze, or whatever it's called?" I asked, baffled.

"The particular current you fell in was composed of so-called airy water," Cameron replied in an explanation that made little sense to me. "Airy water is a magical mix of two elements and adapts your lungs to breathe liquid easily and quickly, much the same way a baby breathes amniotic fluid in the womb. So be at ease. Do not worry. You are almost completely healed. The pain you might feel—"

"Check," I cut in, definitely feeling the downside of having been in a battle.

"—is only temporary, an echo from when you were hurt," Cameron continued like I'd said nothing. "Like last ripples by a stone in a pool, the waves will subside. Give yourself time."

But I couldn't do that, not in good conscience. Guilt swept through my waking mind. "The Water Shard…."

I knew what to expect even before Cameron said, "It was taken."

"Why do bad guys always have badass armies at their disposal?" I raged with my eyes closed and my soul bursting with a mix of righteous indignation and shame born of failure. "Where the hell do they always get these goons and henchmen to do their bidding, goddammit? Fuck, there were so many of them…. I managed to get the woman in white tossed and trapped into one of the water columns. But then there were, like, a gazillion guys dressed in white, swarming at me like evil ninjas, or whatever the paranormal equivalent is."

As I continued to seethe and grouse under my breath, a single touch from Cameron on my shoulder calmed me down. I might not have succeeded in retrieving the Water Shard, but I now knew that our enemies were large in numbers, organized, and capable. A conspiracy.

I finally managed to crack open my eyes, but the light was blinding, forcing me to shut my eyes again. "Why's it so fucking bright?"

"That would be my fault, Finn. I apologize." The female voice sounded sort of familiar, but I couldn't pinpoint the owner from my memory Rolodex.

From behind my closed eyelids, I detected the light around me dimming, and I didn't have to squeeze my eyes shut anymore. I squinted, then blinked hard, and finally managed to sit up, wide-eyed, to get a sense of my new surroundings.

I was at the Grianan of the Undine. The main temple, to be exact. Sections of walls lay in ruin, energy barriers holding the ocean at bay. Burned banners lay on the floor along with stone rubble, pieces of pillars, wrecked furniture—and dead bodies under white silk sheets. I swallowed at the sight, closing my eyes to ward off the ghastly vision.

"No, Finn. This is not your fault. You are not to blame." Cameron sat next to me on the narrow metal bunk.

"Reason isn't helping me right now," I said, shaking out of my self-recriminations as they wouldn't do me or our side much good. "But I'll try to remember that. Thanks, Cam." I turned to him. The mischievous spark in his eyes had faded. His expression was grave, and his stance relentless and rigid. But there was no wound on his chest, which was revealed underneath his immaculate new clothing. "How'd you survive?"

Cameron smiled ruefully. "Muirín saved me with her healing grace."

That couldn't be, my logic told me. "But... I watched her... die. She couldn't have—"

"Rumors of my demise are greatly exaggerated," a woman spoke softly, her figure in the shadows. As she approached, a sense of déjà vu overcame me.

"*Muirín...?*" I'd seen her die, practically in my arms. And yet there she was, her green eyes warm and kind, the way they'd been before. "You're alive? How?"

Cameron nudged my thigh, his hand resting on me. Even through the blanket, I felt his heat and strength. I shivered, hot blood stiffening my cock to the point of a full-on boner. I bunched my hands over my groin artistically, going for casual.

"She is not the Muirín you met," Cameron said after he'd caught my attention.

Oh boy, had he caught my eye! Mentally I waved a hand over my heated face. God, but that piece of male eye candy was smoking hot with his long black hair, like priceless silk, and his teal-colored eyes whispering to me of tropical islands, white sands, and hot lovemaking in the shade....

Then his words sunk in. "Say what?"

"Since the dawn of time, there has always been a Muirín. They are not immortal but all too familiar with every aspect of mortality, birth, and life and death." Cameron gestured toward the woman, who appeared nearly identical to the one I'd known and watched die. "The memories of the previous Muirín are preserved in a sacred vessel and then transferred to the new Muirín. The one you met was the nine-hundredth-and-eighty-third."

My poor head was spinning. For a brief flash, I was certain I was being punked. But as I stared at the serious but sympathetic faces above me, I accepted that the Unveiled world was far more intricate than I ever gave it credit for. "Okaaay…."

"As long as the Water Shard exists," the new Muirín said, "I will exist. There must be a Guardian. Always."

In my honest opinion, I'd waited long enough, and my patience had reached its end. "It's high time you guys share what you know. What happens if the Shards are brought together? And be precise."

Cameron and Muirín exchanged wary glances I had no trouble interpreting. They were going to choose their words carefully, if they uttered anything at all. Cameron especially had more than once demonstrated that he could and would stay tight-lipped.

With a short but deep bow, Muirín excused herself and left the temple, her long robes trailing in her wake, as did her handmaidens. I was aware they were all mermaids, but they exited on foot, showing their shapeshifting abilities.

Cameron let out a long sigh. That spelled bad news in my book. The fact that he averted his gaze confirmed as much. "We rarely speak of such matters with humans."

"Tough," I cut in, my tone sharper than I initially intended. "This is definitely a need-to-fucking-know kind of situation." I took a deep breath and collected my thoughts, reining in my temper since it served no good purpose. "I mean, the way you fear the Shards being brought together suggests it's happened before, with dire consequences."

Somber, Cameron nodded. "Yes. Long before the Veil lifted. Ages ago. The time so far in the past many have forgotten what took place."

"That doesn't sound good," I commented quietly, apprehensive about what I'd learn.

Cameron huffed out an indignant, sarcastic chuckle, sounding more human than ever. "The elves. They advanced on hundreds of kingdoms simultaneously, conquered them in military coups, and took the Shards for themselves. We hoped the theft was merely to display the Shards as trophies, as spoils of war."

I tried to assimilate the news. It was hard. Classic fantasy literature portrayed elves as something refined, beautiful, angelic even, so absolutely good and pure that they practically coined the terms. To hear they had been historical villains? I had a tough time wrapping my brain around the concept.

"The elves used the Shards," Cameron continued, his voice sounding gravelly and dangerous. I hoped I'd never again be at the other end of that voice, as his enemy. Then again, being his friend led me to ignorance often enough. "When I told you before—that if the Shards were brought together the world would end—it was both true and misleading."

I gritted my teeth. This wasn't the first time I'd been treated like a dumb human during this twisted quest of ours. But I set the emotion of outrage aside in favor of finding out what fate potentially awaited us.

"Together the Shards have the capacity to create and destroy," Cameron said carefully. "Sometimes both at once."

That confused me to no end. "Elaborate, please."

"The Shards are connected to the very essence of supernatural beings," Cameron said, though to my ears that sounded like no explanation at all. "Behind the Veil they bound us all as one. So that no one species was naturally greater or more powerful than the others. A balance existed, harmonizing our world."

"Okay, I guess that makes sense," I commented, shrugging.

"When the Shards are brought together, forged into one again, the way they used to be before splintering and safeguarding the world...." Cameron's voice faded into nothingness. I saw his throat convulsing as he swallowed. I assumed what came next was a whopper. "The Shards can affect evolution."

I blinked. I opened my mouth. I blinked some more. I closed my mouth. My brain had obviously frozen as nothing emerged from it to voice. I had no idea what Cameron was saying. Finally I muttered, "Look, uh, though I usually hate being treated like an imbecile... would you mind terribly, just this once, talking to me like to a child, using the simplest possible terms? I'd really appreciate it."

A dry chuckle emerged from Cameron, and a lopsided grin flicked over the corner of his delectable lips. "Yes, I will make the effort. For you, Finn." Then he grew grave again. "Whichever species forges the Shards back together will experience, as an entire species, an evolutionary jump forward. A big one. A huge leap ahead in intelligence and physical abilities, among others. That's why the elves are, of all the mythical species, the most advanced in science, technology, and psychic abilities."

I felt my eyebrows rise to my hairline. "Wow. That's… something." Yeah, it sure was. Something to die for and kill for.

"There's a downside," Cameron added quickly, his expression hard and ferocious.

I snorted. "Isn't there always?"

Cameron smiled shortly. "As one species evolves, another… devolves."

I let out a breath so profound I actually fell backward, my back hitting the wall behind the bunk. *Holy. Fucking. Shit.* Now I started to understand why ensuring the Shards could never be reunited mattered so much. "Devolves…?"

Cameron slumped and ran a hand through his hair. "The single time it happened in the past, it caused the elves to evolve. That explains why they are so much more technologically, scientifically, and intellectually advanced than any other mythical beings in the Unveiled world. They have sky cities, orbital habitats, secluded populations, secret weapons, psionic abilities. The full extent of their knowledge is unknown to us. But the gap is wide indeed."

"Who devolved?" I asked in a rush.

"Orcs, ogres, and goblins," Cameron replied. "They had a civilization once, a great and powerful one. As they devolved, they reverted back to their animalistic, predatory forebears, with their clans, primitive armaments, and hunting-gathering culture. Some tribes even lost their ability to use language. It was a nightmare."

I had to raise a hand to my mouth, or I would have groaned or vomited, or both. "Jesus fucking Christ…."

"A magical evolutionary jump, whether backward or forward, caused by the Elemental Shards would enhance one species and devolve another, perhaps several, at random. Violence would spark, civilizations would fall, destruction would be assured. As it was back then. A great war between countless species raged on for centuries. Our World War. It nearly destroyed us all."

As Cameron grew quiet, I finally understood his stony expression, the mixed feelings of remorse, guilt, and anger flashing in his eyes. "And you're part elf...."

Cameron closed his eyes tight, and his jaw quivered. I wished I hadn't reminded him of the burden of blood he shared with an equally bloody history. "Yes. Yes, I am. A fairy dragon."

"That's why you can never ascend to the throne of the Chinese Empire," I concluded softly.

"Exactly. Hatred and fear toward the elves is justified. Even after all this time, many millennia later, with few survivors left from those dark days." His frown deepened, marring his flawless skin in a way I didn't like. "After the elves used the Shards, they locked the Crystal away in an impenetrable vault. During the upheavals, a union of five nations broke into the vault, stole the Crystal, shattered it once more, and disbanded the Shards to the five winds, under the protection of new Guardians."

I brimmed with questions. "How? I mean specifically how were the Shards separated from the Crystal after the elves used them? You said they were forged together?"

"When five Guardians accept their task, the Crystal breaks into five Shards," Cameron replied. "I was not there. My mother was. Before the troubles began, she was the wife of an elvish sorcerer prince. He was captured by his people and subsequently executed as a traitor for marrying outside his species. Their loving union resulted in my birth, so she welcomed her honored role as a Guardian. When she died of natural causes, I took on her role as a Guardian. I accepted the holy task gladly and proudly."

My throat worked convulsively as I absorbed the shocking news. His father had been killed by his own people? No wonder Cameron despised the elves. "Shit, Cam, I'm so sorry." Cameron nodded in acknowledgment of my sentiments. A curious thought occurred to me. "Wait. According to official records that Griffin let me have a peek at, your mother was a British dignitary and your father a Chinese antiques dealer."

"That information was created for my protection, long before the Great Unveiling," he explained shortly. "Nowadays that sort of trickery is no longer necessary. I must not have updated my files. I'll have to see about that... if we survive this, of course." Then he straightened up, back in control. I admired him. How could I not? "You humans see the Unveiled world as rich and full of mythical beings. But in those terrible times, many species perished into extinction. We lost... so much. Too much."

I had a terrible thought. "Griffin is dead but... there could be other humans involved in this conspiracy. What would happen if humans reforged the Shards together?"

Cameron quirked an eyebrow as his gaze locked with mine. "What do you think?"

Yeah, I already knew what would befall on us. "Humans would evolve—while some, or all, mythical beings would devolve."

Cameron nodded, seemingly pleased with me. I think he appreciated mostly my tone, since mine was fueled by rage. I didn't want humans to advance through the demise of others. It was unethical, amoral, cruel, brutal... wholly inhuman. I believe Cameron sensed my feelings on the subject and approved.

"There's no way to predict which species would devolve," Cameron said, staring at nothing again. "This is the Unveiled world. For all we know, an Earth species could bear the brunt of that evolutionary attack."

I closed my eyes and let my head fall against the wall with a thud, and a painful one at that. As scientists of several fields had proven time and again, our world teetered on the edge of a precarious balance. A single species lost, like bees, could upset that delicate balance and plunge Earth into a mass extinction event and spell the end of humanity. At that point, whether the lost species would be an Earth one or a mythical one would not matter one iota.

The abject terror for the future clinging to my heart made it difficult to think straight. But I tried. "The woman in white? She's not human. Neither were her buddies. Not the way those guys moved, superfast and sort of weightless."

Cameron nodded, pensive as he stroked his short beard. "That suggests a mythical species has joined forces with humans."

"Would that work?" I asked in confusion. "Advancing several species at once?"

Cameron shrugged. "I do not know. It has never been attempted. Last time the elves stood alone, without allies or comrades in arms. Anything is possible, I suppose."

"That's not exactly the answer I was hoping for," I remarked dryly.

Cameron laughed. "No, perhaps not. Do you regret meeting me?" He didn't look at me when he asked his question. Could this magnificent and powerful dragon have insecurity issues? I found that nearly impossible to believe.

"The short answer? No, I do not regret meeting you. With you, I've seen wonders. Amazing things. Beauty beyond imagining. You're one of them. So how on earth could I be sorry?" I decided not to add the part about having the hots for him. Wrong time, wrong place.

Cameron said nothing. His gaze aimed at nothing, wandering around the damaged hall like a pinball. Finally he said, "Finn? I have a confession to make."

Uh-oh. That sounded ominous. "Okay?"

Cameron licked his lips and seemed to focus his whole essence into his next words to me. "You are a human. You are not a Guardian. But you are vital to the success of this mission." He clenched his teeth; I could tell from the way his jaw moved.

"What aren't you telling me?" I asked with bated breath, readying myself for the blow to come.

"If the Shards are forged back together," Cameron started, deliberately slow and steady, "the Guardians are no longer necessary. Their—*our*—bond with the Shards will be broken... and we will die."

I couldn't breathe. My heart skipped a beat, or half a dozen. The cold touch of death brushed over my very soul. There were no words. If the Guardians were lost, then no one would be left to break the Shards apart again.

Except.... Then I had my epiphany. I finally understood my role in all this. And in this instance, ignorance had been bliss as knowledge gave me no comfort.

Cameron spoke the words I already knew would come. "If we Guardians die, you must shatter the reforged Crystal somehow and hide the pieces forever where no one can find them. You alone can do this once my fellow Guardians and I are no more."

Chilled to the bone wasn't even close to describing how I felt at that moment.

Chapter Eleven

"I'm NOT a fan of this plan," I complained, but in a subdued tone since I knew my words would not make a difference to the strategies of an ageless dragon.

"Neither am I," Cameron agreed, surprising me. "But only the Wood and Fire Shards are left. We must warn their Guardians."

"Still think this'd be easier with cell phones," I muttered under my breath.

We trudged through the thick woods of the Zhangjiajie National Forest of the Chinese Empire. The foliage and undergrowth were dense enough to block lines of sight behind impenetrable walls of greenery. The hot weather was heavy and moist, dampening my clothes, over and under. A mist camouflaged the rest of what could be discerned. A fresh earthy scent was carried on the winds that ruffled the leaves. Little critters skittered beyond my field of vision in the underbrush; startled flocks of birds rushed to fly away as we approached; and the sounds of rushing and dripping water from brooks, streams, springs, and waterfalls was ever present.

Naturally, every five seconds I thought about taking a leak.

Above us massive and majestic plant-covered sandstone and quartz pillars rose toward the skies high above. These thousands of rock formations were what made the park so famous. They were lofty and magnificent, lush and imposing. Even I couldn't deny their magical, breathtaking quality.

Despite the fabulous scenery, my mind was on other things. Like why we had to travel all the way here to warn the elves about the Wood Shard being the target of thieves worse than me? Though I'd never met a single elf, I hated them. I loathed them because of the sorrow they had caused to Cameron and his family—and to countless peoples and species throughout history.

Yes, sure, underneath these spiteful emotions, I knew why we were here. Because both Cameron and I had a heart, a moral backbone, and a purpose. Ethics and needs necessitated this meeting with these reclusive elves, who had kept a surprisingly low profile since day one after the Great Unveiling.

In any case, apparently, saving the world from destruction trumped hurt feelings.

Plus, a big part of me was curious to see these creatures depicted in literature, art, and the cultural heritage of numerous peoples.

Nonetheless, I had a sneaking suspicion the woman in white had something to do with elves. Her agility, swiftness, form: they all hinted at superior abilities. If she was indeed an elf, the Wood Shard might already be gone, snatched from under the nose of the Guardian.

Would it be immature of me to gloat if that happened? Yes, probably.

The mist turned into a heavy rain, showering the forest gully around us. I lifted up my hood and covered my head and neck. But it did little good as the wet air sprinkled my face, skin, and clothes anyway.

"Why the heck did the elves choose this place to live in anyway?" I asked, shoving branches and leaves off of me in frustration, only to have them slap me back on their return swing until all I could taste was rain, leaves, and earth.

Cameron glanced at me over his shoulder, an irreverent grin lifting one corner of his sensuous mouth I'd wanted to kiss for days. "The Wood Elves have actually resided in this region for eons longer than humans. In our world before the Great Unveiling, at least. In short, they were here first."

I grumbled under my breath. "Yeah, I get that. But why? This place is inaccessible and rough. No roads, no signs of civilization, no shelter, no cell phone reception, no Internet connection. Just unruly nature. It's practically a jungle out here."

"There are over a thousand species of trees here, about five hundred of them before the Great Unveiling," Cameron explained, stopping in his tracks as his gaze traveled to the lush pillars, scanning their natural uniqueness and beauty. "Also, the word you used—inaccessible—has always been a favorite of the elven nations."

"Let me guess," I interjected sarcastically. "To keep their technological marvels close to home?" Cameron's chuckle answered me well enough. I still had several doubts knocking on the door of the mental chambers of my self-preservation. "Just out of curiosity… what's the likeliest welcome we're gonna receive?"

"You mean will they kill us and ask questions later?" Cameron stopped and turned to me. "The elves value life, so I find it highly unlikely that—"

"Judging from everything you've told me," I cut in, "they value their own lives and species far more than anyone else's." I didn't miss the tick in Cameron's jaw as he gritted his teeth. I knew I was getting to him, filling him with the same ominous dread that encompassed me. Maybe I'd gone too far, so I added quietly, "Of course that was a long time ago. Perhaps they've changed. You know, evolved?"

At first Cameron stared at me like I'd grown another head. Then he got my joke, and his lips twitched as mirth replaced the agitation. "We can only hope."

Before he walked on, his gaze swept over me, nearly too quickly for me to notice. But I did see it. He'd given me the once-over, and it sure wasn't casual or insignificant. I realized he and I had never actually mentioned sex or orientation. But I figured—or maybe it was wishful thinking—an age-old supernatural being like him would have grown bored of one gender and the missionary position as time went by.

I wanted to ask him point-blank, no ifs or buts about it. The words hovered on the tip of my tongue, begging to be let out. But I couldn't find my voice, my throat so dry it hurt.

All my life I'd dreamed of the perfect lover. Him. The one. The man who would be an answer to every one of my questions before I even thought to ask them. I suppose everyone did at one time or another. A romantic fantasy for some; a sweet reality for others. I envied them.

Was Cameron that person for me? Or was this a mere lustful desire to connect with a warm body before the end?

Heck, he might not even be gay. Pondering such a trivial subject when the world was about to end only aggravated me more. And nature around us did me no favors either as I stomped through the thick undergrowth, trying to appear masculine and strong, never complaining, always in charge.

"Are we there yet?" slipped out of grumbling me before I could catch myself.

Cameron's deep-belly laugh cut short when an armed-to-the-teeth group of masked men descended upon us as though falling straight from the sky.

Dressed in tight outfits of gray and green, they concealed everything, head to toe. Even their faces were hidden behind metal mesh masks and shaded visors. On their armor plating was a sigil, a circle with a white tree in the center. They held spears with an electrical charge lighting the tip and bows with arrows that sparked equally lightning blue.

I raised my hands superfast, Cameron following my lead, only slower.

Cameron's voice didn't tremble or quake as he said, "I am Cameron Feilong. I have come to speak with Prince Liro. He's an old family friend."

The sentries nodded us in the right direction, but their weapons didn't lower an inch. I puzzled over their hostility. Surely these Wood Elves could sense Cameron was half elf and thus of their own kind?

No words were spoken as they surrounded him and me, guiding us to a path only they seemed to know. The winding trail gave me no pause to consider our options. I wondered if these folks were this inviting to all visitors to their territory. Because if this was the royal treatment, I'd sooner dwell as a commoner any day.

I'D GOOGLED our national park destination on our flight here—on Cameron's back, of course—so I'd learned about the Bailong Elevator, the world's tallest and heaviest outdoor elevator, made of glass. I'd prepared mentally for the possibility of going on it.

But the elevator Cameron and I, plus our silent sentries, used was nothing like it. The single similarity was the unimpeded view of the tremendous heights surrounding us.

Only a wooden platform, four posts, one in each corner, plus a wire working in a pulley system separated us from a deep plunge to the earth below.

I swallowed hard as I inched to Cameron's side, trying to focus on the distant horizon and not on the ground vanishing beneath us as the launcher lifted higher. "You know what? Walls and railings are totally underrated."

Cameron chuckled and took my hand in his. I'd never felt more protected.

"Do the elves value visibility in all directions?" I asked dryly. "Or do they just have an irrational distaste for safety features?"

Cameron laughed louder. I liked that I could make him laugh, even in such dire straits. "There are protective barriers around us. You just can't see them."

He scratched a fingernail over what I thought to be mere empty space. But a sharp crackling sound preceded a turquoise web of energy that briefly became visible as no more than a flash of bright light after Cameron's touch. The shield seemed to surround the entire elevator.

"Oh, that's so cool," I murmured in surprise and awe. I glanced above, and since there was no roof, I had an unobstructed view to the heavens.

Though I could not see the top of the natural pillars, I did see branches so big and wide they expanded far beyond the edges of the rock face. No tree I knew was that massive, not even the giant sequoia known as the General Sherman tree or the cypress tree of Tule.

"What is that?" I asked, breathless and wide-eyed, unable to look away.

Cameron followed my gaze and smiled. "It's from the elvish world. It's known as the giant golden oak tree. Since the Great Unveiling, these massive trees now top all the charts: they're the oldest, tallest, and widest trees on earth, and the largest living organisms on this planet. Some of their roots hang off the edges of these stone pillars, half of them reaching as far as the ground. This is the only place on earth they appear, and only thirty-eight exist."

"God, I've never seen anything like it," I murmured, gobsmacked.

Then I saw yet another novelty, and I was again blown away.

Wooden structures, resembling pinecones and seedlings and even blossoms about to bloom, were suspended high in the air, hanging from the grandiose tree branches. Some were small and unassuming, while others were huge and intricate. The fair-colored wood gave the structures an airy feel, as though they were light as a feather.

"What the hell are those?" I was starting to feel like a yokel who'd never been anywhere or seen anything, asking these questions and pointing everywhere and staring dumbstruck.

Cameron chuckled. "The elves treasure nature above all else. Their goal throughout their existence has been to live in harmony with the great outdoors. Before our worlds joined, the Wood Elves were naturists, so there would be nothing between them and nature."

"*Nudist elves?*" Try as I might, I couldn't picture it, no matter how big and wide my eyes got. Elves personified physical beauty, but being naked all the time, for all the world to see? Sounded incredible. Then again, they didn't have much to do with the outside world of humans, so perhaps it wasn't a big deal after all. "Are they still...?" I waved a hand about to indicate Cam should fill in the blanks.

Cam shook his head. "Not often, no. Certainly not when company's coming. In any case, since they do not wish to harm the trees in order to live close to them, or on them, they use suspension wires to connect their buildings to trees. Nothing nailed down or directly stuck to the tree to injure it or hinder its growth. They have other kinds of tree dwellings too here at Chún Chéng, the Heavenly Tree Town. They took the name for their tree city to honor the Chinese who live in this region, not wishing to appear inhospitable. Once we get up there ourselves, I hope we'll have time for a tour, perhaps even a guided one."

I turned my back on Cameron, pretending to admire the scenery. But I did it because I didn't want him to see me jealous. "This, uh, Prince Liro... he a close friend of yours?" I might have had trouble imagining a whole elven nation naked—but I had no difficulties picturing some drop-dead gorgeous elf lordling naked in bed... with Cam. I cringed in jealous dismay, wanting to wash out my eyes with acid to make the image disappear.

Silence dragged on as I waited for a response or a reaction, or anything. Why wasn't he speaking out, even if to tell me to shut up? He'd done it before. My palms sweated, and my stomach lurched. Why was he inflicting this torment on me?

Maybe because he didn't know how much I wanted him. Or liked him. Just being with him or close to him.

But then Cameron said, almost too quietly for me to hear, "Listen."

I pricked up my ears, searching for the sound that caused Cameron so much distress. But I heard nothing. Wind rustling in the trees, the wooden platform creaking beneath our feet, the electrical weapons around us humming, rattling and sparking. "I don't hear anything."

"The Wood Elves don't entertain often, but they're usually more hospitable than this," Cameron said, confusing me further. "There's a custom among their kind, a welcome song to their guests. The magical harmonics of elf singing affects brain activity and makes their patrons mellow, docile, suggestible, and nonaggressive. As I'm sure you can imagine, Finn, it's a highly advantageous custom in all the elven nations. Thanks to their heightened sense of hearing, this welcome song begins long before visitors reach their city."

"But I don't hear any singing," I said slowly, and I sure didn't feel any groovier.

Then realization hit me. His next words were unnecessary.

"There's typically an abundance of animals and birds gathered around here. They sense the benign elvish nature, so they congregate near elvish dwellings. But now? There's nothing." Cameron's voice had gone low and dangerous, the deep thrum seeping into my very bones and flesh, vibrating within me. "Something's wrong."

A wooden cudgel or a mace made contact with the back of my head before the echo of Cameron's voice had quieted. Pain and dizziness swamped me, inside and out, leaving me a heap of jelly limbs. Groaning, I fell to my knees.

Through the flashing haze, I saw Cameron being brought down to his knees as well, a dozen weapons aimed at his head, demanding his utter submission and surrender. A metal collar, glinting sharply in the sun, locked around Cameron's neck. The click wasn't loud, but it sure didn't bode well.

My hands were fastened behind my back, the material so hard and tight I feared for the continuity of blood flow to my hands.

Cameron was equally bound. Why wasn't he shifting into his dragon form? No matter what metal the collar was made of, surely his mass alone could and would break it to smithereens. I tried to catch his eye, but he looked away. Yet from his stillness I could tell he was enraged.

As the platform lift rose slowly but steadily toward the heights of the sandstone pillars and the elvish city, I knew we were definitely in trouble. What awaited us above? Interrogation? Betrayal? Incarceration? Torture? Or worse… death?

Chapter Twelve

"*IT'S THE woman in white!*" I stage-whispered.

Cameron and I were escorted from the lift platform to a massive wooden structure wrapped around the trunk of an equally massive golden oak tree. Instead of any part of the construct touching the tree, the multitiered and lightweight installation was actually suspended from the tree trunk and its largest branches. In a way, it hugged the tree rather than smothered it. Like the petals of a blossom, movable canvas sheets shielded the sides of the open-air structure from the elements, like rain and wind.

The configuration was ecologically sound, aesthetically pleasing, and a true wonder to behold. Yet my eyes had a single focus at the moment: the woman in white.

This time nothing concealed her face, part of which was stunningly beautiful but cold and scornful. Long tresses of snow-white hair were gathered in an odd, complex coiffure of buns and braids, none of it hiding her pointed elvish ears. Her white body-hugging and armor-plated outfit didn't sport a single blemish or speck of dirt. Her eyes, so blue they could have been blocks of ice chipped from beneath the waves of Antarctica, sparked as they made contact with mine, leaving me shivering.

She caressed the right side of her face, where her beauty twisted into a jagged scar born of her encounter with the acid stream. She undoubtedly would have killed me with her look if she could. I beamed with no small amount of pride at my accomplishment. I'd injured the enemy. That was worthwhile.

"You," she remarked coolly. "You keep popping up at the worst possible time despite my best attempts at ridding the world of your annoying existence."

"You'll excuse me if I take that as a compliment," I shot back, baring my teeth.

Cameron's hand landed on my shoulder, grounding me as my temper flared at seeing our nemesis face-to-face. "Be at ease, Finn. I'm sure Princess Kamala will explain her actions." He spoke as though no other option existed.

But her name… it rang a bell. I'd heard it, and recently too. I wracked my brains trying to find the lost piece of the puzzle.

But a man's smooth, low voice broke my concentration. "I'd appreciate it if you didn't address my fiancée in such overly familiar terms, Mr. Feilong. Making stark demands from royalty is… inappropriate and indelicate."

The moment the new man walked out from the shadows and into the circle of light, I recognized him.

Anthony Hathaway, a multibillionaire green-tech businessman, known throughout the world as the CEO of a Fortune 500 company.

Tall and handsome, the dark-haired man had a short-trimmed beard, classy spectacles, a well-groomed appearance, and equally flawless business attire that had to have cost thousands of dollars, like something from the cover of *GQ*.

That was when I realized where I'd heard of Kamala *and* Anthony Hathaway recently. In the news, from a stranger's radio, on a boat as I'd made my way to New Shanghai. Hathaway's engagement to an elvish princess named Kamala had been announced. At the time the information had been irrelevant to me. I didn't know either billionaires or any elves in person. Of course, had either owned something precious, I might have made their acquaintance. Or, to be precise, I might have seen them, but they would not have seen me.

Now knowledge of their identities signified everything and explained a lot.

"That's how she's been able to fund her private little army," I murmured to Cameron. "Hathaway's a billionaire."

"Yes, I'm aware," Cameron replied with a twist of the lip, and needlessly gruffly in my honest opinion. "Milady, I'm waiting."

Kamala didn't smile. In fact, she sported no expression whatsoever. "You are one of the Guardians, Mr. Feilong. But that will not afford you any special dispensation."

"If you had no use for me, I would be dead," Cameron said, as though he were baiting our enemies—who outnumbered us in every respect, from weaponry to conquered territory. Was he insane to taunt them so blatantly?

Kamala bowed her head slightly. "You are correct, Guardian. You and I both know why I can't kill you. Yet."

I didn't need a pop-up book either. The bond between a Guardian and his or her Shard was unbreakable. Only death or reforging could intervene and sever the connection. That much at least I'd gathered during our long journey.

Her cool gaze landed on me. "Curious that you should spare the life of the would-be thief, Mr. Feilong. Could it be you... feel for him?"

So that was to be their game, I mused—even as my heart skipped a beat imagining the possibilities of human-dragon love affairs. Our enemies would use me as leverage against Cameron to force him to do their bidding, whatever that was. I refused to be a pawn in their death match, ready to be sacrificed at a moment's notice, so I opened my mouth for an argument.

But Cameron got there first. "Instead of these less than veiled threats, might I ask for an explanation? You are elf-kind; you respect nature, and you know the awesome destructive power the Shards possess. Why take on such a suicidal mission with so little to gain?"

Kamala scoffed, crossing her hands over her chest. "I have no wish to see the world in ruins, if that is what you mean. I was but a wee girl when I first heard the tales of the Watchtowers, the Elemental Shards, and the Guardians. But I do remember them, even after all these centuries."

"She's looking good for her age," I whispered to Cameron off the side of my mouth, and was rewarded by Cameron's muffled chuckle. "Maybe Hathaway likes older women." I had a total Indiana Jones flashback from the days of yore.

Her eyes might have been the color of ice but her glare could burn me to ashes. "How droll. Humans have such a... low-brow sense of humor." Okay, I admit it; I was both offended *and* humbled by her comment, which was made in earnest.

"Being able to laugh in the face of certain death is a human skill I envy," Cameron said out of the blue, surprising the hell out of me. I was but a lowly thief. Why should he revere me in any way, shape, or form?

"Well, I suppose there's no accounting for taste," Kamala said with a drawl, her gaze swiping over me from head to toe. Judging from her obvious discontent, I doubt she saw anything that pleased her judgmental sensibilities.

"What have you done to the Wood Elves residing here?" Cameron asked, switching topics so fast it left my head spinning. I'd forgotten this place had other occupants. None had been in sight, either dead, injured, or imprisoned. Where the hell did everybody go?

Kamala chuckled, an oddly joyless sound coming from her. "You show surprisingly great concern for a people who consider you nothing but a mongrel and who wouldn't grant you the time of day if you begged down on your knees."

Cameron went stone-cold rigid next to me. I could sense his outrage but also how the words stung. To be treated like a pariah by one's own flesh and blood, well, it had to hurt. I wanted to take his hand in mine, to offer comfort and kindness and support. But... no need to give our foes further ammunition.

"They are *my* prisoners," Hathaway interjected, his tone as cold and indifferent as his bride-to-be's. "I've devised a deliciously devious cage for them. If you wish to see them safe and unharmed, I suggest you play ball. Cooperation is key."

Cameron grew quiet, and I worried. Was he close to giving in to the demands of these wrongdoers? But his next words showed he was on to the villains' schemes. "If you had either Lady Vivian or Prince Liro in custody, you would be parading them before me to show how badly you've defeated us. Considering their noticeable absence, I doubt you have as much of an upper hand over the situation as you claim."

Hathaway's handsome face grew ruddy as his anger built until he practically had steam coming out of his ears.

But Kamala smiled mildly. "You are, of course, absolutely correct. Liro and Vivian have barricaded themselves in the Shrine of the Tree of Light."

"Who are these two?" I asked, hating being in the dark and having to ask, showing ignorance in front of our enemies.

Cameron didn't so much as grant me a glance as he replied, "Prince Liro is the leader of the Wood Elves residing here, and Lady Vivian is the Guardian of the Wood Shard, which is kept safe within the Tree of Light, high in the Kuafu mountain range, in the heart of the Enchanted Forest where only Vivian may tread."

Since I'd studied the map of this region on our way here, I recognized the name. Like the golden oak trees, the Kuafu peaks had transferred from the world beyond the Veil to merge with our Earth by displacing a few sections of the Zhangjiajie National Forest. The Kuafu towers were geologically identical with the sandstone pillars natural to the area, only far more massive.

But I'd never heard of any Tree of Light.

"You Guardians are all the same, empathetic and self-sacrificing," Kamala remarked. "You would all fall on your swords to protect each other, the Shards, and the world." She sighed in a show of boredom, which I doubted was real. "You understand the situation, Mr. Feilong, I'm sure. Liro and Vivian might be secure inside the fortifications of the Shrine. But they have no way out and nowhere to go. In effect, they are our prisoners, same as you. I wonder what their response will be once they learn of your capture as well…."

"You can't attack the Shrine," Cameron said wisely, his voice serene and soothing. He had me on my knees, figuratively speaking. Too bad our villainess seemed to have a block of ice where her heart should have been. "Or you risk damaging the Tree of Light. That could destroy the Wood Shard too, the prize you so desperately covet. I have to ask myself why…."

"Tell him nothing, honey," Hathaway said brusquely, crossing his arms over his chest, puffing up to appear larger and taller. His vast resources in conjunction with his obvious corruption were bad enough in my honest opinion. "He's not gonna help us."

"You're human, Hathaway," I cut in for the first time, not bothering to hide my disdain of him. "You do realize if the Shards are reforged, you won't be alone in your evolutionary rise. All of humanity will follow, with who knows what consequences."

Much to my surprise, Hathaway cocked his head, looking confused. "Come again?"

I frowned, and as I exchanged concerned glances with Cameron. His brow was equally marred. "You do know what happens if the five Shards are reforged, don't you?" I asked, baffled at Hathaway's seeming puzzlement.

Hathaway scoffed, rolling his eyes. "Of course I do."

"Anthony, stop." Kamala's command came a breath too late.

"The Veil between our world and the mythical will be restored," Hathaway said, lifting his chin as though he was pleased with himself. "What has been one world in turmoil for over a decade will once again be two separate universes in peace."

I swear I heard an audible click as my jaw dropped. "What the fuck? That's not—"

"Enough!" Kamala stepped forward, her motions so swift I saw nothing but a blur as she transitioned from far away to right in front of me in an instant, smacking me in the face with her backhand, quite effectively silencing me.

Cameron's growl echoed in my ringing ears, and then a thud and a groan of pain told me he'd been subdued. White lights flashed before my eyes, the right side of my face throbbed in pain, and I tasted blood. At least I didn't fall down on my face because that would have hurt more, my fragile male ego the most.

"That the best you got?" I asked in a quivering voice, my knees wobbling like jelly.

Kamala actually chuckled. "You've got spirit, human. I'll give you that."

"I'd prefer you give us the stolen Shards," I shot back, blinking to get my vision to return to normal.

She gripped my chin firmly, her touch so cold frost formed on my skin, and she tilted my head up so her face filled my view. "You've got a lot of nerve chiding me about stealing, thief, when that is all that you are or ever will be. A petty criminal, a small-time felon—"

"I object!" I protested weakly, my jaw and mouth growing numb. She was frigid.

Did she have such a freezing effect on her would-be husband too? Unlikely. Anyway, I figured the cold touch was part of her magical powers rather than a constant state of affairs, or otherwise she and her kind would freeze everything around them, from blades of grass to bones of men. (I think that last part was funny only to me and my teenage-level sense of humor.)

With a contemptuous shove, Kamala pushed me back, forcing me to stagger until one of the guards behind me righted me with another violent shove.

"Pitiful humans," Kamala murmured, sneering at me as she ambled away. "The world will be better off without you in it."

"That include your precious fiancé?" I tossed back. "Has he served his purpose? Given you his time, his devotion, his well-funded private army? Gonna throw him aside now you're done with him too?"

A moment ago I'd begrudged Cameron baiting our vicious enemies, and now I was doing the exact same thing. God, what an idiot I could be!

"She's taking me with her to the other side of the Veil," Hathaway said. He sounded like he meant it too. Was it possible he was a major ignoramus, a brainless puppet being used by a much smarter woman? Wouldn't have been the first time the power behind a man stemmed from a woman, and a kickass woman at that.

Kamala frowned, seemingly displeased, as she cast a smoldering glance at her would-be human husband.

But once again Cameron beat her to the punch. "You said you heard the stories about the Shards as a child, Kamala. What were you told? Surely even the Snow Elves knew the truth of what reforging the Shards could mean." The tension in his being resonated in his voice, giving it a hard edge unlike any I'd heard before.

Kamala quirked an eyebrow and looked thoughtful. Was she actually considering revealing her plans? Unlikely, I surmised. But suddenly she let out an almost defeated-sounding snicker. "It doesn't matter what fairy tales my people spun, whether it's a reconstitution of the Veil or the evolutionary shift forward of an entire species."

"What?" Hathaway asked, his bafflement clearly fighting his rising frustration.

"It's irrelevant," Kamala continued starkly, as though Hathaway hadn't uttered a word. "This world, humans have ruined and devastated it. I am a Snow Elf. I belong to the Ice Dominion, a group dedicated to bringing back the colder days of yore. And this planet is being consumed by global warming as a direct result of human actions, industry, and indifference. You do nothing to stop it. The situation continues to worsen and escalate because of petty human greed and purposeful shortsightedness. You are despicable, unworthy as a species to inhabit this globe."

"So you intend to wipe us out of existence?" I asked quietly, a horrible sinking feeling settling in the pit of my stomach. Not that I thought she was wrong about humans being the cause of global warming, which we were;

but the end didn't justify the means, especially if it meant the extinction of an entire species that could still turn the tide.

Kamala's smile was as icy as her demeanor. "For me and my Snow Elf kin, reforging the Shards is a win-win. Either the Veil is reestablished and we return to our glacial realm, or we gain superior intellect as a species, an advantage we will use to obliterate humanity from this fair world of *ours*." She tilted her head as she locked gazes with me. "Does knowledge of your fate bring you relief, human?"

I wished I had a smart retort to offer. But knowledge of my impending doom did little to aid my cognitive processes.

I had only one shot across the bow left. (Well, truth be told, I had another card up my sleeve, but it wasn't yet time to resort to cheating.)

"Not really," I replied. I stared at Hathaway. "How about you, dude?"

Hathaway ground his teeth. I watched his jaw working. His suspicious gaze shifted to Kamala and then back to me. I think he was developing trust issues. *Stupid man.* He should have asked those questions long ago. I could only hope sowing the seeds of distrust would work in our favor, Cameron's and mine.

But Kamala stepped up to the plate before Hathaway could make his move, whatever it might have been. "Guardian, I will keep you and your thief friend alive for now. But only as long as you're useful to me. Sentinels, take them to the holding cell."

As the sentries, whom I now knew to be both humans and Snow Elves, grabbed us and began hauling us away, Cameron called out to the elf princess, "You can't attack the Shrine!"

Kamala turned away, but her chilly voice reached us nonetheless. "Your opinion is noted but disregarded, Guardian."

Worriedly I glanced at Cameron as we were escorted away. He looked like a lightning rod gathering up a charge. I could only pray he wouldn't explode in close quarters with me.

Chapter Thirteen

"WHY DIDN'T you shift into your dragon form back there? You could've taken them with ease." I waved in the general direction of the palatial structure, now left far behind.

Cameron tapped at the collar around his neck, his features stony and furious. "This is a negation collar. It prevents all uses of magic, including alteration and shapeshifting." He stopped talking and began looking around—casing the joint, same as me.

Our prison cell was identical to the palace, only infinitely smaller and on a single tier, and it resembled a seed or a pod. Made of light-colored wood, the structure collared the tree trunk, suspended in midair. The trunk was smaller than the main trunk of the giant golden oak tree, yet it was still part of the same single tree, as the golden oak had several diverging trunks, spreading to a wide area. Split into three areas—a living room, a bedroom, and a bathroom—the dwelling had little furniture: three lounge chairs and a coffee table occupied the living area, a king-sized bed and a dresser behind a wood-and-paper folding screen composed the bedroom area, and a gray-water shower, a wooden sink, and a composting toilet made up the bathroom. All the basic necessities one might find in a quality hotel suite.

The most curious thing, however, was the fact that there was an empty circular hole around the tree trunk, plus the whole installation was open air. Sure, we were high up, but we could construct a rope....

"How good are you at climbing trees?" I asked, crouching by the round hole to see how far up we were and if the tree bark allowed enough roughness and footing for a trip down.

Behind my back Cameron snorted derisively. I was getting mighty sick of his condescending and demeaning attitude. Nonetheless, his reaction warned me there was something I wasn't seeing.

When I caught what looked like specks of dust in the wind shimmering in the sunlight as the golden orb in the sky peeked through the raggedy clouds, I realized what I was missing.

A single touch, hindered immediately by an electrical rattling sound and a jolt vibrating through my system, told me there was an energy barrier surrounding the whole structure. Despite the visible openings, we weren't going anywhere anytime soon.

I plopped on my butt and surreptitiously observed Cameron. He sat on the bed, his elbows resting on his knees and his head buried in his hands, though he sat stone still, without trembling. Had he succumbed to despair already?

I decided to get his mind off his woes. "I thought these guys were superadvanced. But basically they live in huts in the trees. Not quite the space-age-level tech I was expecting, based on the whole jolt forward in the evolutionary tree thing."

I smirked at the end, hoping to entice even the smallest smile from Cameron. But he continued to brood. I doubted he'd even answer me.

Finally, though, he muttered, "Wood Elves build ecologically sustainable civilizations, and these dwellings are prime examples of their inconspicuous knowledge and craft." He went silent again after that.

My mood was sinking, so I made a second effort to coax an encouraged response from him. "How do they move between the huts and other trees?" Cameron gave me a knowing glance, and his gesture lifted my spirits. I decided to be a prick. "Swinging from liana like Tarzan?"

Cameron rolled his eyes. His rigid expression softened, just a bit. "Don't be ridiculous. They use suspension bridges and elevation platforms."

I considered his sarcasm a win. At least he wasn't quite as depressed as he had been. So I went on, "What I don't get is, why aren't Kamala and Hathaway going for all the Shards at once? It'd be logical, you know. Why snatch them like this, one at a time? They've got the manpower and the resources, but it takes more time and gives us a chance to prepare for an attack." I had the good grace to grimace. "Though we've been a couple of steps behind them so far...."

Cameron grunted as if displeased, but his expression was contemplative, his brow furrowed as he rubbed his jaw, stroking his tiny beard. "I believe they're moving along the creation cycle."

"What's that?" I asked, baffled at yet another new piece of information.

"The elements have a relationship with one another," Cameron explained, his gaze far away, aimed at something in the distance I knew not what. "There's a cycle of creation and a cycle of destruction. Both depict natural progression. In the first, earth bears metal, metal enriches water, water nourishes wood, wood feeds fire, and fire creates earth. In the reverse, earth dams or absorbs water, water extinguishes fire, fire melts metal, metal chops wood, and wood roots part earth."

"Okay," I said hesitantly, not sure if I understood the underlying meaning behind these cycles. "What do they have to do with not gathering all the Shards at once?"

Cameron sighed. I don't think he was impatient with me but weary of the battle. Which I thought was kind of ridiculous since in my humble opinion, the battle hadn't even begun. "I think they're gathering the Shards in the order of the creation cycle so that they can employ their power in the destructive cycle, thus reforging them to maximum disastrous effect."

Okay, that didn't bode well, I mused glumly. It seemed clear that regardless of the end result of reforging the Shards into an Elemental Crystal, Kamala had every intention of completing her grand design. Like she'd said, no matter what, she would come out on the winning side.

If I was really honest with myself, I had to admit that I could think of worse fates than the Unveiled world splintering back into two separate ones. Neither would be destroyed, so that was a positive. But our two universes had been joined for over a decade. Unions had been made, new knowledge had been found, landscapes had been transformed, children had been born. What would be their fate?

Whether I liked it or not, the Unveiled world was committed to a path of joining. What Kamala planned threatened the balance we were only now starting to discover.

No, Kamala and Hathaway could not be allowed to go ahead with their mad plan.

Then again, I seriously doubted Anthony Hathaway would play any kind of role in the events to come. "Hathaway's expendable, isn't he?" I commented to Cameron, mostly rhetorically. "Kamala doesn't really have any need of him anymore. Unless she actually cares for him…."

Cameron had fallen silent as the grave again. His brooding began to grate on my already frayed nerves. Didn't he know he could confide his troubles to me? I'd be glad to shoulder some of his burden.

I made another effort to draw him out of his shell. "I know these Snow Elves are our enemies but, wow, do they have to be such comic book villains? I mean, they must have missed out on orientation, like… how to treat your guests and/or prisoners 101." Nothing. Cameron didn't so much as flinch. It was as if I wasn't even there. I pouted. "How come after all these years, or what I assume to be centuries, you don't have a life partner?"

That did the trick. With a look of disbelief and modest shock, Cameron glared at me. "Is that really a priority right now?" God, but he sounded both bored and vehement as he spat his words at me.

I scowled right back. "Just making small talk. You know, to fill this awkward silence."

Cameron let out a frustrated scoff. "The human penchant for idle chitchat never ceases to amaze me. Idiotic and small-minded people talking about absolutely nothing of consequence. Such a perfect allusion to the human condition."

I stood up in a rush. I was seething with righteous indignation, and pretty justifiably, too, in my honest opinion. "What the fuck, man? Not every goddamn conversation has to be a philosophical debate about the meaning of life."

Cameron stood so slowly it was a miracle he managed to get upright. His eyes sparked like lightning in a summer storm. "I'm surprised you humans ever manage to speak of anything that matters. Perhaps that is because you don't think. You act, and then lament over your mistakes and wrongdoings when it's too late." He took a step toward me. "Need I remind you we wouldn't even be in this mess if it weren't for you and your thieving ways?"

I fisted my hands at my sides, and my head throbbed with fury. "Why the hell are you busting my balls? I was used, same as you, and I've goddamn apologized a dozen—"

"Oh, did I forget to compliment you on that?" Cameron snorted, jeering at me. "Do pat yourself on the back for doing one thing right—after a lifetime of misdeeds and lawlessness."

"I don't deserve that, or your resentment," I countered, so angry I was seeing red. "I've done nothing but stand by you and help you since this whole thing started, though I don't even know you and you've kept things from me, important information I've needed. I've cooperated with you every step of the way. But hey, I'm just a stupid human, right? So no need for you, mister big shot dragon, to say you're sorry. God forbid you'd ever stoop so low as to admit that you're capable of making mistakes, same as us lowly mortals."

I couldn't tell if it was the room that seemed to shrink or if his being, his shadow, his essence suddenly felt like it filled the confined space around us. Either way, I backed off a step or two.

I watched a vein on his temple pulse, his skin flush with the heat of rage, and him bare his teeth as he grimaced. I'd met a whole lot of people in my life who hadn't liked me; heck, I'd even made a mortal enemy or two. But I'd never been at the receiving end of such a glare, a look that could kill. Scared, I retreated another step.

My ire abandoned me. All I felt was fatigue and depression. For the first time, I had to concede to the possibility—no, the likelihood—I wouldn't be walking away from this alive.

In my forlorn state, I murmured in a melancholy tone, "You're never gonna get over me being a thief, are you? No matter what I do, or have done, that's not gonna change. I'm always gonna be… subpar to you. No… subhuman."

Cameron went rigid, his advance interrupted, the flame in his eyes fading. He swallowed hard, and I saw his throat convulse and his Adam's apple jump. He blinked, and his lips parted, as if to speak, but no sounds emerged. Had I struck him silent? I would never have thought that possible.

After breathing laboriously for a minute or two, he uttered in a hoarse voice, "Only because I believe with all my heart that you're capable of so much more. To be a better man." He cringed, as though he knew his declaration wasn't enough. "You are right, Finn. I am sorry. I might be ancient, but as my fears swamp me, I have allowed my basest being to speak hateful words. Please forgive me."

I let out a shaky breath and nodded. "I'm scared too, Cam. But we're in this together. I need you. You can't crap out on me." I waved a hand about. "Pardon the cheap vernacular."

Finally a smile lifted the corners of his sensuous mouth. Why hadn't any of the guys I'd slept with had lips like those? *Sigh.* Due to the sexual flashes cavalcading through my brain, I almost missed his words. "Thank you, Finn. I might not have sounded like it but… I can't imagine doing this without you. Or anyone but you. What you have done for me and the other Guardians…. I am in your debt."

"Pfft." I pursed my lips and rolled my eyes. "You've saved my butt more than once too, you know." The sudden image of his hands squeezing my asscheeks made my breath hitch. Naturally, Cameron gave me a quizzical look. I deflected the inquiry I suspected was to come by saying, "Besides, Cam… to err is human."

Cameron blinked. Then a slow smile crept onto his lips. And then he laughed so hard I worried he'd burst with mirth. "Touché."

I smiled back, delighted I could at least give him this, the gift of laughter. "So… now what?"

His grin was irreverent and mischievous. Looked like his puckish fairy dragon nature had come out to play. "Escape."

Short and to the point, I thought with a chuckle. "I like the way you're thinking, man." I tapped my nose knowingly. "Thankfully I still have some of my gear, plus a surprise."

An astonished expression caused Cameron's eyebrows to rise to his hairline. "But they frisked you. The sentries, I mean."

I snorted loudly and flicked my tongue at him, waving my hand about in a rather drag-queen manner. "Oh, puh-lease. Like I'd let anyone rob *me* blind. Who do you think you're dealing with, a chump?"

With a flourish, I produced a short blade, the tip glittering with a lightning-blue electric glow of magic. The scent of licorice tickled my nose.

Cameron stared at the knife, then at me, then the blade again. "Where…?"

I shrugged, all cool and nonchalant. "I nabbed it from one of the guards." I waved the weapon at the openings shielded by invisible energy barriers. "Let's find out if our cage can handle a little jolt, shall we?"

Cameron cocked his head, his eyes narrowing. "Why didn't you tell me sooner? When I was feeling like we'd already lost the war and was certain we were done for."

I didn't like his tone. "I was planning on waiting till nightfall. We can't try anything until then." Then I glared at him. "Besides… you were a jerk." Cameron's cheeks grew ruddy then, and he lowered his gaze. I smirked, though he didn't see it. "Good thing you were a sexy jerk."

Chapter Fourteen

FOR A while Cameron didn't look up. But I saw his smile appear and widen.

"So, I've been wondering…," I asked, gradually testing the waters. "How come you're alone, without a life partner?" I'd asked before but he'd sidestepped my question. This time I hoped for a better result, namely personal background information. "Do dragons have destined mates like a lot of mythical beings? You know, like werewolves?"

Standing there, astride, hands folded over his chest, Cameron appeared the picture of masculinity. I desired to worship at the altar of his sex. My knees nearly buckled in the wake of my passionate need to follow through on my heated vision.

"No," he finally said, his voice quiet and kind of distant. That was disappointing. My initial assumption was that he was perhaps in mourning for a lost love or was himself a jilted lover. Either way that didn't speak favorably for my chances with him.

"Oh." I had nothing else to give at the moment. It was utterly strange to commiserate a lost love I'd not even had.

"Over the centuries I've had several relationships," Cameron suddenly confessed, his voice echoing a sort of sadness I didn't understand. "Only a small number have included sensuality and sexual relations."

Gosh, but the man could turn even lovemaking—or superhot sex— into a clinical act. "Well, uh, that's okay, I guess. Not every affair has to be, um, you know, carnal." A small chuckle from him only confused me more, so I asked for clarification. "Were your lovers human?"

Cameron shook his head. "No. Dragon-human matings are virtually impossible."

That shocked me as, over time, virtually all kinds of human-mythical being couplings had surfaced into the public eye. "Oh?"

Finally he locked gazes with me, a lopsided grin gracing his luscious lips. "Have you heard of knotting?"

"No." What the heck was he talking about?

Cameron's grin widened wolfishly, giving his stark countenance a savage quality I found stupidly hot. "Some supernatural creatures, such as werewolves and canine shifters, have a penis that expands during climax, making it quite impossible to dislodge. Thus the couple mating stick together for a considerable length of time, and in most cases are able to keep coming for a long time, or go again and again."

Wow, I thought in shock. "Uh-huh. And dragons have this, uh, knotting penis?"

Cameron inclined his head. "In a sense. Our penises expand—and spikes spring up."

"Your cock has… spikes…?" My hole twitched nervously—and my groin burst into flames. I'd never wanted him as much as right then, the lust mixing with fear.

"Yes."

Perhaps the subject required some levity, so I commented, "So… basically you do it like hedgehogs. Extremely carefully?" He snorted. "*Ouch.*" I had moved away to stand in front of the mirror above the dresser to check how much my cheeks had flamed. The mere notion of his spiky dick rammed inside me to the hilt made my stomach clench and my cock jump and pulse eagerly in my pants. "Fuck. I can't think with a hard-on."

I only realized I'd said it out loud when I heard him speak. "You are a most peculiar human. Pain intrigues you?"

Could I confess to a dangerous dragon how much of a pain slut I was? How the idea of him dominating me excited me no end?

I felt him stand behind me, his weight and height all but touching me, encompassing me. A world without touch, yet not void of sensations. "Would you like me to inflict pain on you? Would it feel like… pleasure?"

I snorted derisively to regain control of myself and the spiraling situation. "I bet you never bottom."

Surprisingly, he shoved me forward harshly, my abdomen pressed painfully against the dresser. His hissed words spewed venom. "Don't presume to know anything about me, human."

I could have cowered before him. The thought crossed my mind. But I was getting real sick of being the underdog, so I maneuvered myself around to face him.

"And I'm getting tired of being pushed around," I grunted through gritted teeth.

I shoved Cameron's chest, trying to force him back. But he was an immovable object, like a bolder hindering my path. I couldn't get him to budge an inch, though I used all my strength. *Damn him.*

"You could at least pretend to be intimidated and forced to step back because of my awesome strength," I said grudgingly, pouting and scowling.

Cameron's stern expression smoothed as his shoulders shimmied, and his lips twitched in pent-up amusement. Then his eyes, *qīng* as the green-blue color of nature, darkened like storm skies, he leaned in, and his voice dropped an octave or two.

"And if I don't move back, what are you going to do?" he whispered.

I swallowed hard. My palms, armpits, and groin sweated, but my mouth dried up like a desert. I managed to croak out, "Then I'm gonna kiss you and not let go."

Rather than wait for Cameron's response, whatever it might be, I lunged. I wrapped my arms around his neck and smacked my lips against his. No, it wasn't particularly hot since our mouths were closed and he didn't react. I pulled back an inch, afraid I'd misinterpreted his interest and stepped out of line. Maybe he wasn't gay….

But the pause lasted less than a second. Then he crushed his mouth on mine, as though set on devouring me whole. I happily let him have at me. His lips were soft and firm against mine, but his tongue was hot and insistent, and don't even get me started on the heavenly suction and licking.

There was no hesitation in his kissing, no insecurities, no awkwardness, no stopping. His tongue seemed hell-bent on tracing every inch of my mouth, our teeth clicking slightly, our lips fused, our breaths mingling.

I whimpered into the kiss, going pliant against him. He wound his arms around my midsection and held me tight, compressed against his solid, lean, and muscular frame. I felt too hot for my clothes, and I slipped my hands under his yellow silk shirt, relishing the velvety skin and the corded muscles, the hidden strength and the power rippling inside his body.

He was majestic as a man and as a dragon.

Cameron slipped his hands lower, to the small of my back. His touch was featherlight, but I felt it all the way down to my curling toes. I rose up on my tippy-toes and held onto him fiercely. He pushed his stout thigh between my legs, his brawny thigh muscle pressing potently on my balls and cock.

With one hand he cradled the back of my head while the other slid down to squeeze my buttcheek. I shivered, riding his robust thigh wantonly, losing my self-control.

He shifted to cup my ass with both hands, lifted me into his lap, and a second later I lay on my back on the bed, bouncing from the force of his throw. As proof of the high standards of elvish craftsmanship, neither the bed nor the structure so much as vibrated.

Then he was on top of me, his weight crushing me in a way I deeply needed it to, his heat searing me even through the layers of our clothes, his body trapping me between him and the bed, and his mouth on mine, delving and probing with gusto. His kiss was ferocious but his touch was a mix of gentle caress and rough fondling. I could not decide which I preferred.

I longed to feel more skin, to have our bodies really touch, without barriers. I clung to him, trying to get underneath his clothes, clawing at him. Cameron grunted into the kiss and bit my lower lip, stinging me, a taste of blood flowing over my tongue, and I trembled inside and out.

"God, how you kiss me," I murmured once he'd released me, licking the hurt away and peppering me with soft, wet smooches.

He framed my face with one hand, a lingering brush that left me wanting more, warmed to the core. "I've wanted to kiss you since we met," he said in a sincere, serious tone.

I barked out a laugh. "I was sure you wanted to eat me."

He pressed his forehead against mine, still petting the side of my face. "Only certain parts of you." His smile suggested delectable possibilities for the future.

I answered with one of my own. "Are you going to?"

His eyebrows rose in query. "Eat you up?"

"Make love to me." Funny but I'd never used such a romantic phrase before, certainly not in the sack. Was he the sole reason for my poetic turn of phrase? Or did our dire straits have something to do with my choice?

A low chuckle warned me I'd be hearing a sarcastic remark. But his tone remained soft and tender. "Of course I am, Finn. Sunset is still hours away, and like you said, we can't make a move until then."

"So I'm a mere time-filler?" I added a chuckle to the end to show it was a joke, but my voice still cracked uncontrollably.

A firm chiding look from him and I had my answer. He wanted me. "When you asked me about human-dragon couplings, it occurred to me that I'm wearing a negation collar." I stared up at him in confusion, and he chuckled low. "This unique situation makes it possible for us to indulge in a number of sexual activities that normally might be... uncomfortable with a human partner."

I gulped, my heart lodged in my throat. I imagined my eyes were as wide as saucers as I gazed up at him, mesmerized. "Oh. Well, that's... good, I guess." What the hell was I saying? It was brilliant. He and I could have all the sex we wanted without me having to worry about an ass stuffed full of spikes. Although, I wasn't particularly concerned about that.

Cameron grinned like he could read my salacious mind, one hot thought at a time, and see right through my horny self. "Yes. But just so you know... the spikes will still be there."

My jaw dropped with a click. "O-oh...?" Before he decided to stop, I added in a rush, "I want that. You, I mean. Every part of you. All of you." I had a hunch the pain he'd inflict with his cock would serve to enhance the pleasurable experience.

He threaded a hand through my hair, grabbing it to force my head to fall back. "I know. I sense your willingness to submit."

"Cops and robbers has always been one of my enduring fantasies." I spoke before my brain caught on to my mouth. My mind filled with images of cuffs and riding crops, dominance and submission, pain and pleasure, Cameron and me.

Cameron laughed, but he wasn't making fun of me. I think he liked the way my dirty mind worked. His words confirmed as much. "Tying you up so you can't escape, master thief, and gagging you so you can't talk back, all that tickles my fancy."

Heat suffused me, and my hunger for his flavors grew. "Then shut me up with your cock," I dared him, lifting my chin in defiance, totally goading him.

He gripped my chin, showing his easy supremacy over me. His beautiful slanted eyes burned with a dark fire that excited and scared me. "Giving me orders, human?" His growl stirred across my skin like a vibrating sensual touch. I ached for him. "I forbid you to move."

When he pulled back, kneeling between my legs, his back straight and his position imposing, I nearly creamed myself. I raised my hands above my head and stayed perfectly still as he slowly divested me of my clothes.

Wanting to obey in bed reflected my independent way of life out of bed, I suppose. I can't explain it, but at that moment nothing turned me on more than the idea of following his each and every command.

Cameron took his time, his movements unhurried, his care gentle and exploratory, his smile sweet and beckoning. His unique odor, sort of smoky, hung in the air. I puzzled if that was the scent of his arousal or simply a result of his dragon's fire-breathing.

When I lay on the bed naked at last, Cameron studied me, his expression revealing nothing. I longed for him to like and appreciate what he saw, desire me and covet my sex, even wish to keep me, heart and body and soul.

Cameron placed his hands on my thighs. I jumped at the touch. His skin was rough, warm, and dry, and I needed him to move up and fist my needy cock as it lay heavy, thick, and wet on my trembling belly. But Cameron smiled, as if my frustration only fueled his devilish seduction, so slow it drove me insane.

He slipped his palms down to my inner thighs, the coarse skin of his fingers not only a testament to his beast but abrasive on my sensitive skin. He pushed my legs farther apart, and I gasped. I was open and fully exposed for his viewing pleasure.

I waited with bated breath to find out what he would do with me next.

Chapter Fifteen

"YOUR HAZEL eyes remind me of... acorns," Cameron murmured above me, startling me out of the sensual cloud I floated on.

I chuckled breathlessly. "My, uh, nuts are all yours."

With a quirky grin, Cameron inched his hands up and down my thighs, always skirting past my cock and balls. I had a feeling his long years had taught him a thing or two about the art of edging and other forms of sexual torment. He sure was taking his time.

Cameron slid his hands beneath my buttocks until he cupped one in each palm. Then he yanked me closer till my balls nuzzled his chest. I drew in a sharp breath, which turned into a moan. I fisted my hands above my head as I fought for control. The need for my hips to move, buck, and gyrate till I found something hard to rub against was an urge difficult to rein in.

"Shh, be at ease, Finn. We're just getting started. No need to rush over the finish line." His amused scolding caused my cheeks to flame with embarrassment.

Then again, with my previous lovers—all guys I'd fucked, seeking release over learning their bodies and what made them moan—there'd been no need to take my time. We'd all gone straight for the cock and ass; no finesse required.

I realized with Cameron I wanted to savor each precious moment, not simply because at the end of our journey one or both of us might be dead, but because I believed he was the lover I had always fantasized about and dreamed of, adventurous and passionate, patient and caring, ardent and down-to-earth.

He rested his palms on my hipbones, his touch like fire. I bucked up, unable to help myself. He gently pushed me back down, framing my cock between his splayed fingers. Heat from his body suffused into mine, causing my cock to leak hot droplets of precome over my quivering belly. I groaned, closing my eyes.

"Sigmund told me humans can lack forbearance to truly indulge in the pleasures of the flesh, to delve deep into an ocean of carnality." Cameron's voice made me swallow, my mouth dry, and I quivered. "I'm pleased you're allowing me to set the pace."

A part of me, the dark side of my persona, held within secrets of past sexual acts. No matter how badly I wanted to tell him what I needed, I feared his judgment and disapproval. Most people associated pleasure with sex; few understood how pain could grant an orgasm beyond this world too. For me, being with Cameron had to be enough in itself. I had hinted at being a pain slut, but I couldn't find my voice to beg for my hidden needs.

So I stayed silent, my eyes closed, my body putty in his hands.

Then Cameron raked his nails, sharper than those of human, across my hipbones, from my sides to my upper thighs. Pain sliced through me, and my eyes flew open.

"How like you my brand of loving, Finn?" Cameron asked, his voice low and sinister.

I gasped, staring at him in amazement. "C-can you read my mind…?"

Cameron's eyes narrowed. "I have lived a long time. I had not expected to discover a consort who would be compatible with my sexual appetites." He leaned over me, his sizable bulk menacing as he hovered, a mere shadow as daylight shone above him. "And a human one at that." His gaze swept over me, head to toe. "I have put my mark on you."

He'd drawn blood. "Yeah, you have." My voice was nothing but a whisper.

Cameron dipped his head and licked across the wounds, lapping up the blood, leaving nothing but a trace of red. I took a breath, watching him with a rising concern. Dragons didn't really eat humans… did they?

But as Cameron rose, I saw my wounds had healed. Only thin white lines were left, and even they were fading fast. Cameron chuckled at my perplexed expression. "I wouldn't eat you, Finn. All Guardians have healing powers. Muirín is the strongest of us in that regard, though."

I nodded but my bafflement hadn't evaporated. "You were proud of marking me. Then you make the marks vanish?"

"To show you I can heal you from anything—and to demonstrate I can make new ones whenever I wish." He sounded confident, strong, and self-assured, all man and beast, ready, willing, and able to dominate me in any way he chose.

How on earth could I not be attracted to a man who understood me so well?

CAMERON'S UNBUTTONED silk shirt parted as he straightened above me, revealing long expanses of beautiful, unmarred, tanned skin. What could his lineage be? Asian, surely. Beyond that, I couldn't guess. He was as mysterious as the earth, nature, space. I knew I'd never find out all his secrets.

I was proceeding purely on instinct. That and sexual desire. Plus, lurking in the back, in the shadows, a need for an intimate connection that expanded beyond the physical. I hoped he'd be able to fulfill all my dreams of the perfect lover.

With the fingers of his right hand, Cameron brushed over my balls. I gasped, anxious for more. A dragon's talon scraped the tender sac, and I jumped at the touch. Cameron's eyes grew dark and dangerous. It was mad to want him, a stranger and a mythical beast rolled into one, but I did, so much. God help me, but I did.

He rolled my balls in his palm, a squeeze here, a scratch there. He was driving me nuts all right. Lowering, Cameron took my right nipple into his mouth, a soft suction accompanied by an occasional lick around the hardening peak. I shuddered, a nearly unbearable heat pooling at the base of my cock.

Man, he was good at lovemaking. Slow and steady wins the race, as the saying goes. He must have coined the phrase.

I held on to his broad shoulders, his muscles jumping under my caresses and grips. His long black hair flowed over my skin, a whisper of sensation, a kiss from a breeze. Cameron moved onto my other nipple, this time adding sharp teeth to the mix. I jolted when he sank his fangs into the areola, but a couple of quick licks from him and the pain subsided. The bleeding stopped as well.

Cameron kissed his way up to my neck to suck on the sweet spot just below my ear, his lips and tongue caressing my skin and giving me goose bumps. When he sucked softly, my ears filled with the roar of blood, my heart thudding hard. He made me wish our loving would be never-ending.

Finally, oh finally, his fingers wrapped around my aching cock. But instead of a sweet, leisurely stroke, he fisted the base, staving off my impending release with a steely grip that caused all the blood in my groin to pool at my fast reddening cockhead.

"You fiend," I murmured into his ear. My reward was a seductive chuckle.

Then his hands were everywhere, and his body encompassed me. I felt as though our skin kissed at every single spot, uniting us. His bulk landed fully on top of me, and he rocked back and forth, a sensuous swaying that brought our hard, hot cocks into nuzzling range, exchanging wet kisses of their own.

Cameron kissed me, a savage thrust that took what he wanted, namely me. I answered in kind, sinking my teeth into his full bottom lip till I tasted blood. He grunted, and his hips bucked. So, my beautiful dragon wasn't immune to a little pain play either. Perhaps he'd lived long enough to see all kinds of loving. I definitely approved.

He shoved me down, separating from me. He stared at me, pinning me with his golden dragon eyes and his hands on my wrists. Yet our lower bodies touched, and maybe to punish me, he never stopped moving, his hips snapping fiercely up and down, teasing me with a closeness I craved with every cell in my body.

Then he let go entirely, retreated minutely, knelt between my legs again, and took my cock deep down his throat. He licked, sucked, and swallowed. He pressed the tip of his tongue on the sensitive spot under the mushroom head, and with that single tantalizing touch, he owned me. As he sucked on my cockhead, slithering over my leaking slit, the wet silken heat and enveloping pressure left me a puddle of desire and crying out hoarsely. Anyone within earshot heard me in my most wanton state.

When Cameron added his hand to the mix, using both his fingers and his mouth to get me off, nothing short of a cock-ring from hell could stop me from climaxing.

"Cam, I'm gonna come," I pleaded, my voice all but gone.

Cameron pulled off, a lewd wet pop as he let my dick drop from between his lips. He looked down at me, grinning smugly. "Humans. Always rushing." He leaned over me briefly, his face stern, a warning. "No coming until I say."

I desperately sought to turn the tables on him and take some of his control. But every part of me that enjoyed sex told me to let him do as he pleased. I was certain my delight and release would be far better off, no pun intended.

So I didn't command him to get to it, to the final lap, to the fucking.

Did it make me a sexual "freeek" if I admitted to myself that I wanted nothing more than to feel his spiked, knotted cock rammed deep inside me? Maybe George Michael could tell me.

AGAIN CAMERON left my cock to weep alone on my belly. His hands glided along my body, up and down my sides, gently tickling my nipples, stroking my arms and legs, fondling my asscheeks, groping my balls, and caressing my face, as though he were memorizing my features for the future.

I didn't stop him, with words or deeds.

After a long while keeping me on the knife's edge of delight, he flipped me over to my stomach. I landed on the comforter with a thump and *oomph*. He parted my buttocks, stuffed his face in my crack, and let his tongue travel, making me writhe and mewl. Cameron suckled on my hole, leaving it twitching madly, and stuck his tongue inside, wiggling about.

"Oh, sweet Jesus, don't stop." I felt no shame in begging. He domineered me, in control of my pleasure as well as his own. I think he preferred me entreating him. "God, that feels so good."

It was kinda funny. I was the thief, but Cameron stole my breath away.

Cameron hooked his arms under my hips and yanked me upward a bit, closer to him, as I opened nicely for his talented tongue. He bit my buttcheeks, stinging my fleshy mounds, and then went on to eat out my hole, an unrelenting assault I had no desire to battle against. I buried my head in the pillow and let the waves of pleasure crash over me.

At long last—a few minutes or an hour later, I didn't know for certain—he kissed, licked, and fondled his way up my back till he covered me like a hot blanket.

I liked that he was bigger than me, stronger and more adept. His domination over me rated at the top of my sexual bucket list.

Cameron's hard cock, much bigger than I'd expected, lodged in my buttcrack. And he rocked back and forth, his uncut dick, wet with precome, sliding deliciously between my asscheeks. His balls touched mine, his cockhead tickling over my perineum until my hole spasmed in desperate need to feel him inside me.

"Oh God, please fuck me, Cam," I beseeched him, shameless and lustful, my prick trapped between my belly and the comforter, my body shimmying on the bed in search of greater friction.

"Not yet," he breathed in my ear, his warm breath fanning over the sweaty skin of my neck, making me shiver. His little beard tickled my shoulder till I squirmed. "No rushing, Finn. My pace, remember?"

Gathering me in his arms and spreading his legs to trap me between them, he ensured his motions kept me on the precipice of pleasure. God, but I wanted him inside me. But he didn't grant me anything swiftly. Slow seemed to be the name of the game. I whined beneath him, trying my best to move despite his strong, muscular bulk on top of me.

My impatience must have shown because Cameron pushed off me, and I feared he'd grown tired of my hurrying things along. But as I glanced over my shoulder, I saw him spit on my hole. He used his fingers to get me ready, as if his tongue, saliva, and precome hadn't already done the trick.

He gripped my hips and pulled me up, the backs of my thighs against the fronts of his. The tip of his impressive cock nudged my opening, and I sighed in satisfaction.

Yesss....

Chapter Sixteen

I DIDN'T feel the spikes at first. Cameron's blunt, silky cockhead breached my puckered hole, and I could have sworn I heard the pop reverberate within me. He made a slow foray up my channel. He was big. Bigger than any guy I'd ever been with.

And he was hot. I don't mean his dick was just sexually attractive—it was literally burning hot. Perhaps it was a result of his dragon nature. I had no clue. Hard as a rock and straight as a pole, his cock stuffed me full to the point I panted laboriously trying to accommodate his size.

I finally figured out what he'd meant about knotting. A part of his cock, below the head, felt bigger than the rest of his shaft, sort of swollen. He already filled me to the brim, so an anxious sensation lodged in the pit of my stomach as I imagined him growing further inside me. How would it feel? Would I burst apart at the seams?

Yet he didn't surge inside me, didn't once move too fast for me. In fact, in between heartbeats, he progressed so steadily and slowly that at times I felt as though he hadn't shifted at all. But when he descended to rest on my back again, I knew he was close to being all the way inside.

After a while Cameron whispered, "Like my cock, Finn? You're so tight. But I know your ass loves me."

His words were far dirtier than I'd expected from him. From the beginning he'd come off as a Chinese gentleman of yore, civil and debonair in a way I'd never cared to be. This kind of sexy trash talk surprised me.

"Love it," I murmured breathlessly, tilting my head so Cameron could plant a kiss on my cheek, on the corner of my lips. "Are you all the way in yet?"

Cameron chuckled seductively. "Why? Can't you feel me?" He punctuated his words with a little thrust forward, his cock advancing an inch or two.

I cried out, my voice muffled in the fresh floral-scented pillow. But it was Cameron's smoky, piney odor that pushed all my buttons. "Oh, Cam. God, yes…."

Cameron changed tactics in an instant. Instead of pushing forward, he drew back a bit.

And that was when I felt the spikes. "Oh, yeah. I can feel them now. *Ow ow ow ow.*"

These weren't bone spikes, I could tell. They had to be cartilage or tendon, or similar in substance and structure, for they didn't hurt me as much as they tickled. The scrape did sting, but it was a fleeting perception, nothing like what I'd feared before.

Then the spikes jabbed across my prostate. I didn't so much cry out as howl, a pang of pain and pleasure stabbing me right in my sweet spot.

"Ah, yes, my beautiful human," Cameron muttered into my ear and sank his fangs into my neck, the bite piercing the skin only a bit. "I hear the word echo from your mind, calling out to me. Pain slut." I trembled as he said the words, heat pooling in my groin and my skin prickly with goose bumps. "How do you like me now? Once you go dragon, you don't go back."

I laughed breathlessly at his pun, one I hadn't anticipated from a mind as ancient and powerful as his. But it was true: he got me. He understood what I was all about even though we hadn't ever actually talked about each other's sexual preferences.

When he pushed in next, I felt his balls press tight against my ass crack. He was inside to the hilt. I whimpered, a gust of hot, moist air that my lungs couldn't hold anymore. He filled me so utterly and profoundly, I felt as though the very essence of Cameron now dwelled within me. And fuck, if that wasn't a hot notion. His spiked cock ignited all the nerve endings in my channel, a flash of pleasure spiking in my groin till droplets of precome bubbled out of my slit.

"You humans don't appreciate lovemaking as much as us mythical beings," Cameron said quietly. My eyelids fluttered open, and I looked up to find him staring down at me with a rapt expression full of pure lust and ravenous hunger.

I snorted. "What? Are you keeping records?"

Cameron flicked his tongue at me—and I saw the tip was two-pronged, like that of a snake. So that had been the extra sensation I'd felt when his tongue seemed to be everywhere when he'd sucked my prick and played with my hole.

"I've been known to make mad passionate love for days and nights, and that was just round one." Cameron sounded curiously cool as he said those words, ones that coming from anyone else would have sounded like boasting or exaggerating.

But in my heart I knew he spoke the truth. Cameron wasn't one for hyperbole.

"I wish we could do that," I whispered, glancing warily around us. But the forest green was all I saw, an impenetrable wall of lush vegetation and glimpses of faraway horizons. "But if we intend to escape and free the elves from captivity, we can't indulge in an all-night orgy." I groused about that under my breath. Why'd I have to meet the perfect lover while in danger of death?

Suddenly Cameron pulled back, leaving me bereft of his touch and weight on me. But he merely straightened up, gathered me in his arms, and lifted me into his lap, my back to his chest. I felt his heart beating the same rapid staccato beat as my own, and we were in perfect sync.

He wound his arms around my chest, one close to my neck, the other pressing tight on my belly. My legs parted to bend at the knees next to his, but his hips never stopped moving, showing how strong he was to keep me up just enough to facilitate his special brand of fucking.

"There's always next time," Cameron huffed next to my temple, his breath brushing a few strands of my hair out of place.

"Oh?" I chuckled. "What happened to the pessimist I spoke to a while back?"

"I suppose some of your positivity rubbed off on me," he teased, and I heard the smile in his voice. He planted an openmouthed kiss on my shoulder, on the same spot where he'd bitten with his dragon fangs. I shivered.

"Through osmosis, more like," I taunted right back, wiggling my butt and squeezing my inner muscles, clamping down on his cock lodged inside me.

Cameron laughed. I still had a knack for humor, I thought, pleased with myself. "But I haven't even come yet. Guess I better put my back into it."

He lifted me slightly, straining his arms. I looped my own arms over to the back of his neck and felt his corded muscles, taut and hot and sweaty, with my fingertips. *Man, I love gay sex. Good to be a man and a bottom.* Cameron was bold and able-bodied, holding me in his arms with a relaxed, confident ease.

But there was nothing suppressed or held back in his thrusts as he pounded into me. I brought one hand down and dug my fingers into his brawny bicep, loving the feel of his potency on me and in me. What were shallow thrusts at first soon grew deeper, faster, and harder as he reamed me good. No, better than good; he was divine.

Now his spikes touched me more prominently, scraping sharply across the length of my channel. Yet, it still didn't hurt tremendously. An edge of pain sliced through me but morphed into pleasure in a split second. The sensations blended into a concoction of delight, elevating a sexual encounter into a heavenly experience.

"W-why don't they h-hurt?" I asked, my breath choppy and my voice raspy.

"The spikes?" Cameron sucked up a mark on my neck, then another. My eyes rolled to the back of my head. "They get sharper when I'm close to climaxing, but they also inject a chemical concoction of endorphins, dopamine, and oxytocin into my lover's system. The so-called pleasure hormones."

I laughed. "You drug your sex partners? Groovy. Far out." I tried to make the peace sign, but Cameron growled and took my offending fingers in his mouth, laving them and suckling on them softly. Fuck, but I'd never known getting this much attention on my hands would feel this damn fine.

Perhaps to punish me for my jesting, Cameron slipped his hand between my thighs and tugged on my nuts, his touch on the borderline between gentle and rough. Oh yeah, I was definitely a fan. Then he gripped my achingly rigid, engorged cock and stroked leisurely. For every stroke he pounded into me twice or thrice, the paces sort of matching.

"Oh, you're so cruel," I admonished, out of breath, deaf from my heart beating in my ears.

"Enjoying our time together is cruel?" Cameron nipped at my earlobe to chide me. I quaked, my hips bucking as I desperately tried to follow his motions, to grind myself on his dick. But he merely tightened his hold of me, keeping me in line. "I wish to give you pleasure, Finn. Accept it by savoring this moment. However long it lasts."

Easier said than done. My previous sexual escapades weren't really that. They'd been fast, superficially satisfying, and over quicker than it took to get undressed, on the few occasions we ever got to that point.

So the idea of relaxing into him and letting go seemed strange. I had no experience with that kind of sex. But I did the best I could. I leaned back, gripped his arms, and stopped trying to fight him. His hips snapped back and forth as he moved, and as I rested my head on his shoulder and loosened up, I think I opened up more to him because his pace quickened and his cock entered me more deeply.

I moaned in delectation. And that was when I reached the right headspace. I must have since an intoxicating haze enveloped my brain, silencing everything. Only his body and mine existed in the whole wide world. I sighed, closed my eyes, and let him make love to me.

I couldn't tell how much time passed. An hour, two, half a day? Perhaps.

Cameron's cock felt like hot steel inside me, pulsing with a power coming from his masculinity and beastly qualities? I didn't know and didn't care. His hand rubbed my dick up and down, unhurried, unrushed—perfect.

Finally I understood what he'd been after. How the sex act morphed into something… exquisite, transcending the physical, time slowing to a crawl, space folding in on itself around us. My pleasure grew and built, seemingly without end, always flying me higher till stars exploded around me.

And my dick exploded too. Spasms wracked my body as ropes of sticky come splattered on me, him, the bed, everywhere. I screamed. I almost doubled over as the tremors quaked within me, but he kept a hold of me, his hips pistoning inside me so fast and rough I had no words for it.

Cameron grunted deep in his throat, and he swelled inside me. The spikes stung sharp as they embedded into my flesh inside. Then a wave of pleasure crashed over me, undoubtedly from the chemical overload, and sent me whirling into space.

Teeth clenched, I sobbed, not knowing why. I felt raw and exposed and vulnerable. I was tender, and he held me through it all, whispering soothing nonsense in my ears, though I could not distinguish a single word. I was grateful, for this novelty tore me up inside.

His cock grew impossibly large within me, and I knew we'd be joined at the hip for a good long while. I felt liquid fire burst in my passage as he ejaculated, growing rigid, holding his pose for what seemed like ages, a statue of a dragon god of transcendental sex.

Then Cameron rocked us both slowly, back and forth, a calming manner about him now that the pleasure had crested and ebbed. I clung to him, even as his hips kept swaying a little, keeping us close and in touch.

My sweet spot felt bruised and battered, overstimulated and used. But in the best way possible. Had I been able to move an inch, I would have fallen on my knees and worshiped with ardor at the feet of my stunning dragon and his thick dick.

But sleep beckoned. We had a bed to rest in, a shower in the back, and a bowl of fruit and a water jug on the table so that once we roused ourselves later we could sate our hunger and thirst. Sometimes being imprisoned and forced to sit on our hands had benefits.

Gently, as though he were handling a priceless piece of glass or art, Cameron laid me down on the bed and lay behind me, spooning me in the safe circumference of his strong arms. It wasn't a position I had much personal experience with, as my sexual partners tended to be on their merry way once a climax had been reached.

Now I wondered why the hell I had ever avoided this.

Hot like a furnace, Cam gathered me close, his breath on my neck, his cock stuck inside me. Every move either he or I made sent a shiver of pleasure coursing through my body as his swollen, knotted cock shifted. No wonder Cameron had initially believed a human couldn't handle this.

So out of curiosity, I asked quietly, "How much bigger would you be exactly if you didn't wear that negation collar? Your cock, I mean."

Cameron rubbed his face on the back of my neck, inhaling deeply, as though he could not get enough of my scent. Nuzzling, it was called. "Considerably. Few mythical beings can handle a copulation with a dragon in his full form. No human, surely."

I considered his response. Was he denying such a thing purely out of some protective instinct? Or was there more to it than he was letting on? "But you've had human lovers in the past, right?"

"On occasion," he replied slowly, sounding pensive or maybe hesitant. "It is extremely difficult and time-consuming to attempt to control my form during lovemaking."

Well, that explained a lot. "That's why you like to go slow. Edging and stuff like that."

"I prefer to call it tantric." Cameron did come off a little snooty, but apparently he had good reason. "With other dragons, matters are less complicated. Also, I can stay awake for several days and nights without requiring sleep. But humans are not so fortunate. That is why tantric, or going slow as you called it, is problematic with them."

I glanced at him over my shoulder, his face once again unreadable, even a bit closed off. I frowned. Wow, he didn't even wait to slip out of me before retreating into his inner solitude. "We did okay, didn't we?" I asked, unfortunately rather defensively. I wish I'd been able to keep the hurt out of my voice better. But right after amazing sex, with a man still inside you, it was hard to be unemotional and ignore harsh words.

Cameron looked away, blocking me from seeing the truth behind his fallen eyelids and long black lashes. I hated that he brought a barrier between us. "We did," he said, and I knew there was a *but* coming. "But... I wouldn't try this again without the negation collar."

I turned away, settling my head on the pillow, trying not to feel rejected. "Of course, I understand," I replied. My voice cracked, but only a little. I guess I was a quick study when it came to this emotional detachment thing.

Cameron let out a long breath. Then he whispered in a contemplative tone, "Maybe I need to get my hands on a negation collar of my own. For future... emergencies." I heard the smile and amusement in his voice. His arms tightened around me briefly before he loosened his grip and squirmed, making himself comfortable. Then he kissed me between my shoulder blades, giving me goose bumps and heart palpitations. "Sleep well, Finn."

I lay there on the bed, huddled in his embrace, gobsmacked. Guess he wasn't planning on ditching me after all, sexually or otherwise. In fact, he seemed to have specific designs for round two. On an undefined future date. With me.

Well, fuck a duck.

Chapter Seventeen

"ARE YOU sure that is safe?" Cameron asked, concern tinting his tone.

I glanced at him over my shoulder, frowning in confusion. I assumed he was joking. "I have rubber soles, so… yeah." I rolled my eyes and returned to the task at hand, specifically to the magical electric blade I'd "borrowed" from one of the sentries before they'd locked us up. "Honestly, Cam. You're an ages-old dragon and you claim ignorance about electricity? Come on."

Out of the corner of my eye, I saw Cameron's sun-kissed skin redden slightly, and his lips pursed as though he were vexed. I rather liked the idea of him worrying about my safety and well-being.

As titillating as it was to observe Cameron blushing, I focused on steadying the knife handle between the rubber soles of my black sport shoes. Since rubber doesn't conduct electricity, my shoes were the best available insulation for when I attempted to short-circuit the energy barrier between our fancy cage and the tree trunk.

"Ready?" I asked Cameron, who crouched behind me, ready to yank me away if things went awry. Cameron grunted his acquiescence, but I knew he wasn't a fan of this plan. Perhaps one reason was the fact that I'd devised it. "You told me yourself that Kamala will undoubtedly attack the Shrine in the morning, completing her incursion by noon when the Tree of Light is at its strongest, and the magic within—"

"Yes, yes, I'm well aware of our necessity for haste." Cameron sounded grumpy—and human. I kind of liked that aspect of him but wisely chose not to antagonize him further.

I pressed the button on the knife, and a magical energy blast lit up the sharp tip with blue lightning. Hissing sounded crisp in the air, and I felt the hairs on my body stand up.

I angled the knife to the proper position and lowered it to the ring on the floor around the tree trunk. I swallowed hard, closed my eyes, and dropped my feet, praying there was enough juice to short out the barrier. A harsh rattling sound accompanied a bright flash—and the smell of burning.

"It worked." Cameron sounded awed.

I took his amazement at my talents in stride. I opened my eyes, withdrew my feet, and let the blade clatter to the floor. The metal smoked, scorched. My soles smoked too, but I'd expected them to melt, if only a bit.

The best part, though, was receiving visual confirmation that the energy barrier of our confinement had dissipated.

We were free. Sort of.

I jumped up and hopped in place to ensure my shoes wouldn't catch fire. Cameron and I then hunkered over the round opening.

The drop was considerable. Though we were about halfway up the tree, the fall had to be several hundred feet from my precarious vantage point alone. In addition, the bark was coarse but hardly enough to give us much needed hand- and footholds. Climbing down seemed a task best accomplished by bugs or winged animals.

I cringed at the sight. "I've gotten us this far. Got any ideas, genius?" I tapped at the cool metal collar around his neck. "Any chance of prying this off you?"

Cameron huffed out an angry breath. "Magic locks and unlocks it. No amount of force can rip it apart, as far as I know." He wiggled his fingers underneath to show that no matter how his arms strained and his muscles grew taut, the metal didn't twist, bend, or so much as dent.

"Damn. I see what you mean." I let out a breath I'd been holding, wishing in the back of my mind that his magic could counteract whatever spells kept the collar bound to his human shape. Alas, no such luck. I took an assessing gander at the bed. "You think there's enough bedding to make a sheet rope with?"

Cameron stared at me like I'd grown a second head. Then he burst out laughing. "And here I worried you didn't have a plan."

I narrowed my eyes as I glared at him. "Hey, don't dis the plan unless you've got one in the works. And I don't think you do, buddy." I crossed my arms over my chest, preparing for an argument. But a curious thought occurred to me. "Wait. Didn't you partially shift when we were...?" I rolled my wrist in the you-know-what gesture.

Cameron quirked an eyebrow, most likely as a response to my avoidance of a specific term. "My nails are dragon claws, no matter the size. Therefore it wasn't shapeshifting, not strictly speaking."

"Oh. So you're never 100 percent human?" I sought confirmation.

"No." The answer I was expecting. Cameron inspected the opening with a discerning eye. "There are a couple of branches to hold on to."

"Nah. They don't go all the way down, not enough to help us." I huffed in irritation. "If I still had my backpack, I'd have all my gear, including rope."

"Exactly what kind of gear does a thief have?" Cameron asked in a suspicious tone.

I shrugged nonchalantly. "The usual. A bump key, pry bar, rappelling/ abseiling rope, blowtorch, gloves, screwdriver, lock picks, glass cutter, blackjack, wire cutters, forgery tools, bolt cutters, grappling hook, base-jumping parachute, Swiss army knife, lighter and matches, medical kit, extra pair of gloves, that sort of thing. And that's just the low-tech stuff." I grumbled. "But now I don't have any of them on me."

Cameron smiled at me, as if the world showed only its brightest side to us. "And here I thought you were an optimist. You're a thief, so aren't you also an escape artist by default?"

"Duh." I waved my hand at him, dismissing his suggestive insult. "Dude, that'd imply I ever got myself in a jam or close to an arrest. I never have. I'm the best." I lifted my chin so high it was ridiculous. Humbly, I lowered my gaze. "Your dragon magic, is it the same as the power of the Earth Shard?"

"No." Cameron cocked his head, his expression one of puzzlement, as he continued pensively, "As a dragon, I have special abilities that few mythical beings, if any, possess. As a Guardian, I have a couple of others."

"Any of those such that you can use them in your human form?" I asked, getting excited by the notion that the collar didn't inhibit his skills absolutely.

Cameron gave me a flicker of a grin. "Actually... yes."

Brimming with newfound hope, I gestured for him to get on with it. The sun had set some time ago, so the night gave us the cover of darkness. But that advantage wouldn't last long.

Cameron nodded. He sat down, cross-legged, and assumed a Zen pose, the full lotus, lifting his feet upon his thighs, squaring his back, and resting the backs of his hands over his knees. Clearly not a first-timer to the arts of yoga and Zen, I concluded. His breathing evened out, his eyes closed, and his expression became serene. Like a statue of harmony, he appeared divinely beautiful to me.

I wondered what kind of powers he would be tapping into, how much of them inherent and stemming from within, and what might be borrowed from nature. I kept waiting, anxiously worrying my lower lip, fidgeting in place from one foot to the other, my arms crossed over my chest to keep them from shaking.

The wait seemed to last forever. Then I heard Cameron chanting, his words a whisper, his meaning carried with the winds to hidden places unknown.

Shattered rock and pillars shake,
Stones will grind, ground will quake,
Boulders chip and pebbles flake,
Crumbled soil and mountains break,
Spires fall, disintegrate,
Earth now cracked, wide awake.

I shuddered inside, suddenly afraid of the awesome power these Guardians possessed. Whatever forces they unleashed on their enemies, annihilation was assured.

The ground did indeed quake beneath my feet.

It didn't matter that my feet actually touched a wooden floor, high above the earth. The giant golden oak tree shook from the effects of the earthquake. Somewhere far below rocks ground against each other, a harsh sound echoing all the way up to us. Splinters of stone broke and were hurled from the sandstone pillars down to the forest floor. Thunder and turmoil beneath the soil and rock spoke of disasters ahead.

Cameron's using the Earth Shard.

I wished I knew if his actions would save us—or destroy us along with our enemies.

I DIDN'T dare interrupt Cameron while he was channeling the awesome powers of the Earth Shard. For all I knew, disrupting the dragon's magic might backfire and kill us both. So with bated breath I waited for him to stop. I'm not ashamed to admit that I took more than one step back, just in case.

I had to hold on to the wooden wall when the tree our cage was suspended on started to sway precariously. A booming sound below warned me that the earth might just reclaim the pillars supporting us by crumbling them, and subsequently us, to dust.

"Stop!"

Three sentries dropped from the barrierless opening on the roof, between the structure and the tree trunk, and pointed their weird weapons at Cameron and me. I could tell from their rash, wild gestures and high-pitched voices that they were human and incredibly concerned over what was happening.

I had to intervene to give Cameron time to complete his task. "If you interfere with the chant, you'll kill us all," I told them. I had no way of knowing if it was true, but it was my fear. And that panicky emotion transferred to our enemies.

The sentries breathed hard and fast, their armaments shaking in their grip. Clearly they had no idea what to do or if their instincts could be trusted to tell them the correct course of action.

I raised my hands, backed off to the wall, and let them surround Cameron, who still sat cross-legged on the floor, mumbling magical incantations with his eyes closed, seemingly shut off from the world. The three intruders took positions around Cameron, the shimmering barrels of their pistols aimed directly at his face.

Before they could decide how to proceed, I made my move.

I jumped on the back of the closest sentry, snatched a knife from his belt, and stuck it firmly in his shoulder. Grunting, he dropped his gun.

Unfortunately his graphene bulletproof vest deflected the blade from penetrating his armor. My wrist twisted painfully in the thwarted attempt.

With an angry growl, my foe pivoted, probably to gain speed, and threw me over his shoulder. I landed on my side, aching from the impact, and slid across the wooden floor to hit the wall with a heavy thud. I banged my head on the wall, and red and white sparkling stars danced in my blurry field of vision.

Once I could see again, I found the sentry standing over me, gun back in hand, the barrel aimed squarely at my head. He grimaced. "Fucking thief, you're dead."

I didn't even manage a gasp as yet again I faced certain death.

But movement flickered behind him, and gunshots cracked loudly. The two remaining goons let out muffled screams that cut off midshout. The last sentry whirled around, crouching to ward off a threat. As he hunkered I had a full view of what happened.

Cameron stood now, bigger than he'd been before. His skin… was stone. The bullets from the enemies' weapons did no damage, bouncing off him. The sentry closest to me was hit by a ricochet, and he went down. I cowered in a fetal position to avoid the flying projectiles. Cameron had a death-grip on the throats of the last two sentries as they dangled almost a foot off the ground, gasping for air like fish on a hook.

Then Cameron released them. Both villains fell down, unmoving, same as the third had. I wondered if they were dead or merely unconscious. In the end, I don't think I much cared.

I stood cautiously, staring at Cameron, who appeared to be in some sort of trance, just standing there like a literal stone statue. Should I address him or touch him? Would that help him out of this weird enchanted state he was in, or would my interference make things worse?

A deep sigh emerged from Cameron's throat, and a cloud of dust puffed out with his breath. Then, like flakes from broken rocks, the stone shield on him shattered, falling to the floor in piles of rubble and sand. Beneath, the old Cameron was exposed.

But he looked terrible, his skin wan, his eyes feverish, and his whole body wracked by tremors. His knees buckled, and I just managed to grab him before he fell face-first. I held on to him, as close as I could without us melding into one being.

"You're fucking crazy, you know that?" I chided him, my throat clogged with the pain of nearly losing him.

His arms came around me, and again he exhaled. "I know, Finn. I know." He petted the nape of my neck and my back, and I was close to tears, their emotional weight burning in my eyes. "Using the power of the Earth Shard is…."

"Dangerous? Stupid? Monumentally insane?" I suggested, gripping him tighter.

"Taxing," Cameron finished, a mild chuckle following his words. His jest didn't work; my anxiety levels remained high.

The ground shook still, and the vibrations carried through the giant golden oak tree to reverberate inside us. "Why hasn't the earthquake stopped?" I asked, worried almost beyond reason. I feared that after everything Cameron had done, we were still no closer to gaining our freedom.

"I didn't so much use the Earth Shard as I unleashed some of its natural power. Only a Guardian can do that, since we're bound to the Shard so profoundly. The Crystal reforged, that's another matter." Cameron pulled back, away from my embrace, and glanced around. "I have never before had to resort to this, so I can't say for certain what the consequences will be." He locked gazes with me. "We should go."

I nodded toward our defeated foes. "They came from above, so we should probably try that way first."

"Need a hand?" A familiar face peeked through the round opening.

Both Cameron and I exclaimed at the same moment, "*Sigmund!*"

Chapter Eighteen

"THANK YOU, dear friend," Cameron said in a hushed tone, rubbing his neck.

Sigmund held up the torn pieces of the negation collar, smirking at Cam. "If our situation wasn't so dire, I'd think this was amusing. You, the civilized, prim dragon, and a collar. Kinda hot."

"I agree," I cut in, grinning widely. Cameron gave me a warning look not to take this topic further. Therefore, I turned to Sigmund and pointed at the collar. "How come you could break that impervious collar but no one else can?"

Sigmund shrugged and said nothing, as though he didn't care, so the answer was left to Cameron. "Sigmund is a special case. Due to his curse, which imbued him with divine magic, he is simply teeming with excess magic. Therefore he can use or destroy any magical artifact."

"Huh." News to me. But fascinating facts nonetheless. I turned back to Sigmund. We'd already debriefed him about who and what we were up against. "Thanks for coming. We were in rather deep doo-doo, as it happens."

Sigmund smiled, baring his fangs. "No problem. I figured it was better to save you two than to engage the enemy without knowing their full strength and armaments."

To my ears, Sigmund sounded like a man with extensive military experience. Maybe he was. Who knew?

"Not that I'm not glad to see you or anything, Sigmund, because I am. But... I was under the impression you couldn't join us, you know, what with your curse and all. You still crave ... uh, human flesh?" I was going to ask if he was still hungry for *me*, but I held my tongue.

Sigmund's eyes narrowed, and I gulped. "I guess I'm going to have to play the obedient dog and heel." His grin, with his sharp fangs showing, made me nervous. But if he said he could control his urges, I was willing to give him the benefit of the doubt.

His nose scrunched as he sniffed the air. Or rather… me. His gaze swept over me and returned with a knowing look. I blushed fiercely. Leave it to a lycan to be able to smell sex on my skin.

I cleared my throat. "Where'd everybody go?" I asked to veer the subject away from me, gesturing around us.

Sigmund had brought us back to the palace. No sentries, no elves, no one. The place had been vacated as swiftly as it'd been vanquished. Moonlight streamed through the foliage, leaves danced in the wind, and the night sky was empty of clouds and fog. Stars arched above us, their blinking a sign of peace in an endless universe.

Most of the palace was open air, same as our cage. Wooden surfaces with wavy lines surrounded us, spacious and grand yet light as a feather. Banners and canopies rippled in the breeze, colorful and bright. Simple furniture was scattered about, the pieces few and far between, the area lit by paper lanterns. I supposed these Wood Elves were minimalists as well as ecologically inclined.

No bodies, though. Not even a speck of blood. Maybe the earthquake had scared them off after all. I could hope.

"We must find where the Wood Elves are kept prisoner," Cameron said before Sigmund had the chance to reply to my question. "Hathaway hinted at a fiendish imprisonment for them."

When he and Sigmund exchanged a knowing and worried glance, I knew to expect the worst. "What?" I demanded.

Sigmund spoke gravely, "It is said the Wood Elves must be in contact with trees every day… or they'll wither away and die." While I gasped in shock, Sigmund addressed Cameron. "You thinking what I'm thinking?" Cameron nodded, and Sigmund continued, "Somewhere high in the air, then, out of touch with wood as a final insult."

I snapped my fingers. "Metal cages suspended on the branches that tip over the edges of these rock formations."

Cameron and Sigmund were quickly onboard with my suggestion.

Unfortunately, despite my helpful epiphany, I was left stranded as Cameron the dragon flew off, a mere beacon of light among the stars, and Sigmund the giant wolf dashed off, disappearing into the underbrush. Cursing out loud, I decided to do a little snooping of my own.

I wandered about carefully, mostly out of curiosity but also in search of my stolen gear. I wasn't about to let it vanish into thin air.

The wooden platform beneath my feet still shook every few minutes, proving that the effects of the Earth Shard were formidable indeed. Last time the Shards had been used, the Veiled world had been in turmoil and at war for ages. Humanity was entirely ill prepared for a direct confrontation with even a single mythical species, let alone several or all of them.

Now I was forced to consider what additional dangerous ramifications using all the Shards might have on the world, such as earthquakes, floods, blizzards, storms, or droughts.

It seemed no matter how bad I thought things could get, they could always get worse. The Shards represented the natural world, and natural disasters could very well lie ahead. Another reason to stop Kamala and Hathaway now.

Only... perhaps only Kamala.

I stumbled into what appeared to be a council room, with a curved wooden table in the center and an arched roof above, shaped from branches and twigs. The walls were lined with stacked bookshelves, crammed full of books, vellum scrolls, and large folios. Their existence testified to the erudite nature of the Wood Elves.

In the open space in the middle stood an ice statue.

Except inside the frozen cocoon rested Hathaway in eternal slumber.

I took no pleasure in being right about Kamala ditching Hathaway once she was done with him. After all, her deliberate actions had resulted in a gruesome death, if his shocked, fearful expression was any indication.

The good news, however, was that my gear lay on the table. I immediately snatched up the devices and equipment, put each back in place in my many pockets and pouches, and donned my fingerless leather gloves.

"Hello?"

I whirled around at the sound of a voice I didn't recognize.

A green, glowing apparition of a male elf appeared before me.

Startled, I jumped back. At least I didn't scream this time. "What the fuck?" Yup. Me at my most articulate.

The bare-chested ghost was bent in a most curious position. He seemed to be hanging onto something I couldn't see, and another hand gripped his, someone dangling beneath him, also unseen.

"I don't mean to intrude in any way," the apparition said in a civilized turn of phrase, though sounding somewhat rattled, "but I'm in a bit of bind here. Any chance you might be able to help?"

I stepped closer warily. "Who're you?"

"I'm Prince Liro." He looked down and up at what I could not see and added in a rush, "My companion and I were thrown off the palace edge. And I fear I'm losing my grip."

"Oh shit." I started running but stopped dead in my tracks. "Which way?"

"Off the palace's main reception terrace." I had to admit that, despite his awkward situation, he seemed quite calm and rational, if understandably urgent. "If you could hurry, I'd appreciate it immensely."

Considering Cameron and I had met with Kamala on the main terrace, and thanks to the aid of what I now knew to be an astral projection, it wasn't hard to find the right place. I leaned over the low railing, scouring the lush vegetation for any sign of a fallen prince. The giant golden oak tree spread wide everywhere I looked, with abundant foliage plus white flowers and red fruit that I'd never seen before blocking much of my line of sight.

Finally I caught movement far below the edge of the structure and the precipice of the rock pillar. Whoever was there, they were literally hanging on by a thread.

Grateful for my newly recovered gear, I grabbed my reserve of multifilament Kevlar rope and extended it downward. Thanks to several tree branches around me, I was able to hook the rope over a branch to give me better leverage.

"Can you see the rope?" I yelled at the top of my lungs, praying I could reach them. Where was my flying dragon when I needed him?

"Yes." I started as the voice spoke behind me. Prince Liro nodded his thanks to me, and then the green specter vanished. I could only hope that meant the elvish prince was focusing on grabbing the rope instead of projecting himself here and there, willy-nilly.

I gripped the other end firmly, my hands protected by the gloves I'd put on earlier, and waited for the sudden heaviness to appear. The wait lasted a couple of moments, with me anxious and sweaty.

Finally the rope pulled taut as apparently two people grasped on to it. Constant jerking told me they must have started to climb. I hauled with all my strength, gathering the rope to pool at my feet. The weight wasn't excruciating, but all too soon the exertion began to strain my muscles. I'd only ever had to carry my own weight on the rope. But I didn't stop, even when I began to pant and my arms to feel like lead.

I cursed Kamala under my breath. Why couldn't she have thrown them down a smaller drop, dammit. Stupid complaint, I was well aware.

Finally a hand rose and clutched the railing. It was a man's hand, I could tell, even if it wasn't particularly hairy. A head followed, and a beautiful head it was too. Slim and appealing, the elf showed every lovely aspect of his kind, from his golden-hued, spiky hair, to his tanned skin, almond-shaped eyes, pointed ears, and agile figure clad in nothing but a thick yet soft-looking golden-oak-bark-textile loincloth. A vestige from their naturist days to barely have a stitch on? Perhaps.

I freely admit that I felt a fair amount of dismay upon seeing this beautiful man being *not* naked. Why, oh why did they have to learn stupid human modesty and start wearing clothes? No fair. I wanted to see me an elf dingaling, dammit!

Once the male elf was sitting safely astride the railing, I saw a second pair of hands emerge from the abyss, and this time the owner was definitely female.

As soon as I saw the rest of her, I could tell she was *not* an elf. Though I had zero idea exactly what she was.

Her long, long hair had no color at all, not that I could discern much through the thin tree branches, leaves, flowers, and even antlers that seemed to grow right out of her head. Her green eyes were almond shaped, though, like an elf or most Asian peoples. Her yellowish skin suggested she was Chinese or perhaps Japanese. Her body-hugging dress resembled the finest silk and yet also tree bark, leaves, and grass, and I couldn't tell where her skin ended and her dress began. She reminded me of a wooden puppet, beautifully carved and lifelike.

Who, or what, the hell is she?

The minute both had dropped over the railing onto the solid wooden floor, with listless limbs and rough panting, I let the rope slip and dashed to their side. "You two okay?" Both stared at me quizzically, so I continued, "I'm Finn Grayson. I'm here with two other Guardians, Cameron Feilong and Sigmund. They're searching for your people, Your Highness, imprisoned by this human dude named Hathaway and a Snow Elf by the name of Kamala. You might have met them?"

Prince Liro closed his eyes and sighed in stark relief. "Oh, thank the Goddess. I feared Kamala might have… murdered my kin." He swallowed visibly, his skin growing pale with dread, his big eyes wide and worried.

The woman touched Liro's arm gently. "Not even Kamala would resort to murder so easily."

I gasped. Her voice… absolutely divine, perfectly melodious, sweetly dulcet, utterly soul-shattering. I'd never heard anything like it. The voice of an angel, as a Christian might say.

I cleared my throat. "I'm afraid she might already have." I thumbed over my shoulder toward the council hall. "Hathaway's dead, frozen in a block of ice back there. And judging from his astonished look, I don't think he saw it coming."

It seemed Kamala had at least a few qualms when it came to killing her own kind. But those same scruples apparently didn't extend to members of other species, as evidenced by the murders of Hathaway, Griffin, and Suan Ni. Her track record when it came to murder victims was growing at an alarming rate.

Liro and the woman looked mortified, and I couldn't blame them. Shock was written all over their faces, their eyes glowing with unshed tears, their jaws shaking, their hands clutching one another for comfort and support.

But we had no time for sorrow. "Did they get the Wood Shard?" I asked.

The woman nodded solemnly. "Yes."

Liro shook his head, grimacing in obvious anger. "It's all my fault."

Well, that lament sure rang a bell. A few hours ago, it could very well have been me. In some ways it still was. I had not forgotten the role I'd played in this tragedy and chaos.

"Don't be silly, Liro." The woman's hush worked better than a mother's kiss. Liro calmed, his expression assuming a dreamy quality, his gaze drifting somewhere far away. The woman looked at me, not a hint of judgment in sight. "I am Vivian, the Guardian of the Wood Shard."

"Uh-huh. So you're Vivian in a towering oak tree? I guess the only thing missing is a slumbering wizard." I chuckled at my own jest, made at the expense of the Arthurian legend of Merlin and Vivien. Then I blushed in mild embarrassment and added, "Sorry. Poor attempt at levity."

Vivian smiled like the sun emerging from behind the clouds to brighten the day. Or in our case, the remnants of the night. "Oh, I love Alfred Lord Tennyson and his poem about the Lady of the Lake. Besides... 'A sense of humor is just common sense, dancing.' William James, I believe."

Oh, I liked her. Anyone who appreciated my inappropriately timed jokes was a friend of mine. "Cool. It's nice to meet you. Well, even under these circumstances."

Vivian nodded. Then she grew serious. "If two other Guardians are here...."

I finished the sentence for her. "All the other Shards have now been taken, except for the Fire Shard."

Vivian rubbed a hand over her forehead. She radiated anguish, her eyes downcast and full of dread, her expression pained and twisted. "That is indeed terrible news." She exhaled long, a sob emerging from her throat. "We must retrieve them immediately."

"Yeah. We're working on that." I tried keep up a brave front, but I don't know how well I succeeded.

Vivian locked gazes with me. "If our nemeses don't yet have the Fire Shard, we must alert the Starlet at once."

I studied her face for signs of mischief or joking. When there were none, I had to ask, "Why do I get the feeling we're not talking about a Vegas showgirl?"

Liro barked out a desperate laugh. "Believe me, you're not far off." Then he fell silent again, remorseful, like he wore the weight of the world on his slender shoulders.

I glanced at him, still holding his head in his hands, a woe-is-me soft moaning under his breath. "Um, I don't mean to be rude but, uh... how is any of this *your* fault?"

"My people are responsible for the protection of the Tree of Light, which houses the Wood Shard." Liro's explanation didn't exculpate him entirely, but the theft sure as shit didn't seem like it was all his doing. But then the elf prince said, "They used a spirit snare on me."

I frowned. "I'm sorry, they used… a what now?"

"Banned dark magic." Cameron stood right behind me.

He was with Sigmund and a large group of elves, the men clad only in golden-oak-bark loincloths but the women wearing thin silk muslin brassieres as well. With their scant attire, these Wood Elves appeared more primitive than advanced. There was nothing futuristic or high-tech about them. But, damn, none of them were naked, either. This wasn't my day for hot nudity. Plus, it was night, so….

I started upon seeing them, not having heard their arrival. But Cameron placed a hand on my shoulder, stopping me from saying or doing anything. When he spoke I knew he spoke to me. "Liro's special psionic ability is astral projection. Kamala must have used a spirit snare spell on him, thereby forcing his body to teleport to his spirit, instead of his astral self returning to his body. The spell is extremely dangerous and life-threatening, which is why it is banned by all civilized mythic nations."

Liro appeared crestfallen, his shoulders slumped, tears falling from his eyes, and his voice like an echo from beyond the grave. "I used astral projection so I could leave the sanctity and safety of the Tree of Light and negotiate with Kamala. But when my spirit reached her, she used an illicit trick to trap me and bring my body to her through the air. Then she threatened to kill me and my people unless Vivian gave her the Wood Shard."

"And I did," Vivian cut in, sounding as serene as Muirín. "I relinquished my control of the Wood Shard to save a dear friend and a whole people from massacre. I am not ashamed of my decision, nor do I regret it. I do wish, however, that there'd been an alternative."

Liro's lovely face twisted with fury, and he slammed his fist on his thigh. "How could Kamala do such a thing? How could she master such a dark art? She is a Snow Elf. Nature and life mean as much to them as they do to us of the woodlands."

Grimly Cameron said out loud what I already suspected. "She's a Shadowalker."

Chapter Nineteen

"WHERE THE hell is... what was it? Svartifoss? Never heard of it." I wasn't complaining or whining, per se. I was merely reasonably concerned over our next destination, which seemed to be the icy depths of hell.

As he'd been reuniting with his no-longer-imprisoned people, Prince Liro told us that while the sentries held him captive, he heard them talking. At the time Liro hadn't been aware of who Kamala was referring to with her veiled words, but in light of what I'd told him about the other Shards being taken, Liro had connected the dots and figured out the Starlet was now in trouble. Apparently Kamala had already captured the Starlet and taken him to her fort in Svartifoss. Why? I had no idea.

"Iceland," Sigmund replied, readjusting the straps of the wolf hide on his back. "Been there a couple of times myself." My eyes begged for answers, and upon seeing my puppy-dog look, he laughed. "Before the Great Unveiling, Svartifoss was a simple waterfall surrounded by hanging dark lava columns. Hence the name, Black Falls."

I sighed. "Why do I get the sense mentioning the Unveiling is important here?"

Sigmund grinned, baring his fangs. His eyes sparked, as though he were the predator and I the prey in his sights. I prayed his hunger wouldn't overwhelm him. He had given me his word, and despite a couple of misgivings, I trusted him. "After the Unveiling, the site underwent a transformation. The simple, small spot is now composed of a whole mountain of hexagonal basalt columns—plus the snowbound fortress of the Snow Elves. And as a people, they are not hospitable at all. Needless to say, tourism has suffered in the area since it's now exclusively a glacier, year in, year out. Svartifoss used to be an international attraction for hikers and travelers, with a national park around it. Now…."

"Sweet," I remarked sarcastically, rolling my eyes at the thought of all the possible things Sigmund left unsaid. "The fortress, ever been there?"

Sigmund shook his head, his fair mane waving about him. He was ruggedly handsome. Too bad I'd set my sights on Cam. "No, I've never set foot in that infernal icebox. That lot, they're the most reclusive, unfriendly bunch you'll ever meet."

"Awesome. And we're going there why, exactly?" My cynicism made an appearance, uncalled for to be sure. Sigmund seemed to sense my fears since he gave me a look best described as sympathetic. It didn't suit him. But I appreciated the sentiment.

Cameron ambled up to me, his eyes soft, his touch on my arm almost tender. "Ready?" he asked, his voice low and gentle. I realized he was giving me a subtle way out.

I lifted my chin in determination. I started this; I would finish it. "Ready as I'll ever be. I was born ready. Ready or not, here I come—"

"All right, I got the gist of it." Cameron seemed to fight the amusement threatening to burst out but then he gave up resistance. His smile made my day. Then he gazed up at the sky, which was slowly brightening with hues of red, orange, and yellow as the sun peeked just below the horizon, its rays already in sight. Cameron frowned, his smile a thing of the past. "Kamala is several steps ahead of us. She has all the Shards—"

"Not yet," I cut in. "The Fire Shard is still out of her—"

"No." Cameron's adamant tone stopped me cold. "The Fire Shard is not quite the same as the others. The Starlet has it with him wherever he goes."

That explained a lot. So as far as I understood this, to retrieve the Shard, we needed to rescue Starlet from Kamala, and that meant we had a journey ahead.

Nevertheless, I wanted more clarification. "What do you mean he's got it on him? That seems kinda stupid and careless."

Cameron smiled ruefully. "I'm afraid it's not by choice."

A ton of questions weighed heavily on my tongue. But Prince Liro and Vivian walked up to us, so I didn't get the chance to ask.

"Many of my kin have been wounded and hurt," Liro said. His voice cracked with emotion—anger, frustration, and a desire for vengeance the most obvious.

"I will remain here to heal them," Vivian said nobly, and my opinion of her grew by leaps and bounds. "As soon as you signal me, I will join you and reclaim my place as a Guardian." She embraced me suddenly. I choked at the expression of friendship and hugged her back. Her scent wafted to my nose, a smell of spring, new leaves, and grass, trees and fruits and flowers. When she pulled back, tears glimmered in her green eyes. "Be careful. Both of you."

"We'll do our best." Cameron and Vivian embraced too.

I looked away from the intimate tableau.

That was when I noticed the leery, glowering eyes aimed at Cameron when he wasn't looking. The nearby elves spoke in hushed tones in small bands on the terrace, all of them watching Cameron out of the corners of their eyes. It wasn't exactly like giving him the evil eye, but not far off, either.

My temper flared. "What the hell's the matter with you people?" I shouted, startling everyone around till all eyes were on me. "Cameron's done nothing but protect the world from the mess *you* created. And he still helped you and saved your ungrateful butts from certain death. How dare you look down your noses at him? You're despicable. You ought to be ashamed."

I trembled with righteous fury. It was only the grace of Cameron's tender touch on my arm that stopped me from murdering all these snooty elves with a look.

"Finn, please." Cameron's whisper made me shake more, and I had to bite my lower lip so I wouldn't start screaming at the injustice and racism around me.

I shoved his hand off me, but he gripped me harder, whirled me around to face him, cupped my face, and kissed me silent. No one could resist that, I concluded, winding my arms about his neck and plastering my body against his, molding us almost into one. When he finally released me, or to be precise, when I released him, Cameron stared down at me, his gaze dark and lustful.

"I'm not sorry," I murmured to him, feeling the justification of my speech with every fiber of my being.

"Nor should you be." Prince Liro nodded firmly at his own declaration, peered into the eyes of every elf surrounding us, and watched as they all lowered their gazes, hanging their heads in shame. "Not only is Cameron a Guardian, and worthy of our respect and admiration, but he is also one of us. Our flesh and blood, our kindred spirit and our kin."

Liro extended his hand in an offering of peace. Cameron shook his hand. I don't think I was imagining the glimmer of hope and tears in my dragon's eyes.

Behind me Sigmund stage-whispered, "Now I really wanna eat you. I like my food… spicy."

I flipped him off. He laughed in his booming voice.

I turned to Cameron. "Now can we go?"

"THAT'S THE Elvish Causeway," Sigmund said, pointing down as he sat behind me on Cameron dragon's back.

On our trek through the skies, I'd learned that dragons held the record for speed through the air as we'd whizzed our way from China to Iceland in under three hours instead of thirteen by plane. By the time our destination came into view, I was stiff, cold, and pissed off.

Still, the sight of pitch-black basalt columns, all interlocked to form a sort of road, did impress me enough to give a shit. I beheld the magnificent sight, part of it from our world, another from beyond the Veil, the two now forever joined.

Unless, of course, Kamala reforged the five Shards into an Elemental Crystal and as a result destroyed the world.

"How far does it go?" I shouted my question to Sigmund past the icy winds nipping at my cheeks and causing my breath to appear in moist, puffy clouds.

"All the way up there." Again Sigmund pointed, and my gaze followed.

The area surrounding Svartifoss consisted of undulating hills, sharp ravines, and the occasional waterfall. The green, grassy mounds waved about in the wind, pierced in places by wild, winding brooks with rocky riverbanks. Blue skies above held a few ragged clouds, but the sunshine reached everywhere.

Except for the mighty fortress rising behind and above the Svartifoss waterfall. The black volcanic columns rose far higher now than in all the tourist pictures taken before the Great Unveiling, visually shrinking the once majestic waterfall into a trickle.

The moment I laid my eyes on the massive structure, I had an odd sense of déjà vu.

Though the Orient had never been my favorite hangout as a master thief, I'd traveled that corner of the world extensively. And I recognized the architecture immediately.

Lhasa. The fortress of the Snow Elves resembled Lhasa.

Lhasa's vibrant colors—red walls, golden-yellow roofs, and green lush vegetation—had been replaced by icy blues, stark whites, and pitch blacks. The size of the monumental palace was significantly larger too, towering over the grassy mounds (now blanketed by snow and ice), black basalt rock columns, and a glacier-covered mountainside that had not been there before, now nearly topping the Himalayas in all its bleak glory.

I swallowed hard. Getting into that fortified stronghold seemed like an impossible task right then. I had doubts. But I forced myself to get over them. Kamala had to be stopped.

"How the fuck are we supposed to get in there?" Sigmund growled in my ear.

I glanced over my shoulder at him, dead serious. "There's always a way. Trust me." I swept my gaze over the fortress, searching for weaknesses, unguarded points of entry, anything that might give us the advantage for a change. "You know, according to one legend associated with the Giant's Causeway in Ireland, the hero giant Fionn mac Cumhaill built the causeway."

"Well, maybe our Finn Grayson will topple this causeway and become the hero of the hour," Sigmund said, chuckling against my neck. His fangs scraped over the thin line between my hairline and the winter coat Liro had provided me with.

I scoffed in disbelief. Me, the hero? God forbid.

"Look."

Cameron gestured to the Elvish Causeway. A long line of people ran down the hill, in the other direction from the fortress. I couldn't detect who or what they were from so high above. The fact they wore white wasn't telling in itself.

"I'm taking us down," Cameron dragon said with a growl.

Cameron, with us on his back, whooshed lower in swift sweeping spirals, making my stomach whirl with nausea. Cameron descended fast and dropped down on all fours in front of the runners, who halted at once, midstep. As Sigmund bounced off Cameron's back and I hopped down more gingerly and cautiously, I saw the people were Snow Elves, had to be with their snow-white skin, ice-blue eyes, and white body armor or flowing robes.

Most importantly, though, they reeked of fear, their eyes wide and terrified. Several of them sported bruises, scrapes, and blood smears. Best not to treat them like the enemy, I decided.

I stepped closer. "We're looking for Princess Kamala. Have you seen—"

The first man gestured wildly behind him, back up the way they'd come. "She's gone mad. She conquered the fortress with a human army and told everyone who didn't stand with her to leave or die." He had a slight accent, which told me English wasn't his first or even second language. Then again, we were in Iceland, so… Icelandic? Danish? German?

In any case, it was reassuring to know not all Snow Elves had it in for humanity or the world at large.

Cameron had shifted into a man again. He addressed the elves sternly. "Is there a way in without being seen?"

The elf who had spoken to us nodded, radiating nervousness and agitation. He shifted weight from one foot to the other, seemingly anxious to get back to escaping. "There's a new cave where the old waterfall is. An underground glacial river formed it before the Great Unveiling that united our two worlds. It leads up to the sewers of the fortress. I can't tell you if there are guards. Kamala brought many men with her. Please, let us leave in peace. There are children here."

Behind the backs of the adults, tiny faces peeked, horror apparent on their tear-streaked cheeks and in their wide, weepy eyes. My determination to stop Kamala only grew.

Cameron stepped aside, waving a hand at them. "Go. Be safe."

The homeless band of frightened people started to move again in haste. Their leader bowed, thanked us profusely, and then said in a low tone, "These are precarious times. Balance is lost. The borders between worlds are thin. Poles are shifting. The world is in turmoil. Kamala is a herald of dark times ahead. Thank you for your kindness. Walk ever in safety."

The echo of his prophetic words hung heavy in the air between us. Then he joined the lost and displaced expedition, hurrying the young, the old, and the infirm along.

As the lengthy line of refugees passed by, my hunch that this mission might be the death of us all shone from Cameron's and Sigmund's eyes too.

Chapter Twenty

"WHAT THE devil are these things again? Sins?" I asked, attempting to attach the tiny piece of metal to my ear, with little success thanks to my frigid, fumbling fingers.

Sigmund rolled his eyes. "Psins. Psionic inhibitors. All the elven subspecies have their own special brand of psionic abilities, like Liro and his astral projection. Telepathy is the common feature of elven nations. These psins shield you against several psionic powers, mainly telepathy. They were designed as protection against unwanted mental violations. With a psin, anyone trying read your mind will hear nothing but static, like a radio with bad reception."

Impatiently Cameron swatted my hand aside and gently rested the metal oddity against my earlobe. The thing wrapped itself around my entire ear on its own. I should have been deaf. But I wasn't. Plus, I heard Cameron's and Sigmund's voices inside my head. *Cool.*

Then I glanced at the next step of our journey, and I didn't feel as cool anymore.

Like an ominous gateway to the underworld, with the river Styx running through its heart, the sinister entrance to the underbelly of the fortress loomed ahead.

The only thing missing was the three-headed giant dog, Cerberus.

The basalt columns lined the walls, tinted bloodred and pitch-black, like stone curtains between us and our fate. They formed the cave opening we'd been told about, a crystal-clear, icy-cold underground brook our only guide upstream. Not much ice or snow covered the volcanic rock, hinting at their fiery origins and the hidden heat beneath our feet.

The Svartifoss waterfall gushed above and behind us, nature's force in play. Sprinkles of cold spray landed on our faces as we rounded the cascade to the unveiled cavern beyond it.

I could only hope this wasn't our road to perdition.

"What's our plan again?" I asked, staring up at the imposing cavern entrance, feeling rather insignificant in size and stamina. Like a trapped mouse, I looked into the maw of death.

"Get in, locate and retrieve the Shards, find the Starlet, destroy Kamala, and get out." Sigmund sounded perfectly at ease, like infiltration into enemy strongholds was his daily pastime.

"Who exactly is this Starlet?" I had to ask since no one had bothered to give specifics.

"You'll see." Sigmund's grin and wink aimed at me only infuriated me further. I nearly flipped the guy off again.

Sigmund appeared fearless in any given situation, so predictably he took the lead in our little attempt at a break-in, sneaking into the cave crouched, the cavern wide outside but soon narrowing the deeper we went.

"Abandon all hope ye who enter here," I murmured, praying my words didn't turn out prophetic.

I followed on Sigmund's heels with Cameron guarding our rear. Naturally, the thought of Cameron and my rear end gave me a most inconvenient hard-on.

Sigmund smirked at me over his shoulder. "Humans are such a horny bunch."

"Mind your own damn business," I muttered through gritted teeth, blushing like crazy.

THE WINDING underground passage followed the river, having been carved around it over time by nature. Thankfully the waters rippled rather quietly, forming tiny churning pools here and there between outcroppings. There was ample space on both sides of the stream, but we had to be careful of our footing as the basalt stones were uneven and surprisingly sharp too.

As our reluctant elf guide had informed us, the cavern sloped steadily upward. Soon we were under the fortress, and we continued our search for a door, a hatch, or a gap, anything that would lead us to the sewers.

A chilly wind whisked against our faces throughout, suggesting that the source of the underground river might be aboveground, or at least part of the river uncovered from beneath the mountains in a ravine or some other natural aperture.

My cheeks burned, my eyes watered, and the blasted breeze managed to find a way underneath all my clothes. It was cold and damp, and I sneezed and coughed till I worried pieces of my lungs would be spit out. I cursed the arctic freeze under my breath, my teeth chattering from the cold, and I dreamed of golden sand beaches, green palm trees, and turquoise tropical lagoons. I could almost feel the warmth caressing my face with balmy brushes....

Sigmund snapped his fingers in front of me when I nearly tripped over yet another pointed rock, tumbling against his back as I staggered forward trying to avoid a collision with the earth. "Hey. Focus, dammit," the wolfman growled.

Properly scolded, I murmured a quick apology, my cheeks flaming for a new reason.

We came to a natural junction. Rugged passages separated the path, and water ran from both of them. Apparently the underground stream had several sources after all. No lights flickered from either direction, no smells of cooked foods or anything man-made, or elf-made to be precise, came from the dark passages, and no warmth emanated to suggest living quarters.

"We are relying on your senses here, old friend," Cameron said quietly behind me, his words aimed at Sigmund, whose animal instincts surpassed both mine and the dragon's.

Sigmund crouched and sniffed about. "That way." He pointed toward the left tunnel.

I don't know what he smelled, and I wasn't about to ask. With Sigmund in charge, we followed the left tunnel. Thankfully the ceiling never lowered to the point where we might have to crawl or worm our way forward. But no stink of sewers welcomed us either. If there was a hidden entrance to the fortress, or a backdoor, we hadn't found it.

Until we came upon an ice relief on the wall.

No more lava columns, only gray frozen rock surrounded us. The passage must have moved away from the source of underground heat that had created the basalt columns. I wasn't sure if that was a good or a bad thing. On the one hand, the danger of falling into a pool of lava lessened, but on the other, the cold had increased, and no layer of clothing would protect us for long.

I puzzled over the possibility that the Snow Elves and their magic might be responsible for the added chill.

"What is that? Snow Elf art?" I pointed at the depiction in disbelief.

The relief was shaped in the form of a shield, and bright-colored jewels sparkled under the ice. Had I not been so cold that I no longer felt my numb fingers, I might have shattered the ice and taken the other kind of ice with me as a trophy.

"No. It's a riddle." Cameron stepped forward, serious and intrigued. I wondered if this was something he had come across in his wild youth. Naturally I only assumed his youth had been wild and reckless.

His interpretation caught my attention. "You mean they're some kind of code or—"

Cameron shook his head while his hand traveled across the ice shield, hovering above the thin sheet with a kind of admiration. "No. They're buttons."

"Let me see," I said, pushing Cameron aside so I could take a look. After all, this was my special field of expertise.

"You could have just asked me to move," Cameron whispered in my ear, his warm breath's brush a sensuous experience, heating me up inside. He didn't sound angry or hurt but amused. Perhaps he was growing accustomed to my antics.

Behind the icy veneer, five colors of the rainbow were on display in jewel form. Red, yellow, green, blue, and purple. To my recollection, plenty of other colored jewels could have been represented as well. Therefore the choice of these particular shades must have had special meaning.

I frowned in contemplation. The five elements? No, unlikely. Perhaps they were colors with cultural significance to the Snow Elves? Probable. What might they as a people value? A snort escaped me because I knew the answer: white. And a matching hued jewel, maybe a diamond or a pearl, was nowhere in sight.

Unless… it was.

I practically pressed my nose against the sheet of ice as I peered through it.

And there it lay, almost undetectable under the cover of ice. A white diamond that for all intents and purposes got lost in the glimmering ice. Which might very well have been the exact intention of those who wished to hide a secret entrance.

I chuckled to myself and pressed the jewel under the thin layer of frozen water.

The white diamond embedded into the wall sunk in deeper. When the gem stopped, a deep boom sounded, followed by a chafing noise, like giant boulders rubbing together. A narrow rift became visible as a portion of the wall shifted aside. Silent it wasn't, but beggars can't be choosers.

"Well done, lad," Sigmund said, slapping me on the shoulder as he passed beside me, entering the new tunnel. I hoped his praise wouldn't put me on his menu.

"Yes. Good work, Finn." Cameron took my hand and squeezed gently. I shivered, his touch igniting me in all sorts of ways best described as untimely. Then he let go and nudged me to follow our lycan, who had vanished from sight. Increasing my pace, I snuck after him, Cameron at my back.

In a matter of minutes, the rocky earth changed into a stone floor. The hewn walls told a story of craftsmanship—and the stench warned us we'd reached the sewers.

"WOW. THEY'VE really taken this snow and ice motif to the extreme. Kinda predictable and lacking in imagination, in my honest opinion."

Sigmund chuckled at my words, and Cameron's lips twitched up at the corners.

Frost covered all the walls, floors, and ceilings we came to as we wandered up through the labyrinthine underbelly of the fortress. The snow and frost on the ground scrunched beneath our feet, the stone walls emanated frigidity, too cold to touch, and stalactites adorned the arching ceiling above us.

Even the large round cesspool in the center of the sewer system, to where all the pipes and drains flowed, was covered by a thick sheet of ice and snow. A few cracks here and there gave the hot waters that bubbled restlessly imprisoned underneath the ice a chance to vent in steamy clouds. The domed hall obviously had seen better days, which told me these Snow Elves weren't quite as pristine, clean, and hygienic as they could have been.

I stared at the basin, a soft trickling sound echoing around us, me hoping I could avoid a need to pee.

"I think we should separate for a search," I suggested. "We can cover more ground that way."

Cameron's eyes glinted hard like golden gems. "Absolutely not."

I couldn't believe what I was hearing. "Don't I get a vote?"

Cameron's sculpted cheeks reddened. He must not have been very happy with me.

Sigmund spoke first. "He's right, Cam. Like this, we'll be at this all day, and we might get to Kamala too late. Finn's fate will be the same as the world's if we don't pick up the pace." He cast a warning glance at me not to interfere. Then he proposed, "Finn, you take these lower floors, as they'll be the most unlikely to house a huge guard presence. I'll take the servants' quarters and the barracks. Cam, you check the upper floors, the throne room, and—"

"I thought the elves were supposed to be all democratic and shit," I cut in, curious.

Sigmund shook his head, his bland and mildly dissatisfied expression reading a lot like boredom. "Nah. Despite their unifying feature of loving nature and the various nations being based on the varying aspects of nature they revere, all elvish nations are kritarchies with a limited monarchical sovereign."

I ogled with my mouth open, utterly flummoxed. "What the hell's a k… a krit…?"

"Kritarchy is a society ruled by judges and bodies of law," Cameron said vaguely, his gaze skirting his surroundings, as though the topic was something he'd memorized ages ago, knew by heart, and didn't need conscious attendance to the conversation to speak about.

"So… they are strict about the letter of the law?" I asked.

Sigmund snorted. "They have libraries full of legal compendiums. They value law as well as ethics and morality, which form the basis of laws. They're good, law-abiding individuals, righteous and noble." He gave me an exacerbated, bitter look. "Now that we've covered that, how about we get a move on like I indicated?"

My cheeks warmed at the reprimand. We were pressed for time, that much was true. I was intrigued by Sigmund's description since it seemed contradictory with Kamala and her actions. She didn't appear particularly good, virtuous, or lawful. Some people believe their actions are lawful because they are convinced they know what's best, though from my standpoint that was begging the question. But Sigmund was right too: this wasn't the time for such deliberations.

Sigmund obviously decided not to wait any longer, and he turned on his heels and headed for the stairs in one of the corners of the large hall, the landing above disappearing into shadows. "I'm off to the barracks. Keep your psins on. Later."

As Sigmund fell on all fours, morphed into a gigantic wolf, and vanished into the dark, I wondered at how odd it was that Sigmund used current colloquialisms so well despite living solo in the wintery wastelands.

Cameron's gentle touch on my shoulder caught my attention. His teal-colored eyes glowed misty, as though he were on the verge of tears. With his mouth a thin white line, his brows knitted together, and his stance rigid, it wasn't hard to tell he was fraught with woe.

"You...." His voice cracked, and he cleared his throat, averting his gaze briefly from mine. "You will keep yourself out of harm's way, won't you, Finn?"

"Of course." I smiled back as reassuringly as I could. "You too. Right?"

Cameron gave me a wan smile but nodded quite bravely. I think he feared the worst. Considering the situation we were in, I couldn't exactly fault him for having apprehensions. I shared each and every one of them.

He glanced at my lips but so fast I barely caught it. Then Cameron backed off, gave me one last encouraging nod, and whirled around. He shifted into his dragon form in the blink of an eye, his golden scales shining and flashing even in the gray of the sewers. Cameron moved like the rippling ocean, in undulating waves that created an oddly soothing sight, mesmerizing me.

When he faded into the shadows, I couldn't help the dread filling my heart, grasping at the tender organ with its cold claws. There were a gazillion ways this could go horribly wrong.

Taking a deep, fortifying breath, I collected myself. As I started my search, my only consolation was the thought that whatever else Kamala might take from me, she could never rob me of hope.

Chapter Twenty-One

I WAS confused.

Every passage and every room, each corridor and hallway, were conspicuously empty, as though the place had been vacated for the long haul. It didn't matter if I sneaked or crouched, ambled or ran, the frosty snow scrunching beneath the soles of my shoes, nothing and no one came forth to stop me. No guards, no traps, nothing.

Out on the causeway we'd witnessed the mass exodus of Snow Elves fleeing from the power-hungry madness of Princess Kamala. But in my opinion, that didn't adequately explain the unnerving stillness and unnatural quiet inhabiting the place.

At the very least, a guard or two should have been posted on major entry points and exits to ensure no unwanted visitor, or a devilish rogue like me, could empty the place of valuables, armaments, and inhabitants.

The sewer system felt hollow without anyone there but me. My footsteps echoed from the stone walls, giving an eerie, false sensation of company that had me stopping every few seconds to check I truly was alone.

One level up via the stairs, I found myself on the prison level. At least that was how it looked to me—doors with heavy bolts, solitary chambers without furniture, barred windows, and long corridors with more of the same.

Considering the elven nations valued law above all else, the existence of these cells hardly surprised me. I wondered what the standard punishment for transgressions was among these people and if they ever granted clemency or showed mercy in extenuating circumstances. Because often such details existed, and thus lesser offenses merited reduced punishments.

Nonetheless, the cells gaped with unoccupied space, not a living soul present. In a few I noted stone beds with animals pelts and hides covering them, plus a bowl or a cup on the floor, suggesting at least a couple of the cells saw day-to-day activities and reluctant residents.

Had Kamala set them free? Seemed unlikely she would care. Then again, she had let the rest of her people escape out to the causeway without stopping them. That implied she might have a few compunctions about slaughtering the innocent, at least her own kin.

Chains rattled at the other end of the corridor, startling me.

A magical electric knife in hand, I tiptoed toward the chamber at the back, the only one with its door firmly closed. With snow, ice, and frost everywhere, my approach was less than stealthy. Even a thief had to concede to the elements.

"Who's there?" a soft, weak voice asked. "Is someone there?"

I had exactly two options. I chose to speak out. "Unbidden guest. Who're you?"

A quiet, tired chuckle emerged from the locked cell. "If you are a criminal, I strongly advise you to vacate the premises. Elves do not treat offenders lightly."

I rounded the last corner. "I appreciate the heads-up. But I think I'll stay."

"Your choice." The speaker was a man, his voice revealing even in hoarse weariness.

But he didn't look like any man I'd ever met.

On a stone bed, with rumpled cotton sheets around him, sat a prisoner. His wrists were bound with manacles, the chains attached to the wall. He appeared to be naked, stripped of all signs of civility and robbed of his dignity.

But he was *beautiful*. By far the most stunning being I'd ever laid eyes on. Even more enchanting than Cameron, and I had the everloving hots for Cam.

Long crimson-colored hair flowed down to his shoulders and onto his back. Only... I saw ruffled crimson feathers peak through. And from his shoulders, fan-like green plumes peeked. His chest was white, and I mean white, paler than snow. But... it too appeared to be mostly feathers. His feet were bright blue. Not like they were frozen and gangrenous, but simply... blue.

When he saw me, this rainbow gem of a gorgeous man stood, small and slender like a twink except for the two elongated, wiry tails with emerald-green disk feathers at the tips dipping from his huggable backside.

His legs trembled; he looked about ready to collapse. Yet his big brown eyes studied me with keen interest, long black lashes fluttering. His full, pouty lips I couldn't help thinking about suckling appeared yellow, and I couldn't get over the fact of how exquisite, yet weird, he was.

"Uh…." I had trouble forming words.

The young man cocked his head, apprehensive. "You're not a Snow Elf."

"No. I'm a Finn." I shook my head, blushing. "I mean, my name's Finn. I'm a thief."

He chuckled a little, the sound ending in a gut-wrenching cough that forced him to double over and plop back down on the bed. "I… I must say your timing is either far from fortuitous or just unlucky. The fortress has been abandoned. Though I can't say for certain, you understand, I imagine the place has been emptied of everything precious."

His hoarse voice ended in another fit of coughing, specks of blood dotting his hand and chest when he stopped. It wasn't hard to tell he was close to death.

Because despite his apparent exotic fairness, he'd been roughed up, badly.

The corner of his right eye was swollen, an ugly bruise forming. Similar marks marred his arms, chest, sides, back, and even his legs. No wonder he couldn't stand for long. Had Kamala tortured him? If so, why?

Without waiting to hear more, I fiddled with the lock on the door with my trusted set of lockpicks. "Don't worry about a thing, okay? I'm gonna get you out of there in no time. I'm with two Guardians, so they can heal—"

"Guardians?" He raised his head, his eyes huge and full of dread. "Here?"

I fumbled with the tumblers inside the lock, listening and feeling for the right position. "Yeah. Cameron and Sigmund. They're searching the upper levels of the fortress as we speak."

"Oh no." He coughed, covering his mouth with his shaking hand. He appeared so frail and worn. I felt for him, wanting to hold him in my arms and comfort his battered body and achy soul. Blood droplets clung to his yellow lips. "You… you must warn them…. Tell them to leave…." His coughing grew worse, wracking his whole body.

"No, we're not leaving you behind," I countered, increasing my efforts to pick the lock. "Besides, we're also looking for someone called the Starlet, another Guardian, who's—"

"I'm the Starlet," he said in a weak voice.

MY HANDS stilled as I stared at him. "You? You're the Guardian of the Fire Shard?"

He nodded, his face a mask of disquietude. "Yes. My name is Paris Ellery Baird. They call me the Starlet because of my profession. I'm a drag queen in a lavish, exclusive night club in Sydney, Australia." How come I hadn't been to this club? I lived in Sydney after all.

Nonetheless, the explanation made sudden sense to me. Sigmund's vague words, the faint traces of makeup on the Starlet's face, the feathers. Funny, though, how the feathers appeared to be a part of him instead of parts of a costume.

"Cool," I said, gesturing up and down over his lovely figure. "I mean, those feathers look totally authentic. When I first saw you, I thought you were naked." I returned to the lock, my focus intent, my goal of freeing Paris as quickly as humanly possible.

Paris laughed a little, his voice ragged. "The feathers aren't part of any garb. They are a part of me. I'm a king bird-of-paradise shifter."

Again my hands grew stationary as my focus shifted to Paris. "A what?"

A quirky smile raised a corner of his lips even as he lay down on the bed, sideways so I could see him. "Surely you've heard of shapeshifters?" he asked, amused.

But quickly his breathing turned shallow, his eyes grew glossy, and his whole essence seemed to leak life and vitality. He must have been seriously hurt, probably had internal bleeding or another fatal injury I couldn't see without X-ray vision.

"Yes, sure," I replied, going back to work. "Never met a bird shifter before. Or heard of them. Sorry." A question plagued me, so I asked, "How does that connect you with the element of Fire?"

Paris's smile, sunny despite his fatigue and ailments, made my heart flutter. "I'm also a phoenix." I glanced at him, curious beyond belief. He intrigued me almost to the point of morbid obsession. Perhaps it was due to his extraordinary loveliness and sweet disposition. "I was born a king bird-of-paradise shifter," he explained. "When I accepted the role of the Guardian of the Fire Shard, I magically transformed into a phoenix."

"An immortal bird of legend," I whispered, stunned at how I'd manage to live in the Unveiled world for over a decade and knew next to nothing of the vast wonders of that world.

Paris smiled, the expression fading as his eyes fluttered closed. "Yes. Of a kind."

I saw he was on the verge of fainting or dying; I had no way of knowing which at this distance. "Hey, stay awake, Paris. I'm almost there." The damn tumblers were frozen, which made it hard to pick the lock with any ease. Thankfully I was the best. One by one the tumblers snapped in place, giving way to my open-sesame touch. "Tell me more about you," I asked, my voice louder to keep him awake.

The Starlet's dove-like eyes opened but into mere slits. He was fading fast. But a ghost of a smile flickered across his sensuous lips. "You must tell them… the other Guardians… that Kamala is gone…." His voice dropped, disappearing into a muttered whisper every once in a while.

One tumbler left. I worked as swiftly as I could. This had never taken so much time in the past. Guess I had only my frayed nerves to blame. "Gone? Where'd she go? Paris?"

A long exhale from Paris, and I knew time was slipping through my fingers like fine sand in an hourglass. "She… she said…. Wu Yue…?" A raspy explosion of air puffed out of his lungs, along with new specks of blood. "Finn? You must…."

"I'll tell them," I promised in haste, afraid we'd lose him. Would that mean the loss of the Fire Shard too? From what Cameron had told me, the bond would indeed break. If a Shard was destroyed, the Guardian would die; did the same occur if the roles were reversed? *God, I hope not.* "No, you know what? You're gonna tell them yourself," I called out to him, feigning cheer in a loud, perky voice.

"No," Paris whispered, keeling over into a fetal position, groaning in agony and pain. "You must… touch me. Please, hurry…."

The last click and the following screech told me I'd succeeded in my lockpicking. In haste, I whooped and yanked the cell door open.

A chill warned me of another presence when a breath of icy air wafted over the hairs on the back of my neck. The smell of smoke told me what hovered behind me.

A revenant.

I TWIRLED around, standing between the revenant and Paris, who let out a shrill scream, in part a repetitive whirring sound, with an occasional croak. *How peculiar. A warning vocalization of the bird's, maybe?* An occasional wingbeat and flapping of feathers followed the noise.

Not that I had time to ponder that for longer than a split second.

Revenants were creatures of shadow, nothing tangible to them, useful as guards and with a taste for death. They had sharp teeth and nails, though, and they were always hungry. It was like being devoured by a cloud made up of blackness and smoke, razorblades and absolute zero. They were extremely rare, perhaps one to every ten million people. But it was true that shadows should be feared, especially after the Veil had lifted.

"Man flesh…. Tastyyyyy…," the creature hissed, starting to surround me, a blinding and suffocating vapor that I had no means of fighting off.

Chills ran up and down my spine, but I steeled myself against the confrontation. This wasn't my first shadow fight. Of course, last time I'd had a flashlight handy, and I'd been pointing it at the thing by pure chance.

This time my hands were busy with trying to save a life, me still holding the lockpicks with one hand and the cell door with the other.

A blow to my midsection came out of nowhere, literally. I couldn't see the blast. But it threw me across the cell against the wall. Pain shot through me as I slipped down the freezing stone, but I didn't have the opportunity to enjoy the respite as another gust of dark wind from the creature drew me hurling back toward it. I was pulled right through the swirling black cloud, and a kind of cold immersed me till I knew I'd die a Popsicle.

I was getting all too used to mortal danger these days, I thought glumly, as once again I foresaw my own death. Unfortunately, it looked like this time I might have company escorting me to the pearly gates, or wherever. Honestly, that bugged me the most.

A bright spinning whirlwind of rainbow-hued lights crashed against the churning blackness that made up the revenant, nearly blinding me too.

The creature screamed loud enough to break glass and withdrew rapidly back into the shadows, disappearing into the night, smoking and withering as it went.

The hallway stood empty again.

I staggered onto my feet and turned just in time to see Paris standing steadfast behind me, his beautiful plumage all fluffy and pointing up and out. This magnificent king bird-of-paradise shifter shone in the colors of the rainbow, each feather glowing with inner brilliance.

Talk about shining with an inner light.

As Paris's coat faded in brightness and hue, he trembled and swayed, apparently in distress as he'd probably used what remaining strength he had left. I rushed to catch him just as he collapsed, all but unconscious, weighing practically nothing. Paris was quite literally as light as a feather.

Gently, I laid him down on the tangled sheets, careful not to ruffle his feathers.

His steely grip on my arm forced me to bend till our faces nearly touched. A feverish fire burned in his brown eyes. I tried to dislodge his fingers, but he refused to yield his hold.

"I have a... a cousin I'm close to," Paris murmured, his brittle voice barely audible. It seemed to take great effort for him to form words, so I stayed silent and waited for him to finish. "His name... is Rome... Garnett... Baird. Tell him my lasts thoughts were of him."

Desperate not to lose him, I rushed to beg, "Please, don't die. The other Guardians are here, and they can heal you."

"It's too late." He coughed. I smelled something rotten in his breath, sickly sweet and nauseating. "I am dying."

Then I saw it. His perfect feathers changed color to gray. They crumpled inward, like dry husks withering, and one by one turned to cinders, a silent rain of ash falling from his body.

Paris was right. Our time had run out.

Tears singed a path down my cheeks. I didn't know what to do. If he died, could I give him mouth-to-mouth or chest compressions to keep him alive when it seemed his very essence was disintegrating? What would be left of him to aid? A pile of ashes?

Paris looked up at me, the feverish blaze in his eyes waning. "When I pass... the Fire Shard will be alone.... Please, Finn. Help me...."

"What can I do?" I asked him, my own voice tremulous. I'd never watched anyone die before I'd started this quest of ours to save the world. First Muirín, now Paris. Who would be next? Sigmund? Cameron? Me? "Paris, what do I do?"

His lips curved into a smile, a radiance undoubtedly matching his former glory. "Kiss me," he whispered, his weak, quivering hand releasing me.

How could I refuse a dying man his last request? Even if blood clung to his yellow lips like rubies. I bowed to get closer and pressed my mouth to his. His lips parted against mine, and his hot breath puffed into my mouth, the smoky flavor lingering on my tongue and his burning incense filling my lungs.

I gasped. My nerve endings scorched with a liquid fire infusing into my very being, choking me, incinerating me from the inside till all of me was aflame.

The human I'd been was lost as I was immolated from within. A new me was born out of fire, flaring into life, my first breath born of smoke, my first touch seared in flames.

His last whisper confirmed my doubts. "I was the carrier. Now it's up to you."

As I watched Paris Ellery Baird fall to ashes and crumble away in dust clouds, a surge of pure wildfire roared within me. Bright shining colors surrounded me, blurring my vision in a blaze. A power hitherto unknown to me coursed through my veins like magma. Was this the prismatic mana Paris had demonstrated when defeating the revenant? Paris truly had been a gem of a man.

A coat of black feathers sprung up through my skin, scattered here and there without reason or rhyme. My new plumage, dark all over, felt soft and silky on my fingertips. On my back, twinges of pain warned me of the beginnings of my transformation.

What am I?

A new voice of confidence answered me from within, from a well of magical insight I was not privy to. Until now, anyway.

Paradise-crow.

Could I accept the mysterious and mystical reply at face value and pretend everything was fine and dandy? I had never heard of bird shifters till today—and now I was one of them?

With the pangs of discomfort on my back intensifying, I had to ask myself awkward questions. Would I grow wings on my back? Would I one day be able to hover, glide, or fly? Could I soar through the clouds, sunshine bright on my face, fresh air hugging me in its cool embrace?

Paris had been born a bird shifter and then become a phoenix. I'd been born a human, but now I was both a paradise-crow shifter *and* the Guardian of the Fire Shard?

My brain told me that line of thinking and being was impossible, that I was imagining things, that Paris's horrid death had broken something fragile and sensible inside me, and now I was overcompensating with a fictional transformation. I was losing my mind… and my shit.

But my soul sang a song, a tiny little *whup* sound that sort of reminded me of a dog's woof. *My birdcall?*

A moment ago I'd suffered the freezing temperatures and frost clinging to my skin, as usual nipping at any exposed parts. But now a fire stoked to life in my heart and soul. A heat arose through my skin, steaming up the chamber. My breath had come out in soft puffs, but now a flame almost burst into the air from my mouth.

I couldn't deny the truth any longer. I wasn't insane. I had my answer.

I was a paradise-crow shapeshifter. I was a phoenix reborn.

And I was the new Guardian of the Fire Shard.

Chapter Twenty-Two

"FINN? ARE you all right?" Cameron's concerned voice sounded like it came from far away, reaching me over a great chasm.

Kneeling on the cold stone floor, I couldn't feel past the blaze within. I looked up, only then seeing Cameron and Sigmund clearly. Had they stood there, on the threshold of Paris's cell, for long? I had no idea.

"The Starlet is dead." I stared down at the soft mound of cinders, not a single ember in sight to suggest life. He was gone. And yet, somehow, he lived on inside of me. The new phoenix.

Sigmund growled. "That can't be. His Shard.... His power...."

"I... I think it's... inside me," I murmured, unable to veer away from the heap of ash that used to be a person, and a pretty amazing one at that. "Paris asked me to kiss him. I did. And... now there's a force within me. It's burning...."

Cameron knelt next to me, brushing his fingers under my jaw till I faced him. His skin had gone pale, fraught with worries I had only an inkling about. "Paris is a... *was* a phoenix. Fire flowed through his veins. If he was unable to be reborn...."

Anger twisted my gut into fiery knots. "Kamala tortured him."

Snarling loudly, Sigmund smashed his fist into the icy stone wall. The whole structure shook from the concussion, a testament to his physical prowess. "That bitch. I'll spay her. Then I'll flay her and make a little white elf rug of her skin, trampling it under my boot every damn—"

"Sigmund, please," Cameron cut in, vexed. I could tell his irritation wasn't born of his old friend's use of crude vernacular as much as it was his need to maintain control before our overheated emotions swamped us all. Cameron locked gazes with me again, empathy softening his features. "It is called the Kiss of Light. A transference of a phoenix's fiery essence from one living being to another. I've never heard of a cession to a human, though. A phoenix has traditionally always been a bird shifter."

I nodded, working out most of what Cameron said. "Paris said he was a carrier. Now I am. He was referring to the Fire Shard, wasn't he? That's why Kamala abducted him. Because Paris carried the Fire Shard inside himself and thus Kamala could only get her hands on it through, what, torture?"

Cameron nodded with a sigh. "A phoenix's fire is indistinguishable from the magical blaze of the Fire Shard. They merge and are as one. Only an overshadowing death or the destruction of the Fire Shard can separate the two. Paris was—I mean, now *you*—are the only Guardian with such an intimate connection with his Shard."

I frowned. "Shouldn't that mean the Fire Shard is inside me now?"

Sigmund inhaled and started to speak, but Cameron beat him to it, probably to phrase it diplomatically enough to calm me down. "A Guardian has to accept his role before the Shard. As long as the Fire Shard remains apart from you, you are a Guardian in name only."

"But…," Sigmund interjected, raising his voice to be heard, "you are the phoenix now, so you should be able to call your Shard, to hear its call to you, to find out where it is being held."

"Not as long as we're in here," Cameron cut in again, scowling at his old friend. "This fortress has been imbued and ingrained with blackfire spells. We can't hear the summons until we leave this place."

"We might as well do so now," Sigmund said with an unusual smooth purr, as though he were trying to seduce or persuade Cameron into seeing his side and conceding to his logic. "We've searched this hellhole from top to bottom. No one's here, and definitely not our Shards."

"I know why," I said swiftly, catching both men's attentions. "Paris told me Kamala is gone. She's gone to… oh fuck, what was it? Wu Yue…?"

Cameron grabbed my shoulders and shook me, not roughly, though. "Wǔyuè? Are you sure?"

"Uh, to the best of my recollection, yeah," I replied, glowering at his manhandling of my person. "Why? What is this Wu Yue?"

"The five sacred mountains of the Chinese Empire," Cameron replied, radiating apprehension and upset. "The Center Great Mountain, Sōng Shān, is called the Lofty Mountain; the Western, Huà Shān, is the Splendid Mountain; the Northern, Héng Shān, the Permanent Mountain; the Eastern, Tài Shān, the Tranquil Mountain; and the Southern, Héng Shān, is called the Balancing Mountain. As you can see, the Five Summits correspond to the five cardinal directions of geomancy and the five compass points of geography."

"So?" I asked, confused. "Is Kamala going to all these places? Why?"

Cameron rubbed a hand across his forehead, marred with worry lines and a droplet or two of sweat. "The five sacred mountains also correspond to the five elements."

"HOLY. SHIT." I plopped down on my butt, gobsmacked.

"According to legend," Cameron continued. "The five Elemental Shards were created on top of the five sacred summits. But that happened in times immemorial, the event going so far back to primordial ages before the Great Unveiling that there's no way to know for certain."

I struggled to remain composed. "You think maybe you should have told us before now, so we might have anticipated Kamala making this move? I mean, we've been one or two steps behind her strategies from day one."

"Hindsight is always twenty-twenty," Cameron remarked quietly. He looked ashamed and crestfallen, and I didn't feel like kicking a man when he was down.

"Okay, I got this." I collected all the tidbits of information to form a logical, cohesive whole. "Let's assume the legend is correct. Would it therefore be reasonable to deduce that using the Shards works best from those five scared mountains?" Both Sigmund and Cameron nodded, so I continued confidently, "Would it therefore be rational to conclude that Kamala is likely taking each of the Shards to the top of the corresponding sacred mountain to gain the full effect of the Shards' power in order to reforge them into the Elemental Crystal?"

Sigmund snapped his fingers. "If Kamala is the type of person I think she is, she's not gonna give the task to an underling. She's gonna want to arrange each Shard in its proper place herself, alone. That means she might not be done yet. Traveling through the Empire takes time. She's no teleporter. We've still got a window of opportunity."

Cameron straightened, hope rising back to his eyes with a vengeance, their golden glow pure magic. "Agreed. But not a huge window." He stood, determination written on his face, and smoothed his golden silk clothes till not a thread, button, or a cut of fabric was out of place. "We must go at once."

"Wait." I stood as well, grabbing Cameron's arm to stop him hurrying off. "You told me the five elements have two cycles, one regenerative, one destructive, right?" Cameron bowed his head slightly, patiently waiting for me to finish, so I added, "Considering Kamala's goal, it's probable she's gonna proceed in line with the baneful cycle?"

Cameron let out a breath, apparently understanding my point, and his eyes sparked in eagerness. "Yes, of course. If we follow that train of thought, the overcoming order is… the East is Wood, Center Earth, North Water, South Fire, and West Metal. So… first and foremost of the Five Summits is Tài Shān, then Sōng Shān, Héng Shān, the other Héng Shān, and finally Huà Shān. The ancient imperial pilgrimage to pay respects, *cháoshèng*…. It has been far too long since I have last walked that trail…."

"We must gather all Guardians for an assault on the five peaks," I suggested, since in my opinion that solution provided us the best chances of success. Divide and conquer. "If even one of us gets a Shard back, Kamala will have an incomplete set, and so she'll be unable to consummate her plan. She'll be out of luck, and we'll live to fight another day."

Chuckling, Sigmund gifted me with one of his rare toothy—or should I saw, fangy—grins. "You know what, Finn? I like the way you think. For a human."

I grinned back. "Don't you mean pet?" I barked out a doggy sound. Sigmund laughed, not even mildly insulted. I turned my attention to Cameron, who stood there, eerily silent and grave, his gaze glassy, aimed at nothing. "You don't approve of my plan, Cam?"

Cameron blinked, seemingly caught off guard midcontemplation. He stretched to his full height, as if squaring himself off to face whatever calamities came his way. "What? Oh no. On the contrary, Finn. I agree with your scheme. It carries with it an element of surprise. I'd say we have a relatively high probability of success."

Dammit. Cameron had reverted back to his overcivilized manner and speech patterns. I was no longer a fan. At first it had been appealing. Now, to me, his behavior spelled a distancing from the situation, its ramifications—and mainly, me. And I needed his support if I was to survive with even a shred of hope. Did he not need me anymore? Had I been useful to him in the least? Like Hathaway, had I outlived my usefulness?

"Kamala will probably have at least the first, the Wood Shard, in place already at the top of Tài Shān," Sigmund stated pensively, rubbing a hand over his fair beard. Surprisingly, the look suited him—and reminded me of The Thinker statue. "The Earth Shard is next." He regarded Cameron with narrowed eyes. "You think you can handle Kamala on Sōng Shān on your own?"

Baffling me to no end, Cameron hesitated. When he spoke, his words came out slowly. "I think it might be better for me to backtrack Kamala's movements, enter a summit she's already been to, and secure a Shard she's left behind. Dispatching her petty underlings shouldn't prove too much of a problem, I dare say. You two, on the other hand, can get ahead of her, stage an ambush, and regain control over your Shards."

I stared at him in complete amazement. Out of the corner of my eye, I saw Sigmund in an equally flummoxed state. Neither of us had foreseen this kind of hedging from Cameron.

What was he doing? What the hell could he be thinking? Was he... afraid? Surely not. An ancient dragon like him with virtually limitless powers? Yet his gentlemanly reticence gave me pause.

A melodious female voice broke in to the argument. "Dear Cam, you know that is not how it works. A Guardian of one Shard cannot touch another, even with good intentions and in the name of protection."

We all swiveled around to find Lady Vivian and Muirín standing in the hallway.

LIKE BEFORE, Vivian possessed a curious duality about her; she appeared simultaneously a fine human lady and an exquisite wooden creation. Her eyes glowed green, suggesting she was using her magic. I could confirm that with ease, since the ice, snow, and frost around us began to melt.

Muirín walked on two legs. Like her warrior priestess handmaidens, she wore silver-black armor over a glimmering blue shirt and loincloth. Her long black hair no longer cascaded down her back but was held together by a moon-hued helmet with a black-and-blue crest.

Now all five Guardians stood together, I thought, relieved. Now we had a chance.

"Vivian. Muirín." I bowed before them because that seemed the proper thing to do. "How did you find us down here in the cellblock?" I asked, dumbfounded but extremely pleased at their fortuitous arrival.

"I was in the neighborhood," Vivian replied. "I work with the Svalbard Global Seed Vault in Norway, so this remote enemy location was on my route, so to speak. I provide seedlings for their projects to preserve plants in their seed banks in the event of a global crisis or the worst case scenario."

"Vivian doesn't appreciate the cold climate, but I do my best to aid her," Muirín said at her side, smiling and proving without a shadow of a doubt they were close friends. "That is where my high tolerance for cold seas comes in handy."

Vivian took Muirín's hand in hers. The gesture appeared intimate, and I couldn't help but wonder as to the true nature of their relationship. Not that it was any of my business.

"Paris is dead," Sigmund grunted, sullen, his arms crossed over his chest. He exhibited his animal tendencies by snarling under his breath, anxiously shifting his weight from one foot to the other, and in general showing impatience, ferocity, and roughness, all emotions depicted on his face as he grimaced and scowled.

Both Vivian and Muirín stared at him in abject horror, eyes wide, tears forming, their lips parted for silent gasps and prayers. I proceeded to bring the ladies up to speed as quickly as I could before Sigmund could remind us how we were wasting time. After all, despite the losses, he wasn't wrong.

Muirín gave me a warm, empathetic look, a flicker of a smile, a gentle touch on my arm. "You're the new Guardian, Finn? I am at once proud of you and sorry for you. If there is ever any advice, comfort, or solace you need, I will stand at your side."

I swallowed hard, an emotional lump lodging in my throat. Were those tears itching at the corners of my eyes? "Thanks, Muirín," I murmured, grateful and blushing. She and the former Muirín were so alike it was uncanny.

"Our plan is as follows...." Cameron outlined my plan for us to split up, travel to the corresponding elemental summit, retrieve our Shards, escape at our earliest convenience, and meet up again at a safe location. This time Cameron had to acquiesce to a potential confrontation with Kamala, who likely was finished with the Wood Shard and could thus be with either the Earth or the Water Shard.

But there was still the question of how to get to our respective destinations swiftly.

"Um, I hate to break it to you, guys, but we're stuck on the other side of the world from Kamala," I said morosely. "Any of you got wicked speed, or beam-me-up-Scotty powers, or—"

"Union of the Five Phases," Vivian cut in, her tone regal and lofty, yet her expression soft, comradely, even mischievous. Next to her, curiously, Muirín seemed more down-to-earth. "It is an ancient ceremony of primordial magic where the five Guardians join hands and meditate, and ideally—"

"We'll be transported to our own Shards, wherever they may be," Sigmund finished, his skeptical pout evidence of his doubts. "It's never been done. It's just a legend."

"Much has happened lately to challenge our views on what is and isn't possible," Muirín said kindly, her words of reason resonating within me. "I vote in favor of the attempt."

"I agree," I said. The four mythical beings cast glances at me, causing me to cringe and redden until I got quite needlessly defensive. "I might be a de facto Guardian only, but Muirín's suggestion seems like a good plan. What have we got to lose by trying?"

I expected counterarguments. None came. Apparently we were all of the same mind. Nice for a change. The five of us joined hands. My left hand vanished into Sigmund's huge paw, but he held me unexpectedly tenderly. Perhaps he was used to being bigger and stronger than everyone else, and so he took great care with others when in close proximity.

Cameron grasped my right hand. His trembled noticeably. I surreptitiously observed him. A frown marred his high forehead, not even a ghost of a smile graced his beautiful mouth, and he appeared wary, squirming in place, licking his lips, and at times worrying his bottom lip. Clearly he was on the verge of a nervous eruption.

I squeezed his hand tenderly. Cameron jumped, gulping and staring at me, eyes wide and fearful. He really was afraid. For us… or for me?

I let go of Sigmund, pivoted on my heels, wrapped my arm around Cameron's neck, and closed my mouth over his. I felt him start at the sudden gesture, but then he relaxed against me, both his arms winding around me as he pulled me near. He opened his mouth, our tongues touched, and our breaths mingled. We shared a soft sigh, a sign of contentment, as the kiss deepened, and for a time the moment consisted of only him and me.

Sigmund chuckled. "Get a room, you two." Both ladies laughed as well. And just like that the depressing mood lifted, and we were all back in high spirits, confident of our abilities, and ready to take on the world. Well, take on Kamala, at least.

When we rejoined our hands and focused on our Shards and elements, live wires fired and connected us to each other and to our Shards. A charge filled the air, and all my body hairs rose to the occasion. My skin prickled, and my senses grew unbalanced, making me careen. A dizziness came over me as I pictured wildfires, candle flames, and the sun's potent shine, focusing as best I could on the element I was now tasked with protecting.

Next thing I knew, I stood on a windy mountaintop—alone.

Chapter Twenty-Three

THE TRIP from Iceland, even though completed in the blink of an eye via magical teleportation, had cost us timewise. The night had waned, and the eastern sky shone in purple hues, growing redder with each new glance.

Much to my astonishment, Mount Héng was more a gentle hill than a mountain high in the sky. In fact, the whole mountain range appeared lower than the majestic peaks at Huángshān, or Yellow Mountains.

Nonetheless, the mountain air was fresh and cool, the temperature in the midsixties, and the pastoral scenery of Mount Héng blew me away.

Distant rolling hills, with thick primeval woods and vast meadows dotted with flowers, were blanketed by thin sheets of mist, a serene ocean of clouds. The white-gray hues were slowly replaced by an orange tint from the rising sun, still asleep beyond the horizon. Eerie lights flickered warm but tiny, far down on the fishing boats gliding on the Xiangjiang River. The whole scenery shone in verdant shades of green.

Long shadows still dominated Zhurong Peak—which I now knew by name, thanks to Google and my iPhone—as the darkness of the night had yet to disappear in the wake of the day. I could see three of the so-called "four oceans"—trees, flowers, and clouds; the only one missing was snow. Wrong season.

A small Taoist temple, Zhurong Gong, rose on the highest peak. The rising sun bathed the drab gray granite walls with rich golden light, the orange hues tinting the temple with the fiery touches of the sun. A long and wide stone terrace led to steep stairs flanked by two stone dragons, the thirty steps rising to the Zhurong Shrine's arched gateway and temple. Above it were engraved three red Chinese characters—*zhù róng fēng*—in honor of the Fire God, Zhu Rong.

So, this was the birthplace of the Fire Shard. *My Shard.* God, I was gonna have to get used to calling it that, after a fashion. The beauty of the monument and the natural panorama gave me the gift of understanding the roots of the five elemental objects. A part of me, though I hailed from another corner of the world entirely, felt a kinship to this enchanting site. I couldn't explain it, so I merely stared at everything in awe.

The existence of the stunning shrine wasn't the problem; the group of hiking tourists with their backpacks and the line of Buddhist monks in their yellow robes were. The former were chatting away merrily and taking pictures, while the latter chanted quietly, bells in hand, ambling forward with heads bowed.

As soon as Kamala showed her resplendent but wintry face here, these folks would be in mortal danger. Collateral damage? Unacceptable. But how the heck to scare them off? Without violence and threats, hopefully.

Why did they have to be here so goddamn early? Dawn still dwelled beneath the hazy horizon, the first rays warming the air, casting brilliant lights into the sky and heralding the birth of a new day.

Unfortunately for me it looked like my day was well on its way to sucking big hairy donkey balls.

I wished I had some warning as to the overall scores of the game. My moves were part of the strategy, but I needed to know how my teammates were faring. I tried to tap my psin, but all I received was static, the screech nearly deafening me.

Was Kamala the culprit in my failure of communications? Or was it this holy site, with its innate magic, that interfered with my attempts at reaching my fellow Guardians?

Who knew. Who cared. All I knew was that my mojo was being crapped all over by the universe. And these people were still here.

So I went for my number-one trick when I wanted to get rid of people fast.

I started to cry. Loudly. And profusely. Then I increased my volume to wailing. Add a couple of long, unending rhetorical lamentations, and I quickly became the center of attention. The Chinese did not appreciate public displays of emotions, and certainly not big embarrassing shows with mental meltdowns.

Their eyebrows raised, the tourists snapped some photos of me, and then whispered among themselves, heading for the path down the mountainside. The Buddhist monks, however, approached me, sympathy flowing from their faces and words as they hugged me, told me in barely passable English everything was going to be okay, and then left to wander downhill, me with a few yuan in my pocket.

Once I stood on the summit alone, I whooped, did a little end-zone dance plus a moonwalk, and congratulated myself on succeeding without resorting to criminal activities.

"I rock. That's right. Uh-huh. Oh yeah."

Yup. I did every humiliating thing except crown myself king of the hill. And I wasn't far from that, either. Believe me.

As a seasoned thief, I cased the joint, such as it was, and came to a quick conclusion. I had precious few places to hide. And equally few ways of influencing my surroundings. No high-tech gadgets, alarm systems, motion detectors, thermal imagery, surveillance systems, etc., etc. I could toy with and make inoperative for long enough to rob—ahem, borrow— what I needed. That was the trouble with historical structures and cultural sites. Sooooo low-tech.

Sunrise was imminent, and on Zhurong Peak only the Shrine offered enough cover. I seriously doubted the spot for the Fire Shard could be inside a man-made building, and from inside it would take me too long to get to Kamala, if she was wary, on alert, and/or had an army of goons at her side.

So I rechecked. The long terrace was absent of stone railings for the most part, and all around on the hillside grew greenery, namely trees and shrubberies. Some could provide adequate shelter. The woods had to be old since a lot of them had lichen and moss growing on their tall tree trunks and wide branches.

I hopped over the edge of the terrace, found a hidey-hole behind a tree, and set out to wait for our nemesis to appear.

APPARENTLY KAMALA'S arsenal included a henchman with teleportation abilities.

That wasn't good.

It seemed, however, that said henchman couldn't bring a lot of people through, as only Kamala, the Snow Elf teleporter, and two other sentries appeared out of thin air.

That was promising, if not altogether perfect.

But as icing on the cake, Kamala was drenched, her white attire and armor dripping in rivulets, like she'd taken a swim with her clothes on. And she was cussing up a storm.

I grinned. Kamala's disheveled looks told me her last stop had been with Muirín, and the mermaid had given the encounter her all, attacking her foe with her element, drowning Kamala in water. Too bad Kamala still lived.

She punched her teleporting companion on the arm, forcing him to stagger backward, a litany of apologies filling the air. Kamala seemed enraged as she stormed toward one of the higher terraces, her three underlings following meekly on her heels.

On top of a white-gray stone terrace, with stone inscriptions and reliefs on the railings, stood a cylinder-shaped stone pedestal, with Chinese writing on the base, whitewashed plaques that gave the impression of paper. I had no idea what they read, as it had been years since I'd studied Chinese characters.

On top of the pedestal rose a granite boulder, now tinted by the orange glow from the rising sun. The shape of the boulder resembled that of a mountain. On it were carved in four golden Chinese characters, Héng Shān and Nányuè, both signifying the exact same thing with different phrases: Mount Héng or Southern Heights Mountain.

Kamala hustled toward the boulder, which told me it was meaningful.

My nemesis confirmed as much as she pulled a nutmeg-colored leather tube case from behind her back, popped open the top, and shook the tube until out onto her gloved hand fell....

The Fire Shard. Mine.

Unlike the two Shards that had resembled jagged fragments of a larger crystal, the Fire Shard appeared as a perfect sphere, with flames licking the inside of their confinement, spark showers dotting the inner whirlwind of wildfires, and fierce bursts of heat making the air around the round shape ripple and smoke.

Kamala began a terrifying chant, not unlike the spell I'd heard Cameron utter when he called upon the powers of the Earth Shard.

Savage flames, burning heat,
Walls get charred, fiery feet
Marching on to blazing beat.
Black and seared, melting meat,
Man will fall and face defeat.
Fire, arise to choke and reap.

The sun-colored boulder shook, swaying side to side, and cracked like a stone egg. I'd never seen stone do that. The rock splintered into five pieces, opening like the petals of a flower, exposing the inside. Within, a swirling pool of liquid lava roared, sparked, and flamed.

And in the center of the fiery pond rose a golden holder, as though untouched by the raging miniature inferno around it.

Evidently the Fire Shard functioned as some kind of activator for an old, intricate magical machine. The holder was the lock; the Shard was the key. But I didn't really need to guess what the contraption was for. I only knew I had to act.

WITH EVERY prayer and invocation I knew, I called upon the Fire Shard. I was technically kneeling before it, with the shining sphere in sight, so I vowed sincerely and from the heart that I would do everything and anything, sacrifice or battle, to defend the Fire Shard from its enemies, and safeguard the world from it.

In short, I swore an oath to be the Guardian of the Fire Shard till my dying breath.

If a magical force or a living entity dwelled inside the Shard, I hoped I could and had reached it in time. Surely the destruction of the world was a fate not even a magical object would wish to inflict upon the unsuspecting.

Besides, Kamala would have me for a terrible Guardian.

Kamala carried on chanting her horrid tune with creepy words. I was running out of time and windows of opportunity. I couldn't afford to wait for miracles or divine intervention. I had to make them happen on my own.

I snatched a pebble from the ground, said a sincere, though somewhat desperate prayer to the Earth Shard and to any divinities within earshot, and then tossed the thing as far as I could throw.

Thanks to the terrain and wildlife, the tiny stone hit some rocks, then some bushes, and caught the attention of Kamala's underlings. They pulled out their weapons in haste and, after a curt nod from Kamala, ran toward the noise.

I skipped over the railing, my rubber soles not making a sound, and dashed toward the stairs leading up to the small terrace. Kamala was too busy with her singsong spell to destroy the world to notice me. Even her eyes had drifted closed.

I snuck up right to her side with the intention of grabbing the Fire Shard midchant.

"Kamala, look out!"

The teleporting Snow Elf whose presence had slipped my mind, the man as thin as a twig, had not chased after my distracting clamor but had remained in place, conveniently masked behind the stone pedestal, vanishing from my line of sight. *Dammit.*

Kamala swiveled around fast, as swiftly as a twister. I was a mere five steps away. Recognition sparked in her eyes. "You! Blasted thief. Be gone!"

I perceived a contradiction in her between her race and her powers. But Kamala had no such problems adapting her blackfire magic with her Snow Elf heritage, it seemed.

Kamala's hand extended in a flash, and a smoking ball of fire slammed into my chest, knocking me off my feet and about fifteen feet in the air. I hurled through the skies and landed painfully on my back on the lower terrace. I slid across the stone slabs till I tumbled over the side, rolling downhill through bushes, rocks, grass, twigs, flowers, and an assortment of trash, most likely pieces of red prayer papers blown away with the wind.

I managed to grab onto a small tree. The yank tore at my sides, flashes of pain making my eyesight blur as red stars danced in my field of vision. Moaning, my fingernails broken, I succeeded in stopping my rapid descent.

"Fuck," I murmured as I struggled to get back on my feet for the return climb. "Shit, if this is a typical day for a Guardian, I'm gonna demand hazard pay."

I pressed at my side. A wet heat coated my fingers. A bleeding gash had appeared where her blackfire spell had hit me the hardest. Plus, I think at least one of my ribs had broken. Every breath hurt, and my lungs felt like they were on fire.

As I started my floundering ascent, I had to accept the fact that my track record as a Guardian sucked. Was the cause my lack of serious encounters with law enforcement and criminals other than my fence? I'd never needed to resort to my fists in combat before.

If I survived today and was accepted as the new Guardian of the Fire Shard, I required some serious practice in the art of combat. Too bad Bruce Lee was dead.

As I climbed—well, crawled—my way back up toward the terrace, a commotion resounded in my ears. Shots rang out, the noise much louder than I'd expected from my years of experience—watching action movies. A deafening roar followed, the mountainsides echoing with the sound, and the earth quaked under my feet.

That could only mean one thing….

Cameron.

Chapter Twenty-Four

CAMERON'S ALIVE. A fever of hope gave my feet wings. I panted and sweated through my rushed climb up to the terrace. I peeked over the side, cautious but anxious to get a move on.

My eyes grew wide with shock as I took in the scene.

Apparently new goons had followed Cameron from Sōng Shān onto the site here since the temple terrace swarmed with new bad guys.

Only… the men, big stocky guys with loads of body armor and carrying full-automatic weapons, were dancing and singing. Loudly too. They hopped and swirled about their partners in crime, shaking their booties (butts, not boots) and waving and swishing their arms about as they danced and whirled. The dance was the Charleston, I believe. For huge buff baddies, they sure had a lively rhythm going on, all light on their feet.

Their off-sync and off-key singing, however, was atrocious.

"Hello, my baby. Hello, my honey. Hello, my ragtime gal! Send me a kiss by wire. Baby, my heart's on fire!" This cute tune came from a goon well over six seven in height and massive with bulging muscles, his weapon tossed onto his back with a strap clinging to his chest.

"De Camptown ladies sing dis song—Doo-dah! Doo-dah! De Camptown race-track five miles long—Oh! Doo-dah day!" Another golden oldie from a surprisingly nimble little underling doing a mashup of the foxtrot and swing, kicking rather high for a man wearing full-body armor.

Four others were singing a children's song in perpetual canon and endless repetition. "Row, row, row your boat, gently down the stream. Merrily, merrily, merrily, merrily, life is but a dream." Yeah, what an earworm.

Add to that the ridiculous fact that they held hands while circle dancing, in merry-go-round style, and I was hard-pressed not to laugh and break another rib or puncture a lung.

The two henchmen I'd driven off with a noisy distraction had also returned. But they were equally preoccupied with their own dilemmas, as one was reciting the Gettysburg Address in true Abraham Lincoln fashion, back ramrod straight, his hands clutching at a nonexistent collar, and his expression solemn and devout. "Four score and seven years ago...."

The other spouted the same kind of nonsensical gibberish as I had back at Cameron's penthouse. "I thought a thought. But the thought I thought wasn't the thought I thought I thought. If the thought I thought I thought had been the thought I thought, I wouldn't have thought so much."

It was utter, superb, brilliant chaos. I think the likes of Lewis Carroll or Terry Pratchett would have appreciated the madness. I know I sure did. Ahh, Cameron's mischievous mastery at work. I couldn't help but grin and chuckle at the ludicrous sight.

On the upper terrace, however, Kamala hadn't stopped her evil chant to ruin the world.

That sobered me up pretty quick. I clambered over the edge and searched for Cameron but stayed low to the ground.

I spotted him on the highest terrace where the small stone temple, Zhurong Gong, was.

He was battling the teleporting Snow Elf.

Cameron's dragon powers came to light in all their magical glory as he spouted fire and smoke, his stomping feet causing the ground to tremble. He flung blocks of earth, stone, and soil against the fiend.

Unfortunately his adversary proved damned elusive. With his special psionic ability, he blinked in and out of reality, there one millisecond, gone the next, teleporting so fast he got in several strikes with his katana before Cameron could react.

But Cameron was no fool, and he still had tricks up his sleeves.

Instead of flames, he breathed out puffs of smoke and steam until the clouds cloaked him entirely, as though he'd vanished into thin air. I was certain his golden scales could be detected even through heavy layers of fog.

But then I realized where he had derived his name. Cameron. For chameleon and for camouflage. His scales could actually reflect their surroundings, like mirrors, until he became invisible to the enemy.

The male Snow Elf whipped up into the air when Cameron's dragon tail struck against his body, sending him flying until he hit the temple's orange-tinted stone wall and skidded down, falling to the ground bruised and bleeding.

I couldn't spare them another glance. Kamala had to be defeated. Cameron was busy; I could only hope the other Guardians would join us if at all possible. In the meantime, I was the only one left undisturbed and unseen.

I stalked through the throng of dancing and singing foes, grabbed a holstered weapon from one of them as I passed by, and headed straight for Kamala. I dashed up the stairs, stopped at the landing, and pointed my gun at Kamala, the red light at the end shimmering dangerously.

"Stop! I will shoot."

I wasn't sure how effective my threat was. I'd never killed anyone. I was a thief, not a murderer. Last time I'd held a man at knifepoint, Cameron had saved me from having to make the call and end someone's life. Now... I stood alone.

Kamala read me well, much to my chagrin. She halted midchant and swept her gaze over me, assessing. Her lopsided grin told me I wasn't fooling her. "No, little human. I don't think you will. You're not a killer. And I stand before you unarmed. Could you be so callous?" She let out an icy chuckle. "Could you be... like me?"

What did it mean to be human? I couldn't shake that thought. Were we all animals in human disguise, selfish and cruel, ready to do anything it took to survive? Or did we have a choice, reason and conscience to decide to put others before ourselves and to follow a simple creed—do no harm and do not kill?

I wavered. In hindsight, I probably shouldn't have. But what was done, was done.

Kamala laughed, the sound like clinking pieces of ice, a surprisingly melodious sound, quite harmonious. "That's what I thought. Every time we've met, I have bested you. Foolish mortal. I am centuries your senior and wiser. The basic truth of the universe is—"

"Let me guess," I interjected, my tone sharp and sarcastic. "Do unto others before they do unto you?" I smiled back at her, her own grin fading at the rise of mine. "Nah. It's too… mean."

Kamala stared at me as though I were a two-headed freak risen from under a rock. Her scorn radiated to me like toxic fumes. "Not at all," she said slowly. "It's enlightened self-interest." She turned her attention back to the ceremony.

I couldn't allow her to finish, so I said, "The thing is, lady… I *can* kill you." Kamala sighed impatiently, clearly not believing a word. "Since you like simplistic explanations, I'll be brief. It's a case of mathematics."

Frowning, she glanced at me, obviously vexed. "What are you droning on about?"

"Like Spock said, the needs of the many outweigh the needs of the few or the one." I was quite proud of myself for remembering the immortal line. "If by shooting you I can save all the people on the planet…? Well, in the end it's not a tough call."

Kamala's brow cleared as she smiled. "Looks you like you have balls after all. For a petty human, that is." From her tone, she wasn't going to lay down the Shard and surrender.

Apparently she and I had ourselves a good old-fashioned Mexican standoff.

"*Put down the gun!*"

Or not.

I glanced to my side as swiftly as I could without taking my eyes off Kamala. When I saw what awaited me, I froze in fear.

At the foot of the stairs stood Cameron—with the teleporting Snow Elf holding a knife pressed to his throat, the rattle of magical electricity eerily loud in the startling silence.

IN MOVIES and books, someone or something always saves the heroes from death.

But I had no time to wait for some *deus ex machina* to do its fancy trick. Probably because I didn't believe one might be forthcoming. Not even in the form of other Guardians, who undoubtedly had their hands full on other mountaintops.

To say I didn't have a clue as to what to do would have been highly misleading. I knew what I had to do, and it broke my heart.

Cameron stared at me, his expression serene and beautiful, the look in his teal-hued eyes kind and loving.

I actually felt my poor heart shatter to pieces. Unshed tears clouded my vision, forcing me to blink furiously. My jaw trembled, but I gritted my teeth to prevent my pain and sorrow from being seen by our enemies.

"Cam?" My voice cracked as I said his name. I could barely push the words out past the sizable emotional lump in my throat. Was it my heart rising to call out to him? "Cam… I'm so sorry."

Amazing me yet again, Cameron smiled. "It's all right, Finn. Do what you must. I will see you again in the great beyond."

My tears overflowing and my hands shaking, I fired the gun directly at Kamala.

The bullet ricocheted off her armor. Her low chuckle was scorn turned into sound.

I shot again, twice this time. A wave of her hand, and an ice twister caught the bullets in its wake, sending them flying to heights unknown.

I kept shooting till the gun clicked, signaling an empty magazine and chamber.

Whether she defended herself with ice or fire, the bullets disintegrated upon impact with her magic, the metal rounds melted or scorched, frozen or liquefied, in the end destroyed and ruined. I dropped the gun, now useless.

Fuckity fuck fuck. I closed my eyes, chastising myself. Of course Kamala controlled fire; she was a Shadowalker. Add to that her cryokinetic powers, and I didn't have a leg to stand on.

Kamala laughed at me. "Pathetic." Wow, so she really did kick people when they were already down. Shaking her head, she started to resume the chant.

But she stopped short when she realized her hands were empty.

Frowning in confusion and rising anger, she searched the pedestal for the Fire Shard.

"Lost something?" I asked politely.

A moment ago I had felt utterly helpless to save myself, my dragon, or the world.

Now, a fiery weight had settled into my heart. My body roared from magical flames, immolating me from within. Invigorated and reinforced, I grinned, in my mind already the victor.

Kamala snapped her head up, stumped, when she heard me speak. My smile did the rest. "You…?" Her disbelief in me being the new Guardian of the Fire Shard was sweet as sugar. "Impossible."

I shrugged. "Why should you be so shocked, Princess? I am a phoenix, after all."

At first stunned, she then growled. "Give the Fire Shard back, you miserable thief."

I smiled. "Actually… it ain't stealing when you take something that already belongs to you—like the Fire Shard belongs to me, its rightful Guardian."

This was surely the crowning achievement of my illustrious thieving career. Stealing without moving an inch. Only… it wasn't really stealing, now was it? Possession's nine tenths of the law. So sue me.

My grin widened into a grimace, as anger and retribution boiled inside me. "Paris may have died in my arms. But he died by *your* hand. And for that, I will show you no mercy."

FOR A badass supervillain, Kamala was damn quick to react.

Before the echo of my words had spilled out, she shot at me with icicles and ice balls, snow hurricanes, frozen winds, and icy breaths. Cold spikes passed within an inch of my life, a blizzard blinded me, and moisture arose from the earth to freeze my feet, pinning me literally where I stood.

But none of it lasted.

Flames struck out through my skin till a cocoon of fire surrounded me, and every dried-up leaf, blade of grass, and parched piece of soil ignited into a blazing wildfire, spreading its wall of flames around Kamala. A light as bright as the sun emanated from my eyes, dazzling Kamala till she had to close her eyes and shield herself with her arm.

Well, what do you know? I was a pyrokinetic. A fire-starter. *Cool.*

Her ice was no match for my fire.

Then again, my fire was no match for her ice.

Both our powers waned, vanishing in an instant. We glared at each other, both aware we were equally matched.

Out of the corner of my eye, I saw Kamala could no longer hold Cameron's fate over my head either. While Kamala and I had engaged in our magical duel, Cameron had broken free of his captor's clutches.

Instead of using his dragon might, though, Cameron had engaged his elven foe in martial combat. And, *hot dayum*, Cameron had moves! Swift blows and hard kicks, steadfast strength and elegant agility—all masterfully honed with skill and composure.

Cam knows kung fu? Wow. Hawt.

Cool as a cucumber, Cameron stood his ground but stayed light on his feet. I think he could have fought with his eyes closed. The male elf teleported in and out, trying to punch or kick Cameron into submission.

But wherever he struck, Cameron was no longer there. Instead, wherever the elf appeared, Cameron was there to greet him with a slap, a blow, a kick, or a hop and a skip.

In short, my dragon was wearing his enemy down.

All that assessment had taken but a few seconds. If her upset expression was any clue, Kamala had reached the same conclusion: she was losing. Her right-hand man was in trouble with a dragon, and her goon squadron remained busy with the effects of Cam's playful spells.

I tried to reach Kamala one last time because that was what good guys did. They gave their enemy a second chance to choose a different path.

"Kamala, stop this now," I called out to her, gaining her undivided—and absolutely furious—attention. "Give up the remaining Shards. Don't throw your life away on this futile battle. You can see you're outgunned."

A cold laugh broke the standstill as Kamala threw her head back and let it rip. "You're wrong, petty thief. Don't you know what you owe us, my kin and my world and our powers?" I was struck silent, struggling to figure out where she was going with this. "Glaciers shape not only the world but evolution itself. Humans wouldn't even exist without the last Ice Age. You owe your lives and your very existence to us. Our glacier magic is what gave your sad little race the chance to be born and to thrive."

"Huh." I cackled, finally seeing the humor in the situation. "So basically what you're telling me is that you already had a chance to wipe out all living things on the planet, then botched it up by not managing to keep the process going, and now you wanna do-over? Nuh-uh."

Kamala snarled at me, snarky like a vicious beast. "You humans are so shortsighted and small-minded. Think my offer through, Finn, and give it some serious thought. Why not join me? You're a thief. The Great Unveiling must have hurt your business ventures. Let me reforge the Shards with you at my side. Whether the Veil is lifted again or we hop ahead in the evolutionary scale, we can do it together."

Much to my own surprise, I gave her proposition a thought or two. For about a second. "You're right. The Unveiled world is chaotic and messy and unpredictable. But the damage is done. Like we humans did with the atom bomb, we learned to live with the ramifications and the weight of fate on our shoulders. We paid the price for our mistakes; you Snow Elves have to learn to live with yours."

"You are a fool, Finn," Kamala whispered, her tone threatening. "I could have made you rich beyond your wildest dreams."

"Nah. Fanatics make unreliable partners." I snorted cynically. "Besides, call me crazy, but I wouldn't trust you to keep your end of the bargain. I doubt you'd allow humans to gain such an advantage. As evidenced by your prompt, premeditated murder of Anthony Hathaway." Her eyes widened, and I shook my head rather theatrically. "What? You forgot the poor dude already? Shame on you." I *tsked* at her.

Kamala stared at me, at first with pure unadulterated hatred. Then she grew cold and calm. "As you wish. I shall undo the mistake of humanity by wiping you and your kind away from the face of the new Snowball Earth."

Chapter Twenty-Five

WHEN KAMALA attacked, she held nothing back. A storm of magic and blades, she came at me with the force of a bulldozer or a battering ram.

Ice magic in one hand and a katana blade in the other, Kamala screamed and charged at me, forcing me to back off or get sliced and diced. Her ice balls whizzed past me like ammunition, and her sword swung over my head, cutting a few strands of hair clean off.

Like throwing punches, I blasted my own fireballs at her, singing her hair and searing her armor. That only made her madder.

And God, she was wicked fast. Must have been the elf in her. I kept missing her as she swerved and ducked and in general avoided getting hit by anything more than the heat of my missiles. Damn her.

Her ice spikes, however, kept bashing against my black armored vest, pushing me off balance. I staggered backward—and rolled right over a stone railing to land in the bushes.

As I climbed to my feet, struggling with branches and leaves more than with my foe, Kamala jumped over me to the lower terrace, doing a rather impressive flip midair.

During her flight through the air, the tip of her blade cut across my left arm, piercing my suit, my skin, and my flesh. Hot blood flowed down my arm, slipping under the fabric. Searing pain sliced through me, making everything wobbly. My arm started to shake.

Good thing I was right-handed.

Not that I was doing so well anyway, which became all too apparent when she pelted me with ice balls. Only by the grace of God and the Fire

Shard did I manage to stave off defeat. The flames burning inside me thawed every blast of ice and snow she hurled at me, most even before they hit me. Her katana was something else.

Defensive fighting wasn't working for me. I had to get on the offensive.

With a sharp shout, one I couldn't quite believe I'd made, I stormed at her. Surprised, Kamala brought her blade up, probably with the intent of hammering me to pieces with it. I got to her first. I grabbed her wrists before she could bring the blade down on me and cut me in half. The move brought us nose to nose.

Kamala snarled at me. "I will kill you, thief. And I will destroy everything you hold dear in this world."

"Not if I get you first." I admit, not the most creative response, but I was kinda too busy to think of a smartass retort. My left arm was killing me.

Kamala barked out a laugh. "Unlikely."

I'd assumed her physical prowess comprised agility and nimbleness, like mine. But as she wrenched her hands free with a show of superior force, I had to concede she'd held much back.

Kamala smacked her palm at my face. I tilted back an inch and avoided a collision that would have broken my nose and sent me flying backward, dizzy and disoriented. Still, she brushed against me, stinging the tip of my nose. At least there was no blood.

She swung her sword like a hurricane of steel. Thanks to my acrobatic line of work, I ducked and dodged, retreating toward the steep stairs up to the Zhurong Gong stone temple. I used every trick available to me, be it backflips, cartwheels, parkour jumps, somersaults, or capoeira.

As I stepped onto the lowest step, I yanked out my magical knife, the blade glimmering with lightning-blue energy.

Kamala scoffed. "Thief." Not much of an accusation. I'd heard it before. Besides, from my point of view, I'd liberated the lethal weapon from a villain.

As her katana clanked together with my knife, a blue spark shower spread about us, and the resulting clang rang in my ears. My injury made it hard for me to preserve my stance and utilize counterforce to block her sword from piercing my body.

I allowed Kamala to shove me down, back against the stairs. I bent my knee between us and kicked her off me. She tumbled backward and rolled around, on her feet again in less than a blink of an eye. *Damn her.* I hadn't bought more than a precious few seconds at best.

"Strike like you mean it, human, or you will lose." Kamala's advice I didn't need to be told. I was already doing my best.

But she clearly knew what was in my mind as well as I did. I avoided direct confrontation with her because I didn't want to kill her. To be precise, I didn't want to become a murderer. Taking a life was bad juju and even worse karma. I'd never even had to consider the possibility I might have to kill to save myself, another, or the whole wide world. Now… it looked like I had to.

I hopped backward up the stairs as Kamala ascended with me, a few levels lower. There was no hesitation in her eyes. If she got the drop on me, she would take it.

Behind her, out of the corner of my eye, I saw something that defeated my spirit in an instant.

Cameron disappeared.

And it wasn't the Snow Elf's doing, judging from his stunned expression. A billowing dust cloud told me in no uncertain terms that Cameron had camouflaged, made himself invisible, and taken flight, basically dusting himself off and fleeing.

The concussion wave of his sudden departure spread outward, like a ripple in a pond. The breeze was so strong it knocked all the bad guys around him down, pushing them back until the lot rolled over the edges of the terrace, down the steep hillside where I had already ventured. I doubted I'd ever see any of them again.

But they didn't matter. Cameron did. I could scarcely breathe, my heart threatening to splinter into a million pieces.

He left me…?

KAMALA GLANCED over her shoulder. When her gaze returned to me, her smirk grew in confidence. "Aww, looks like the poor little dwagon got scared. Hope you didn't bet big on him."

I swallowed hard, unable to breathe. Why would Cam leave? He had to understand the fact that if we didn't triumph over Kamala today, the world would be lost. None of us got do-overs.

Unfortunately, I didn't have time to worry about Cam's motives. Kamala crept up the stairs toward me, her katana balanced, her expression serene. She probably knew that now she could dispose of me without interference from my comrade-in-arms.

I backed up slowly, keeping her in my sights while simultaneously checking out my surroundings. None of the goons reappeared, so that was positive. But none of the other Guardians appeared either, and that was definitely negative.

Kamala chuckled, the sound menacing in the worst way. "What's the matter, Grayson? Lost your nerve?"

An unbidden image of Paris rose to the forefront of my mind. A burst of vengeance erupted inside me. Cam might be gone, but I had my own score to settle.

"If I were you, I'd be more worried about myself," I growled out.

A flicker of surprise showed in her eyes and her stance, a flash of uncertainty, as she stopped for a second before advancing on me again. Kamala said nothing. I supposed the time for words was at an end.

Grimacing, Kamala dashed up the last few steps as I retreated to the highest terrace, the stone temple at my back. The sun turned the gray stone golden. It reminded me of Cam—who wasn't here anymore. I stood alone.

Kamala brandished her katana at me. I blocked with my knife, the electric rattle stark in the air, echoing off the stone walls. The smell of burning attacked my nostrils.

Bombarding me with a series of sword strikes, Kamala aimed to corner me. I jumped, using the stone railing as a springboard, and vaulted out of harm's way. On a hunch, I suspected my dodging efforts wouldn't work for long.

She kept coming. Her katana lashed and cut through the air, every time missing me by less than an inch. Maybe elf kids were taught fencing the moment they could walk. Who knew? I was in trouble. She'd cut me to red ribbons in no time at all.

But I remained steadfast. I could only hope the other Guardians, and Cam, would soon come to my rescue. They were my only chance of living to tell the tale.

With a swinging kick, I disarmed her, the katana winging into the side of the temple, a sharp clink heralding its impact. I surprised even myself with the successful move.

The act surprised Kamala too. But her vehement reaction came faster than mine. With a sharp shout, she rammed into me, her shoulder slamming into my diaphragm. We both tipped over the stone railing. I managed to get a grip, my arm wrenching badly, and not fall. She didn't, but the drop wasn't steep, so she was on her feet in an instant.

I climbed up to the railing. By then she had stormed up the stairs, and we faced off yet again. She came at me. I jumped over her, knocking her on her belly against the railing. She *oomphed* but didn't appear any worse for wear.

Growling, she reached for her belt—but came up empty-handed.

"Looky what I got," I singsonged, dangling her own knife in front of her, the magical energy glowing blue.

Kamala charged at me. I had two knives; she had nothing. I fended off each punch and blow aimed at me. I slashed her clothes to shreds, but the blades did no damage to the armor.

With an almost aerial ballet-dance move, Kamala hopped to the spot where her katana lay. In the blink of an eye, the weapon was back in her hands.

A whirlwind of steel, Kamala whipped and stabbed at me. I avoided death by the skin of my teeth. She overwhelmed me, even with my two blades to her single one.

Finally she kicked me in the gut. I grunted in pain, folded over, and landed on my butt on the terrace floor. Clearly I wasn't meant to be a warrior.

Kamala approached. The tip of her blade shone in the bright sunlight. She jabbed at me. I rolled backward to avoid the stab and to disengage from the fight. The move hurt like hell, my stomach roiling and nausea rising in my throat.

I hadn't gotten far. Kamala stepped up to me, her feet making no sounds. Ice emerged from her hand and glided down the katana, covering it with a frosty sheath. My breath came out in frozen puffs as the air chilled around me.

"Time's up, thief," she said, advancing with determination. "Say your prayers."

With my fingertips, I felt one of the knives at my back. I slipped it into my hand and tossed it, figuring Kamala was close enough for me to hit something.

The magical blade sunk into her left side at the tiniest rift between two armor platings. I gasped in shock. How lucky was that throw?

Moaning, Kamala staggered and tripped, fell backward, and dropped the katana, which landed at her side with a clink. She pulled the knife out, grunting in pain. Blood trickled down from the open gash, though she tried to cover it with her hand.

Still in agony myself, I fumbled to my feet, snatched the katana, and stood over her, the blade aimed at her exposed throat. "Surrender, Kamala. I don't want to kill you. But... I will, if you persist with this folly."

Hunkering on one knee, Kamala grimaced, staring up at me, a peculiar winning smirk on her face, as though sure she hadn't lost. "When I tortured him, Paris squealed like a pig brought to the slaughter. The more he screamed, the more I hurt him. His anguish made me laugh."

My hand shook. Rationally, I knew what she was doing, trying to aggravate me to the point of murder.

Images of the past couple of days rose in my mind: Cam dying and buried under the seabed. Muirín lying dead on a cold marble floor with the smoldering ruins of her serene palace around her. Paris in chains, his tortured and frail body and haunted eyes an everlasting testament to the horrors he'd endured....

I had so many reasons to kill Kamala. And only one reason not to.

My voice trembled as I said, "I could be like you. Call vengeance justice and be done with you once and for all. I could kill you and believe I was doing the right thing."

It took every good part of me to pull the blade back from her jugular.

"But I am nothing like you," I finished, feigning most of the determination I put in my quivering voice. "And you aren't worth the bad karma."

Pivoting while crouching, Kamala struck me on the shin with her booted foot. The blow knocked me down.

Only... instead of falling, I floated, my feet no longer touching the ground.

When my clothes incinerated and rained down from my body in a thick black cloud of smoke and cinders, I realized I was on fire. Literally.

Chapter Twenty-Six

HUGE SPRAWLING wings expanded from my back, each feather burning with red, orange, and yellow flames. I gathered I had somehow completed my transformation into a phoenix. Tiny fiery explosions seemed to function as catalysts for further growth spurts for my wings until they expanded far beyond the length of my body.

Nifty. And not a moment too soon.

Oddly, I felt no pain. I mean, wings had sprouted from my back, literally out of my body, but I experienced no agony or torment, not even any discomfort. The wings seemed… like they'd always been there, a part of me from birth. Like they simply… belonged.

I didn't know how better to explain the ease of my metamorphosis. But I had no extra time to dwell on my emotional well-being and physical transformation at length.

Kamala hissed, standing at the foot of the stairs. She swiped the katana at me but missed by a mile. I floated too high above, a bit farther from the earth with every breath I took. I think my wings did that on their own, the heat essentially lifting me.

"Coward!" Kamala howled at me, unable to reach me. "You know what I'm going to do if the Veil won't unlift and I get an evolutionary boost instead? I'm going to invent a freezing machine that will send your precious world into a new Ice Age."

Though this was hardly her first threat aimed at me personally, this fabulous invention of hers sounded like a declaration of war on humanity. Could she actually accomplish such a feat with her newfound intellect?

Probably. Her people at Svartifoss hadn't wanted anything to do with her, but that hadn't even slowed her down.

"If you want to stop me," Kamala yelled from below. "You're going to have to drop back down here to do your dirty work. Or are you truly a lowly yellowbelly? Is that the naked truth, human?" Her stark laughter should have told me something was up.

Flames rippled over my figure like a second skin, covering me head to toe. My clothes had completely burned off. Beneath me, on the whitish terrace, lay a pile of gray ashes. As a result, I'd also lost all my thieving gear, including weapons. Phoenix's fire was apparently quite sturdy stuff. Dissolving-chemical sturdy shit. Was that a thing?

Then, as the true reality of my situation struck my consciousness, I realized I hovered above my enemy—*buck naked*! That was what Kamala's scornful laugh had indicated.

The sudden shock hit me like a freight train.

In distress, I felt the fire leaving me. My wings vanished. Naked, I flailed in midair. Then I fell. No amount of flapping saved me. I screamed.

Something soft cushioned my fall to the terrace at the foot of the stairs. A sharp grunt came from beneath me, followed by a long whimpering exhale. Something sharp pierced my shoulder. At first it felt like a little pinprick. But soon the acute ache grew into a splintering stab of pain.

I opened my eyes, unaware of when I had closed them. Probably during the inevitable descent through the heavens.

Under me, twisted into an awkward position like a broken doll, lay Kamala. Her eyes wide and her mouth agape, she stared up at me, blinking in disbelief.

Through her chest pointed the katana, the tip embedded and lodged into my shoulder.

Blood trickled from her mouth as she drew shallow breaths. "You...," she murmured, her voice astonished, likely at the thought of her impending death.

Not much of the blade could have stuck into my flesh. I would have felt that for sure. I could pick myself up and be free. The wedged handle of the katana peeking out from under Kamala meant there was no such easy way of pulling it out of her.

I found it hard to breathe. I had caused this terrible accident. Would I be the cause of her death too?

"Please, stay still," I urged her, struggling to breathe and remain calm in the face of the sheer panic that had me trembling like a leaf. "I'm gonna get help, okay? You're gonna be fine. It's not so bad." My voice disappeared into gurgles at the end when I couldn't even convince myself.

Kamala's lips twisted into a cynical smile, and a hoarse chuckle followed. "No. I'm going to die. You did well, human. Before you, no human has managed to slay an elf. You'll go down in history… killer."

Tears welled in my eyes, distorting my vision of the elf maiden whose mirth murdered me. My jaw quivered, my throat clogged, and my heart pounded so hard I could barely hear a thing.

"I didn't want to kill you," I whispered, able to do so because I still lay partially on top of her. Whatever scrapes or bruises or gashes I had from the fall, they no longer mattered. "I'm sorry." I had to tell her that, even if she made fun of me or died then and there.

Kamala stared up at me. Her smile faded. Her eyes narrowed in suspicion—and in part, confusion. "You would apologize for defeating me in combat? I would not be so apologetic were I in your shoes."

I let out a dry chuckle. "I'm not wearing any shoes." A short laugh wracked her whole body. New droplets of blood spattered on her face. "I've always believed everyone deserves a second chance and that none of us can take the life of another. Bad karma. And we're not gods."

Kamala sighed. "You would have made an excellent elf."

I heard a noise close-by. I whipped my head in the direction of the sound. On the small terrace, the rock that had opened up like a cracked egg had closed again, none of the torn seams in sight.

That spelled the end of Kamala's dastardly plan to end the world.

"Tell me how to alert your people so I can get you the help you need," I pleaded with her. I needed to have faith that she still stood a chance of survival. Even with a broken sword stuck through her chest.

Kamala shook her head slowly. Perspiration appeared on her forehead, her cheeks held a feverish blush, and dark circles surrounded her haunted eyes. "I… I want to go home…. I'm tired. And I despise your world. I hate what you humans have done to it. Every precious gift nature has given you, you've ruined and destroyed in your carelessness and indifference. If I still could... if I still had the energy... I would kill you all. It's what you deserve."

"Not every human is like that," I said in weak defense. "Most ordinary people do care."

Kamala's gaze grew dark and dangerous. "It's too late. You've gone too far. Sooner or later someone will annihilate you. You'll most likely do it yourselves."

Her cold snicker told a story of relentless rancor, a venom that had poisoned and withered the good within her. All that was left was icy barren soil, too late to plant the seeds of trust or friendship.

"You can teach us," I argued—though I could see her eyes growing glassy. "If you let go of your hatred, you could show us how to be better."

Kamala blinked, trying to focus. Her chest didn't rise so much anymore. "I wish... I do wish I had met... you sooner, thief," she muttered, her words becoming a jumble. "Perhaps I might have... chosen a different path." A decisive spark ignited as she locked gazes with me. "Be a good Guardian, Grayson. Be a good human. You're a better... elf than me. Maybe I won't... haunt your... dreams...."

Her voice faded with the wind. Her chest stopped moving. Her eyes lost their glow.

Kamala was dead.

I started to cry.

I STARTED back to awareness of the outside world when a warm rug was placed over my shaking shoulders. I dried my tear streaks with the back of my hand and looked up, a total mess.

All the Guardians had gathered around me—and Kamala's corpse.

Sigmund had tucked me under the gigantic dire wolf rug he carried on his back. The strong pungent odor of smoke and roasted meat reminded me of his cavern, where I'd been safe for a while. Sigmund patted my head clumsily, as though I were a pet dog, which I found kind of funny. Muirín knelt next to me, taking my hand and squeezing. Her soft, soothing touch grounded me, as though I'd immersed myself in a bath and washed away the suffering and loss. Vivian knelt on my other side, her warm arm coming to rest over my shoulders, her fingers caressing my temple almost absentmindedly. A fragrance of flowers and summer trees surrounded me, and for the first time in years, I thought of home.

And then there was Cameron. Of all the Guardians, he was the only one who didn't so much as brush up against me. That stung. But no more than his desertion from the battlefield had. His face was impassive, as though he had no feelings about me, the overall situation, or the outcome at all.

If I hadn't known he was a dragon, I would have likened him to a robot.

"Finn? Are you all right?" Muirín sounded deeply worried about me. Too bad Cameron didn't seem to give a flying fuck.

"I killed her." I sounded alien to my own ears, detached and defeated, as if I didn't care one way or another.

"All life is born with the expectation of an eventual end." Vivian's words weirded me out. She was an immortal being. Who was she to speak to me about life and death? What could she possibly understand about mortality?

I barked out a derisive laugh. "What the hell does any of that mean to beings like you who cheat death and make a mockery of life on a daily basis? Nothing. Everyone and everything is transient and irrelevant to you."

The women gasped. Sigmund growled. I felt them start at the sound of my vehement voice. I knew I was being unfair, and I regretted my words instantly. I hated myself for killing someone, and I lashed out at those around me, people who didn't deserve it.

But how could they console me? They hadn't killed Kamala. I had. I stood alone. As a vile murderer.

"You didn't mean to kill her." Cameron's voice seemed distant, as though it came from far away, beyond the horizon, or maybe deep underground. "You are not a murderer, Finn. You are a good man who fell victim to circumstance. Kamala chose her own path to ruin. None of this is your fault."

Remembering to clutch the fur on my back so it wouldn't drop and leave me exposed in my birthday suit, I jumped up, wrath distorting my vision and sensibilities. "No, this is *your* fault! You ditched me, left me alone to fend for myself. It must have crossed your mind, that humongous ancient brain of yours, that this might happen. That I might murder her. Or that she might kill me. And you left. You didn't care."

Cameron's lashes fluttered as he blinked. Now there were emotions on his face. His composed expression crumbled as I went on. "Finn, that's not true. I did care. I *do* care." He took a step forward, his arms rising to… what? To knock some sense into me? To shake me till I calmed down? To embrace me as though my serenity depended on his actions?

"No, Cam. *That's* the lie. That you care." I backed off fast, and he stopped, his hands dropping to his sides. His rejected, disappointed look did little to appease me. I was too mad to listen. I shook my head, drowning in enmity and ill will. "I'm just a poor stupid human. Good enough to fuck to distraction when the world's about to end. But nothing more than trash after that."

Cameron's features hardened. He must have gotten furious too. "Finn, I know you're sad and angry right now. But I beg of you. Stop."

"Beg?" I repeated, so caught up in wrath I shook from the force. "No! *I* begged. When you vanished into thin air. I begged then. I prayed, I pleaded, I wished. But I guess you had better things to do, more important than—"

"I am the Guardian of the Earth Shard," Cameron cut in, his voice gruff. He fisted his hands at his sides as he stood there, back ramrod straight. "I heard its call. I had to answer. I had to save the Shard."

I blinked back furious tears. "What about my call to you?"

Cameron opened his mouth, but nothing came out. He closed his lips without a word. I knew better than to expect anything. He didn't look away, a steadfast figure of responsibility, an oath taken, a duty to follow. His obligation would always come first, I realized.

Worst of all, I was well aware that was as it should be.

The same way the Fire Shard now was my first responsibility.

No room for love.

I closed my eyes, the pressure behind my lids tight and pounding. I felt like a cloth worn so long it had become thin and frayed. I needed rest. I needed to be by myself.

"I want to go home," I said to them, weary to the bone and tired of more shit than I could name.

Chapter Twenty-Seven

A month later

ANOTHER LETTER from Cameron. Sitting in front of the unlit fireplace at my home in the suburbs of Sydney, I stared at the letter in front of me on the wooly rug.

I didn't dare touch it, for I feared somehow Cam's magic would ooze through the paper and ink, mesmerize me till I felt dizzy and went to him.

I'd burned the previous letters. A new one came in the mail every two, three days.

On the one hand, I was well aware my behavior was childish and foolish. A huge part of me longed to read what he had written to me. Would he apologize? Would he explain? Would he entreat me to come to him and be his—

That was the point where my curiosity usually ended. I couldn't see that scenario come to fruition. I had hurt him; hell, I'd hurt the other Guardians too. I'd insulted them, accused them of being insincere and indifferent, and I'd walked away without a backward glance.

I buried my face in my hands. If I was totally honest with myself... I missed Cam. In the span of the couple of days I'd spent with him, I had been someone new, a better version of me, a kind of a hero.

And sometimes heroes had to kill.

Every time I thought about contacting Cam and reading his letters, a stark, cold visual of Kamala's glassy eyes popped up before me. And I couldn't bear it. It was too much. I couldn't get past the notion of Cam betraying me by abandoning me at my darkest hour. And I couldn't forget I had caused Kamala's death.

I crumpled the letter and tore it to shreds.

As expected, that didn't make me feel any better.

I missed Cam.

LOUD BANGING on my front door in the middle of the night startled me awake, making me tremble in panic. Disorientation waned as I decoded the cause of the noise.

I stumbled out of bed in my black boxer briefs, managed to grab a black T-shirt from the back of a chair, and headed toward the front door. My brain was still woozy. I'd lived in Sydney for years, and I still didn't know the names of most of my neighbors.

As I grabbed the door handle, a brief notion of the cops lurking outside, ready to bust in and arrest me, crossed my mind. Been a long time coming, that eventuality. Nonetheless, I unlocked and yanked the door open.

A growling Sigmund was an unexpected sight. "Took you long enough," he grunted in his hoarse tone, the one that sent shivers down my spine. Instinctive fear of predators as my addled brain warned me.

"What the hell are you doing here?" I asked, bleary-eyed and barely standing on my wobbly knees.

Sigmund scoffed, shoved past me, and headed for the liquor cabinet, probably thanks to his sense of smell if his sniffing was any indication. He gripped one of the bottles, bit off the cork, and tossed back a mouthful. "Mmm, smooth," he murmured with no small amount of delight.

I blew out a breath. "It should be. That's 1937 Glenfiddich. One bottle costs $20,000. Thank you so much for drinking the one bottle I actually acquired legally."

"Oh?" Sigmund didn't seem upset at having deprived me of my pricey whiskey since he shrugged and took another gulp of the rich walnut-hued liquid. "Nice. You can really taste the toffee and cinnamon."

I plopped heavily down on the couch and wiped a hand over my tired face. "I wouldn't know." I looked up at him. "Why are you here? To eat me?" I spoke jokingly, but a nervous feeling crept into my mind.

As usual, Sigmund was striking in his appearance. He liked his fair beard trimmed, as far as I could tell, and the fluffy fur on his back made him seem taller, broader, and definitely more dangerous and animalistic. His blue-and-silvery gaze bore holes into my self-confidence.

"When we met, thief," Sigmund said, his head tilted and his voice rough. "Did you get the impression I like company?"

I frowned, confused about the course of our dialog. "Um, no?" Living in a cavern in the middle of a frozen wasteland didn't meet the criteria of being a people person in my honest opinion.

"As fond as I am of Feilong, his constant wallowing in my best ale is starting to grate on my nerves." Sigmund stepped closer, sat on the edge of the coffee table that creaked under his weight, and kept me in his sights, baring his teeth. He leaned closer, and I could smell the cedar and cloves from the whiskey in his sour breath. "I live underground beneath the tundra. Typically that means I don't get many visitors, I don't entertain guests, and I don't do sleepovers. That's how I like it."

I swallowed hard. "Wh-what's that gotta do with—"

"With you?" His fangs dropped fully, and his one good eye turned into a silver moon. Like looking into a mirror, I could see my own reflection staring back at me. "Take a wild guess, Grayson. I dare you."

I blinked and looked away. Sigmund scared me. He could kill me easily, like swatting off a fly, without even thinking about it. I couldn't speak. My tongue glued to my palate, I tried to find the right words to deflect his targeting me. But I had nothing.

Until his words pierced through the fog of self-hatred clouding my judgment.

"Cam's at your place… wallowing?" That seemed utterly impossible. Cameron was the most disciplined person I knew, the wisest and the strongest.

Sigmund growled. "Yeah. Because of you."

Though I controlled my facial expression, I couldn't stop my heart missing a beat. It was hope, I recognized. "M-me…?"

Sigmund rolled his good eye, back to blue again. "How the hell can that come as a surprise to you?" He shook his head, his hackles rising, his mane much like a wolf's fur. "You better come get him, Grayson. I'm down to my last ale caskets. And you ever seen a dragon drunk? Let me tell you, it ain't pretty. I need to restock on fire extinguishers."

"Oh." I was at a loss for words. I couldn't even imagine Cameron intoxicated.

"Would it kill you to get him off my territory?" Sigmund asked, his voice a testament to the frustration he must have felt.

I bristled. "Poor choice of words, I'm sure."

Though Sigmund looked abashed, I had a hunch he wasn't going to back down. "Finn, are you really gonna blame him for doing what a Guardian is supposed to do, which is to protect the Shard at all costs? You have to know he did the right thing, acted in the name of the greater good. As long as the sacred mountains were activated, the threat was real and imminent."

"I know." I said it because it was the truth. Cam had performed his duty as a Guardian well. He'd made it possible for the world to carry on, unaware of the devastation that almost took place. I rubbed a hand across my forehead, again hot and sweaty, the pounding headache on the rise once more. "I just... I can't help but think that if Cam hadn't left me to face Kamala alone, she might not have... died."

Sigmund sighed. "That death weighs heavily on your conscience, does it?" I nodded, so he went on, his tone surprisingly level and his words slowly seeping into my consciousness. "I've been around longer than the recorded history of man. I have killed many. And thanks to my perfect lycan recall, I remember each and every one, their names and faces etched permanently into my brain."

I looked up. His eyes were dark with a glow I'd not seen before. "D-do you regret them?"

Sigmund shrugged, but I could tell the gesture was far from nonchalant. "Some. Not all. They weren't all good men. And... a few didn't die after my bite. They transformed and became a part of my bloodline, inheriting my curse."

That sounded strange to me, so I asked, "Lycanthropes don't eat humans, do they?"

A lopsided grin lifted a corner of Sigmund's mouth. "No. They change but they don't share my, uh... craving."

Sorrow compressed my chest, a brutal, hollow reminder of my dark deed. "How can you sleep at night after all the atrocities you've committed?"

"You mean, do I think I'm a monster?" Sigmund's good eye flashed intently. "If there's one thing I've learned in all my years, it's that things are rarely that black and white. Most of life is shades of gray. There's a huge difference between murder and self-defense."

I chuckled without joy. "Is there? I killed her."

"And you're gonna have to learn to live with it." Sigmund sounded calm and rational. I prayed for even an ounce of his beastly serenity, the ability to accept what I couldn't change. At least, not without a time machine. Sigmund touched my knee, his big hand sending shivers through me. "Let me ask you this. If Kamala had lived, do you think *you* would have?"

"Lived? Probably not. She was pretty intent on destroying me." I touched his hand on my knee, as though I could partake of his prowess and power through osmosis. "To you that spells justification. To me... I don't know."

"You can continue to blame yourself, or Cam, or me, or anyone if you wish," Sigmund said. "Just be sure you're doing it for the right reasons. After all, you must have done plenty right too, since the Fire Shard chose you as its new Guardian."

Flummoxed, I asked, "Huh? What does that mean?"

Sigmund barked out a laugh. "What? You don't know? Did you think that teleporting elf just got lucky enough to get a drop on a dragon as ancient as Cam?"

A flash of the male elf, Kamala's right-hand man, with his blade against Cameron's jugular came to mind. "I... I don't understand."

Sigmund grinned. "He surrendered on purpose. Well, I mean he allowed himself to be captured. For you." I stared at him, utterly dumbfounded, my mouth agape. Maybe Sigmund took pity on me because he added, "To become a Guardian, one has to perform an act of sacrifice. One has to make the right choice."

"The right choice?" I parroted, totally lost.

"A choice between the Shard and something one holds dear." Sigmund's words flew about in my head like a flock of wild birds. I couldn't catch a single one. "You had to make a choice between the Fire Shard and Cam. You could only save one. You chose the Shard."

"And I became the Guardian...," I whispered as understanding dawned on me at last.

Sigmund straightened up and stretched his bulging arms. "Aye. Cameron always was a great teacher. No one is as in tune with the wisdom of the world as he is." His eye was sharp and smart as it pierced through my veils of self-loathing, guilt, and anger. I had an odd feeling that his milky eye wasn't as blind as I assumed. Maybe he could peer deep down into my soul with it. "In the end," he went on, "the only two questions are: Which troubles you more—taking a life or the perceived betrayal by Cam? And can you learn to live with one or both?"

I didn't need to think or feel my way through the quagmire of doubt. I already had my answer. "Cam did what he had to for the greater good. I can't blame him for... for what I did to her, to Kamala. Nothing short of death would have dissuaded her from carrying out her plans."

Sigmund winked. "Sounds like you've learned a lesson tonight."

"When Cam left me...," I said slowly, letting the full weight of my revelation tear my mind asunder. "He knew the Fire Shard would choose me, exactly the same way I chose it. Cam left me because... he knew I could handle it. Even though I had consistently lost to Kamala in all our previous encounters. Cam believed I would become the Guardian *and* a phoenix— and that I could defeat Kamala alone. Cam didn't desert me; he had faith in me to survive on my own."

Sigmund studied me, seemingly pleased with my deductions. "Innocence and death are not mutually exclusive. I believe it was Graham Greene who wisely said, 'innocence is like a dumb leper who has lost his bell, wandering the world, meaning no harm.' Death is similar, don't you think?"

I smiled, for the first time in a month. "Why, Sigmund, you aren't at all as you appear at first glance."

Sigmund grinned back. "Who is?"

Chapter Twenty-Eight

"GOD, CAM, why do you have to live at the top of the Yellow Mountains?" I grumbled and cursed under my breath as I made my slow, arduous trek uphill on one of the massive, outward-jutting granite peaks of the region.

Yes, there were stairs. Steep and narrow stairs carved directly into the winding granite rock formations. The railings reached my ankles, providing a hazardous joke on any voyagers who dared to traverse the trail.

An aide of Prince Liro's had kindly teleported me to the edge of Cameron's territory. Apparently I couldn't simply pop up at Cam's place at the mountaintop, or I'd risk angering an already edgy and brooding dragon. That was my fault, so I acquiesced.

Beautiful pine trees lined or overshadowed the trail rising upward. I recalled the Yíng Kè Sōng, or Welcome Pine, with its outstretched side branches that looked like welcoming arms ready to embrace a weary traveler.

In fact, most of these Huángshān pines appeared the same, stout and straight but also kind of crooked and twisted too. The Chinese valued the oddly shaped the best, and I could see their ancient appeal. They grew vigorously and with fortitude out of even the tiniest cracks between the rocks and even thrived in such harsh circumstances. Some were hundreds, even thousands, of years old.

The scent of pine resin floated strong around me, and I inhaled deeply. Alongside the pines, leafy trees and ferns, mosses and tiny flowers completed the abundance of natural beauty. A moist mist clung to my skin, clothes, and the undergrowth around me, spreading to the fog between the mountaintops, showing me why these views and expanses were called seas of clouds. The hazy view magically transformed every tree and peak into a dreamy painting of a picturesque paradise. The scenery surely stunned me to silence and awe.

To this stupendous scenic experience, the Chinese had through history added their special touches. The Chinese characters engraved on smooth granite walls inscribed poems and phrases that told visitors the names of various peaks or sights.

I could definitely see how and why this region had influenced the Chinese culture so.

I came upon a small landing, with stairs below and above me. I stopped there to draw breath, plopping down on my butt and leaning my elbows on my knees. As I sat there quietly, with the whole world spanning below me and the man I dreamed of above me, I recalled the teachings of Lao Tzu, the creator of Taoism: "A journey of a thousand miles begins with a single step."

How apt and true. Wise man.

WHEN I reached the top, noon had passed long ago, and the far-off horizon gathered hues of purple, red, and orange, settling in to wait for the inevitable sunset.

But the view was lost on me as I came face-to-face with a wondrous sight.

A palatial structure crowned the mountain peak, the building resting against the tallest rock formation. Glazed tiles of the pyramid-shaped roof glimmered emerald green as though kissed by recent rain. Upward curving roof corners, overhanging eaves, and a multitude of lit paper lanterns and wind chimes gave the construction its classical Chinese characteristics. The round red paper lanterns, with golden Chinese characters imprinted on them, hanging from the corners of the eaves enhanced that perception.

I admired the harmonious way the palace blended into the nature around it.

On both sides of the front building—for I could see additional symmetrical structures behind it, separated by courtyards and trees, rising on several elevations—stood ancient pine trees, their branches extending over the roof and casting shadows over the grassy and rocky terrain.

Under the left pine tree, resting his back against the trunk, sat Cameron, one knee bent as he read a book perched on it. His usual yellow silk robes glided over his steely, strong body. His long black hair flowed freely behind him and at his sides, masking his face from me.

The tranquil vision after the hectic adventure we'd shared gave me heart palpitations. I hesitated even approaching him, disturbing his rest and relaxation. For he appeared to truly belong in this rare and wondrous site.

Would he have a place for me here?

I stepped forward. A twig snapped under my foot, the sound stark in the silence.

Cameron's head whipped up. I could see the exact moment when he recognized me, his eyes growing wide as he stood suddenly, the book dropping from his clutches.

I waved at him awkwardly. "Hi." My voice cracked, and I coughed to clear my throat. When Cam said nothing, my nervousness rattled like dry seeds inside a gourd. "Uh, I would have called first. Only… you don't seem to have a cell phone or a landline, or… anything really. Smoke signals…? You know, fire-breathing dragon, and all…?" My jesting tone and faint smile caused his brow to wrinkle, so I stopped, swallowing hard, sure that I had made a huge mistake coming here.

Cam blinked. Then he squared his shoulders, schooled his features, and came closer. Every determined step he took brought him nearer to me, sending the butterflies in my stomach into a frenzy.

Finally he halted before me, out of touching range. Up close, he was far less serene than he had seemed from a distance. A host of emotions flicked over his animated face.

"Finn." His voice shook just as mine had.

I struggled to say everything storming within my mind and heart. But they brewed so fast and elusive I couldn't find a single word that would have made any sense. Except for a quote by someone who wasn't me. "Wanting what's precious, you do what distorts your being. The sage knows this in his gut, and is guided by his instinct and not by what his eyes want."

Cam's eyes flashed. He cocked his head, assessing me. Then his features softened an inch, and I exhaled in relief. A small smile ghosted his lips. "Lao Tzu. Wise man." I smiled, as that had been my thought a while ago. "I knew him." At his words my eyes damn near bugged out, and his smile widened into a grin. "He understood the world, this and the one beyond, quite well. When he rode his ox through the pass at Hángǔ Guān and left for his Celestial Home, I missed his absence. Had he known, he would have told me to empty myself of that emotion."

I worried my lower lip. "That's kind of... harsh."

Cameron shrugged. "As Lao Tzu himself said, 'Heaven and Earth are not like humans. The Tao does not act like a human. They don't expect to be thanked for making life, so they view it without expectation.'"

I puzzled over Cam's philosophical views. "So, you're a Taoist?"

Cameron grinned. "Knowing others is intelligence; knowing yourself is true wisdom. Mastering others is strength; mastering yourself is true power."

I chuckled. "For someone who claims not to follow doctrines, you sure do quote great minds a lot. That's Lao Tzu again."

I caught a glimpse of Cameron's mischievous nature when he winked at me and out of the blue said, "Why did the dragon cross the road?" I ogled, eyes wide, mouth agape, disbelieving he'd actually made a joke. Cameron laughed and replied, "The road is Tao."

I blinked in bewilderment. Then I blinked some more. Finally I closed my mouth with an almost audible snap. "Huh? Does not compute."

Cameron waved a hand between us. "Lao Tzu would have found that funny—and true. He had an uncanny way of seeing beyond and through the veil that separates worlds." Cam smiled fondly at me. "In that kind of smarts, he reminds me of you."

I grew hot as I flushed, undoubtedly red as glowing embers. We were getting closer to the topics we needed to cover if we were to get past our... well, past and look forward to the future. Together.

Cameron seemed to sense my discomfort and trepidations. He waved toward his formidable, aesthetically pleasing, south-facing abode. "Forgive me. Where are my manners? Will you join me in the second garden for a cup of *mao feng cha*." I frowned, not having a clue what he meant. Cam chuckled and added, "It's the green tea of the Huángshān region, also known as Fur Peak tea. Have no fear, I guarantee there's no actual fur in it."

I laughed, perhaps a little too loudly—because shooting the breeze by discussing Lao Tzu's teachings was a hilarious novelty for me—and then I followed him in.

The dark red front double doors were flanked by door god statues of the Azure Dragon and the White Tiger. Across from the doors, a paper screen wall stood to ward off evil spirits with its depiction of three personified ideas of prosperity, status, and longevity in the form of three men. Beneath them read in Chinese characters *sān xīng zài*. I didn't need to be able to read it to know what it meant. A lot of Chinese houses, temples, and even official state buildings had them.

I guessed Cameron was a follower of the old way with its traditional superstitions. Or maybe he simply showed these out of reverence for the past, acknowledging his personal history.

"I thought the three stars appeared mostly in Taoist temples," I commented.

"While I have no need for status, and longevity is guaranteed by my dragon blood, I do have an affinity for prosperity," Cameron replied, a modicum of self-deprecation and irony in his tone. "Dragons, no matter what corner of the world they hail from, have always loved shiny things."

"Hmm, as evidenced by your penthouse in New Shanghai." I smiled at him, hoping he recalled every detail of our first meeting. Judging from his surprisingly shy smile, he did. "Speaking of which… where's the Earth Shard now?"

"Safe here, in the third garden." He glanced at me. "I'll show you in the morning."

I loved what he was so willing to divulge: that the Earth Shard was secure—and that he planned on keeping me for the night, and hopefully longer.

Cameron faced me, but his gaze darted around before settling somewhere in the region of my jaw. "I wanted to thank you for attending Paris's memorial service despite… our situation. It was kind of you, and I'm positive Paris would have greatly appreciated you being there when his ashes were spread to the winds and the desert surrounding Ayers Rock."

I nodded but said nothing. My presence at Paris's funeral had felt both reverent and rude; he was dead, and I was alive, having taken his place. But his family showed nothing but gratitude because thanks to me a part of Paris survived. So I had mixed feelings about the whole thing, and the company of the other Guardians had only made things worse. I hadn't stayed long.

Perhaps sensing my reluctance for that particular subject, Cameron bid me to enter with a sweeping gesture. I observed he'd taken his shoes off, so

I followed suit, not wishing to be rude. Then again, he'd only worn a kind of flip-flops, while I had on sneakers. Once I'd removed my footwear, looked up, and saw his bright smile, I was mightily glad I'd followed his example.

The narrow corridor surrounding the first courtyard was supported by ornamental red columns. The windows were covered by paper shutters, and the carved beams, complex yet harmonious brackets, and painted rafters above were also colored with bright splashes of vibrant red, yellow, blue, and green. From the beams above floated banners, and on the walls between the windows hung paper scrolls, both with Chinese calligraphy on them.

"Are those poems?" I asked, pointing at the calligraphic writings.

Cameron barely glanced at them while sauntering forward. "Some are philosophical proverbs and inspirational phrases. But yes, some are indeed poems. Famous poems by wonderful writers. That one, for example"—he pointed at the closest—"is by Dù Fǔ. It's a fragment of his poem "Sighs of Autumn Rain." 'The rustling rain hastens the early cold, / And geese with wet wings find high flying hard. / This autumn we've had no glimpse of the white sun. / When will the mud and dirt become dry earth?'"

I stared at the aesthetically written words. Had I understood Chinese characters better, I would have come to my own conclusions, for the interpretation of such poems is always unique to the reader. The meaning of the individual words vanished to the background as I only focused on Cam's artful scriptures. His penmanship was a thing of beauty.

"Any of these poems yours?" I dared to ask.

"Once, long ago, when I was but a young rake of a drake," Cameron said, smirking at me. "I wrote an ode to the autumn moon."

Excitement bubbled inside me, intensifying at the thought of getting a peek into his inner workings. "Will you share it with me?"

Abashed, Cameron looked away, coughing. "I… it wasn't very good."

In an effort to encourage him, I quoted one of the most famous of the Three Hundred Tang poems, "To your hermitage here on the top of the mountain I have climbed / Without stopping, these ten miles. / I have knocked at your door, and…."

Cameron smiled as he finished the sentiment.

You have become my meditation —
The beauty of your grasses, fresh with rain,

And close beside your window the music of your pines.
I take into my being all that I see and hear,
Soothing my senses, quieting my heart.

The spark in his eyes was almost whimsical, the way it had been before all the unpleasantness. "'After Missing the Recluse on the Western Mountain.' Great choice."

"I'm sure yours is on par with theirs," I dared to urge him to share his secrets.

Cameron shook his head with a chuckle. "I think not." I started to argue, but he raised his hand to silence me. Then he spoke.

After the evening rain, the moon illuminates my shadow.
Beyond the five hallowed peaks, my wyvern nature in awe
Of the hills and valleys, shrouded in pale mists,
Hidden beneath the moonlight.
I ride on the cool wind, my soul taking flight.
Fairy figures dance under the pine trees.
Tempestuous dragons swim in the streams.
A lone lantern glows pallid and wan.
A solitary scholar in his moonlit pavilion,
Lets down his black hair, watching through the window,
Awaiting the arrival of his... *fènghuáng*.

Cam's poem. I could scarcely draw breath. Not only because of the vivid, even kind of sad, imagery evoked by his melancholic words and bereft tone, but because I recognized the last word.

Fènghuáng. The phoenix. The mythological counterpart of the dragon.

As yin and yang companions, the two halves and two animals complemented each other and belonged together. Who cared that the phoenix represented the feminine principle while the dragon symbolized the masculine? All that mattered was that Cameron had changed the poem to match our circumstances and the latest addition to his life: me.

In essence, Cameron could not have spoken more plainly. *He loves me.*

Chapter Twenty-Nine

THE SUDDEN epiphany didn't magically transform the situation to one less awkward.

Cameron turned away, ambling down the few steps to the first courtyard. As he made his way, he recited another poem.

The autumn air is clear, the autumn moon is bright.
Fallen leaves gather and scatter, the jackdaw perches and starts anew.
We think of each other. When will we meet?
This hour, this night, my feelings are hard.

I blushed at his words. Though the poem by Li Bai probably initially hadn't referred to sensual or sexual encounters, I couldn't help but interpret his words thus.

"Yeah, I bet they're hard," I murmured under my breath, the rise of my libido evident in the bulge beneath my pants. I had to shift to ease the pressure.

Naturally, with his heightened dragon senses, Cameron heard me. He laughed, tossing his head back and letting it rip, holding on to his belly. I joined him because his joy was infectious.

"Come, my beautiful phoenix," Cameron said and guided me past the first courtyard.

To my surprise, it was a Zen garden. Raked gravel between various-sized boulders symbolized waters and mountains, with little pruned pine trees and mosses adding splashes of green amid all the gray.

"Not what I expected," I remarked, gesturing to the rock garden.

Cameron nodded with affection. "When I return from my travels, I feel drained and empty, so seeing this when I step inside my abode matches my mood."

Cameron continued to look at the rock garden fondly as we passed it on our way to the second building. It appeared my dragon preferred his home be constructed in the old way, with symmetrical structures and consecutive courtyards in ascending elevations. The circular moon doors added lovely curves to the otherwise straight lines.

As we walked through another corridor to the second courtyard, I was welcomed by a wondrous sight, far more like Cameron in my honest opinion. A natural rock formation that resembled the Yellow Mountains rose as the center of the arrangement. From the top a water feature in the shape of a waterfall flowed. Surrounded and framed by twisted pines that had been trimmed to mimic weather-beaten trees in the wild, the natural scenery was completed by smaller bamboo groves, damask-hued blossoming winter plum and peach trees, with white lotus flowers floating in a koi pond and yellow jasmines dotting the mossy and grassy areas.

While I'd traveled in Asia a dozen or so times, I had to admit Cameron's palace was the most enchanting I'd ever seen. I swear I could hear history whisper along the corridors and mythical magic sing through the shutters from the surrounding Yellow Mountains.

The big garden spoke volumes about Cameron's true nature, about what he treasured despite his assertions to his dragon only being fond of gold and all that glittered.

"This place is amazing," I commented in awe. "You've got the three friends here. So beautiful." I referred to the pine (and peach), both symbols of longevity, the winter plum for its boldness to blossom in the dead of winter, and the bamboo for its straight shape and sturdy build. "Did you build all this yourself?"

"Alas, no." Cameron looked about, his love of the place evident in his pleased smile and adoring gaze. "Initially, only the first building existed—as a simple, vacant hermitage. Over the span of many years, I received assistance from notable architects of pagodas, palaces, and gardens of their time. Among them were Wang Xiancheng, who created the Humble Administrator's Garden in Suzhou, Kuǎi Xiáng, who engineered the

Forbidden City in Beijing, and many of the architects who constructed the Imperial Summer Palace in Suzhou. I was fortunate to call them friends." He inspected his lands and abode with affection. "According to their designs, I built several sections with my own two hands. They considered it important that my home should have my marks on it. I admit, though, that when it became time to upgrade to modern plumbing, electricity, and Wi-Fi, I resorted to the aid of professionals."

I laughed. "Hmm, probably best."

Cameron smiled, an attractive trace of bashfulness in his gaze. "I confess, Finn, that you continue to surprise me every time we meet. You told me that post-Unveiling Asia wasn't one of your favorite places. And yet you know a great deal about our cultural heritage."

I looked away, my turn to be bashful. "The reason for that is simple."

"Yes?" Cameron said encouragingly, prodding me softly.

I shrugged, as though the topic of our discussion was nothing. But in truth I felt anything but casual. Too many bittersweet and sour memories were attached to the heights I could have achieved had I applied myself.

"Despite growing up without a mother and being raised by a violent ogre of a father," I started, "I rocked at school. I earned high grades, aced every test, and excelled in my studies. I got a full academic ride to a prestigious university. I got away from my dad, who didn't shed one tear to see the back of me. He's dead now, got himself stabbed in prison, the bastard."

"Oh, Finn." Empathy made Cameron's voice quiver, and I loved him for it.

"My mom...," I went on with my life story. "Though there's no accounting for taste and I still don't get how she ended up with my dad, Mom had an impact on my life even from beyond the grave. She was an elementary school teacher. She loved books, especially travel guides to faraway, exotic places." I took a deep, shaky breath. "She never went anywhere. She lived and died in the same town she was born in. I knew, right from the start, that that wouldn't be my fate."

Cameron smiled. "Your wanderlust, a son's love for his mother."

I nodded. "Yeah. She saw language as the key to the secrets of other cultures. She wasn't wrong. At university I studied languages and humanities: culture, history, geography, literature, mythology, religion.

Everything I could get my hands on. She was the one who adored Asia. In her honor... I simply packed up and left, never officially finishing my studies. I used the last of my money to fly to Cambodia and then to Beijing. There I learned to appreciate all things Asian, but also how to live—and how to steal. Even after the Veil lifted and Asia grew chaotic, I traveled to all the other places my mom had only dreamed about. And I haven't really stopped since."

"But... you have a house in Sydney," Cameron cut in quietly.

I scoffed. "Yeah. But I never stay there too long. Never long enough to put down roots." I looked up at my beautiful dragon and hoped I might do that here, with him—to finally stop my endless wandering and settle down.

Cameron gifted me with a warm gaze and a soft smile, and I chose to interpret them as a good sign. We continued ahead, the mood between us still fragile but growing stronger.

In front of the third two-story building stood an open-air pavilion, its green columns and hexagonal shape supplemented the courtyard's natural scene with the only man-made structure.

Cameron bid me enter, and I walked up the five stairs. A round wooden table and two chairs awaited me there, with a steaming teapot, two plates, and two cups. Had Cam anticipated my arrival? Or was this a demonstration of his hope? I smiled goofily at the possibility as I sat.

Tucked in one corner, a wooden bookshelf sported Chinese classic texts, both the five Taoist and the four Confucian ones, such as *Great Learning*, *Classic of Poetry*, *I Ching*, and *Book of Rites*. But no longer to my surprise, I also saw other classics, like Shakespeare, Dickens, Austen, Orwell, and Yeats. I recited a quote from "The Second Coming" by Yeats with ease since it was so well known.

Things fall apart; the centre cannot hold;
Mere anarchy is loosed upon the world.
The blood-dimmed tide is loosed, and everywhere
The ceremony of innocence is drowned.

Cameron nodded in a slightly abashed way. I could see his smile vanish and his eyes grow sad. He sat across from me, a whispery sigh leaving him. He didn't look at me. "Finn, I... I have to say... to tell you that... I am truly and deeply sorry for what I put you through. I can only beg for your forgiveness but—"

"What are you talking about?" I cut in, frustrated that the soft, tender mood between us had been broken, and for what I couldn't guess. There was nothing *he* needed to apologize for.

"I'm deeply ashamed of the hurt and pain I have caused you." Cameron looked utterly defeated and miserable, his anguish coming off him in waves. His shoulders slumped, his smile had turned into a frown, and his eyes glistened with tears, with a few worry lines around them. "Your lost innocence, which I can never restore. Forgive me, please."

I gritted my teeth and fisted my hands under the table, in my lap, as I fought for self-control. His self-recriminations did neither of us any good. "Please, stop and listen to me. First of all, I thank you for giving me the time and space I needed to figure my shit out. Secondly, *I* was the fool, not you. When you vanished from the battlefield, I thought you left me because you wanted to punish me for choosing the Fire Shard over you." Cameron started to speak, but I waved him silent now that I was on a roll and could still focus on rationalities. "I believed I was wronged by you—when in fact I was merely... wrong. About so many things. I projected my own hurt feelings on you, and that was immature and unjust of me. So it is *me* who should be sorry and beg for *your* forgiveness. I should have had faith in you *and* in me. And that's why I know that in the grand scheme of things, we both did the right thing and acted for the greater good. You when you left to recover your Earth Shard, and me when I accidentally killed Kamala. I... I'm not yet completely at peace with what I was forced to do but I... I'm coping."

Wow, it was becoming easier to say the words. Perhaps over time the guilt wouldn't be so all-consuming anymore either. Something to look forward to.

Cameron sighed, his gaze still lowered. "I could feel myself growing close to you, and our shared intimacy proved as much. The thought of losing you... someone I had become fond of and whom I had grown to respect. I distanced myself from you on purpose so that I could learn to trust in your abilities, that you could take care of yourself without me when push came to—"

"I know," I interjected again. But this time I was in control of my emotions. His words weren't news to me, thanks to an interfering wolfish friend. "Sigmund explained as much."

Cameron's head whipped up, and his slanted eyes narrowed. I guessed I had his undivided attention now. "Sigmund? When have you seen him?"

Well, well, well. Did I detect a hint of growling jealousy in Cam's tone? Be still, my heart. "Oh, didn't I mention Sigmund's visit? How silly of me." When Cameron's expression began to resemble that of a foreboding thundercloud, I decided the joke was over. "He advised me to try and see the situation from your point of view."

Cameron frowned, seemingly teetering on the edge between suspicion and gratitude for his friend's involvement in our affairs. "I see." He swallowed; I could see his Adam's apple bobbing. "And, uh… to what conclusion did you arrive?"

"That I need to keep an open mind—and not be afraid to open my heart." Though I felt decidedly nervous at the confession, I had a feeling he would catch me if I fell. "After Sigmund left, I discovered a curious power."

Cameron cocked his head in obvious puzzlement. "What do you mean?"

I fidgeted on my seat, anxious about the upcoming topic. "I know you sent me letters. I didn't read them. I tore them up or burned them. Sorry."

Cameron blinked and leaned back, exhaling deep and putting on a brave face. "Yes, of course. I understand." He did try, but his polite smile cracked.

"When I touched the ashes, already regretting my hasty acts, I learned that my phoenix didn't like to leave things unsaid, either." Cameron gave me a weird look, and I smiled. "The burned letters… reconstituted themselves, somehow, the cinders dancing and whirling until I held the intact letters again on my palm."

"Really?" Cameron's eyebrows rose to his hairline. It was kind of satisfying and quirky to realize he was ancient, but that I could still surprise him. That boded well for our future. The one I was confident now we were going to have.

"Yeah." I pulled out a stack of five letters from my pocket and placed them gently on the table. "Kinda felt like Torch or Pyro." Cameron quirked an eyebrow. "You know, the characters from *Fantastic Four* and *X-Men*? Comic strips, graphic novels, webcomics?"

His look remained blank. "Are those pop culture references?"

I rolled my eyes and blew out a sarcastic breath. "Geesh. We seriously need to update your knowledge of current events and fads. 'Cause one day soon we're gonna go see a movie on date night, and I don't want you asking people what stuff means, like who's the sparkling vampire. You'll embarrass us both."

"A sparkling vampire?" Cameron repeated, his expression borderline between dumbfounded and dubious. Guess he wasn't on Team Edward.

I decided to move on before his head exploded. "Back to the burned letters that fixed themselves with fire. I didn't know I could do that. Kind of freaked me out at first. But I suppose my phoenix wanted to help. And… to be close to you. Cam, my fair dragon. We are *lóng fèng*, the dragon and the phoenix. Aren't we…?"

Finally Cameron smiled. Not like he had done previously, sort of shy and small. No, this time his smile was broad and true, purest golden sunshine. He let out a long breath, relaxing and unwinding before my very eyes. "Yes, Finn. We are."

"Good." I leaned back too, musing over our rejoining and rejoicing. "So, what kind of tea were you going to offer me?"

Cameron laughed, a breathy sound mixing happiness and relief. He lifted the tea cozy and poured steaming-hot, green-colored liquid to the brim of my porcelain teacup. A distinct scent of orchids wafted to my nose. After blowing on the tea, I sipped it slowly. The floral flavor was there, but a taste that reminded me of sweet peas also lingered on my tongue.

"Not bad," I commented, liking that the zest wasn't too overwhelming. In fact, the taste was a bit underwhelming, so I focused on my dragon.

Cameron's slow movements were trancelike. He'd done this before so many times his hands needed no rehearsals and his conscious mind didn't need to be involved. I wondered if this was one of his ways of meditating. He used a white silk cloth to wipe any wayward droplets off the edges. A bit pedantic, I thought, but watching his handiwork soothed my spirit.

"You know," I said to fill in the quiet, quite needlessly in the end. "I've been puzzling over your Western name. I would have expected something else. I mean… why Cameron?"

"I've been known by many monikers, but I took the name Cameron during the British occupation of China," he explained softly.

"Cool," I commented. "I have a sort of a theory as to why you chose Cameron. But I'll let you do the honors."

Cameron chuckled. "I am a fairy dragon, translucent and invisible at times—"

"I freaking knew it!" I whooped out loud. "Camouflage and chameleon, am I right?"

"I admit, yes, I was thinking of both of those when I chose the name," Cameron said. "I didn't realize until much later that the name actually means crooked nose." He tapped the side of his nose knowingly.

I narrowed my eyes, leaning closer to inspect the part of his anatomy in question. "But you have a perfectly straight nose. Totally symmetrical and aesthetically pleasing, I might add."

"Thank you. But like I said, I didn't know the actual meaning at the time. I merely chose it for how it sounded in my ears." Then his expression grew distant as he became lost in memories. "I had a different name in the beginning. Shòushān. It means longevity mountain. An honorable name with a proud history."

"That's beautiful," I said in admiration. I liked the way the name rolled softly off my tongue. It would probably sound like a sensuous sigh in bed.

However, a grim shadow passed over his handsome face. "Being what I am—a fairy dragon—the elves soon began calling me Shòushàn. A minor difference, one macron in a single letter changed to a grave accent, but full of meaning and… venom. A derogatory nickname." He let out a breath full of ennui. "For you see, it means to accept abdication. I might be the Yellow Dragon Emperor's nephew and the Guardian of the Earth Shard, but because of my fey bloodline, I can never inherit the throne."

I frowned in puzzlement. "Did you *want* to ascend to the throne and rule the Chinese Empire?" I found it hard to believe domination over others was something Cameron desired, even in the back of his mind.

Cameron laughed mockingly and shook his head. "Heaven forbid. Absolutely not." His smile faded slowly. "When I was young, the name reminded me I didn't belong anywhere. Not among the dragons, not among the elves. That kind of burden is hard on a child."

"The elves still look down on you, I've seen that with my own two eyes," I said, still furious about their shameful acts of derision and arrogance. "The dragons treat you as badly?"

"Oh no. They're wonderful. They have always accepted me for who I am." The smile was back in force, and I loved seeing it. Plus, the news wasn't bad either. "I am part of the imperial family, have been from the start. I just can't take the throne. But that's never been my dream. For a child and a youth, it's far more important to belong."

"Yeah, that's true."

Cameron's eyes sparkled as he grinned. "You know, if your intentions regarding me are serious, my uncle will wish to see you and speak with you himself."

I gulped, eyes wide. The Yellow Dragon Emperor wanted to meet me? *Oh. My. God.* I panted, slightly out of breath. Nervousness assaulted me again, with vigor. "O-oh…. O-okaaay…." No pressure.

Cameron leaned over the table, reached for my hands, and took them gently. "Have no fear, Finn. He will love you. Like I do."

My anxieties vanished as the warmth of adoration and the heat of sensuality blossomed in my chest and groin. I smiled because that was what you did when you were insanely happy. "I… I love you too, Cam."

Funny how easy the heartfelt confession was in the end.

Chapter Thirty

CAM TOOK my hand as we strolled toward his bedroom on the second floor. Walking hand in hand was a new experience for me. I kind of liked it. Had we been in public, I might have puffed my chest with pride. Just a bit, though, because I wasn't a gloating dickwad.

His private chambers surprised me again. Instead of the master bedroom, Cam had occupied a smaller bedroom in the left wing.

In the back of the room stood a five-part folding screen with typical Chinese Wŭ Xíng paintings, where the five elements, one in each rice-paper panel, were depicted in five simple brushstrokes in black against the white canvas. The most distinctive were the Yellow Mountains with waterfalls in the center panel and the flying geese and bamboo trees in the leftmost.

"Did you paint those yourself?" I asked Cam, enchanted by the beauty of the art.

Cameron came to stand by my side, his hand still holding mine. "Yes. Long ago."

"I love them." And I wasn't lying. Throughout my time in Asia and my study of the native cultures before the Great Unveiling, I had felt strongly drawn to China, its beauty and mystery. Now I knew why those instincts had existed. Because I was meant to be with Cam. Lóng fèng. The dragon and the phoenix.

Against the right wall, a gentle burned-cream color for that majestic ambience, flanking two sliding paper doors, stood five black wooden pedestals, with copper bells hanging from dark ebony struts. Instead of finding Chinese characters on them, though, I saw the six-syllable Sanskrit mantra often dubbed the jewel in the lotus.

"I thought '*om ma ni pad me hung*' prayer wheels were Buddhist," I remarked.

"They are. Which is why mine, two in Sanskrit and three in Chinese—*ăn ma ní bā mī hōng*—are inscribed on bells instead of wheels. More Taoist, if you ask me." His voice, teasing and flirting, gave me ideas that had nothing to do with learning foreign languages or meditation with repetitive mantras.

On the left side of the room were sliding paper doors, similar to the ones on the right, that must have opened up to a balcony. The room must have been cold in winter. Then I noticed the fireplace on the wall next to the main door, the one we'd used to enter. I supposed a lively fire and a hot dragon by my side would keep me plenty warm.

However, in the center of the room I expected to see a bed. And I did. Sort of.

"A futon...?" With poorly disguised distaste, I stared at the thin brown-hued mattress placed on a low-rise platform. Sure, there were two pillows—*in anticipation of me?*—but they too were slim, the mellowness barely there.

At my side, Cameron chuckled. "Not a fan, are you?"

I shuddered, grimacing. "I, uh... I like my mattress thick, my pillows plump, and my covers fluffy. Sorry...." I'd wanted to love or at least like everything about Cam, his home, his way of life. But this was no good. I foresaw sleepless nights, crooked necks, and stiff backs.

Cameron leaned in to whisper softly in my ear, "Then you'll be glad to learn this is *not* the bedroom we will be using." I raised my eyebrows in question, and he laughed. "You're easy to read, my beloved Finn. Would I leave a pampered Westerner like you—"

"Hey!" I yelled, slightly insulted.

"—to suffer the slings and arrows of an outrageous mattress?" Cameron finished, his jesting so gently made the barb didn't sting.

"I'm pretty sure Shakespeare didn't use the word *mattress*, like, ever," I murmured in feigned indignation, flashing him my tongue.

With a laugh, Cameron slid open the doors to the right, to the actual master bedroom. And it was definitely more to my tastes.

Ancient stone and wooden statues of gods, goddesses, spirits, and immortals were situated around the room, illuminated by unseen overheads. On the back and front walls, bamboo curtains had been lowered in preparation of the coming night, though that was hours away. White silk scrolls hung from the rafters to depict poems in Chinese characters.

Bamboos and tiny, colorful round pebbles in transparent glass jars, along with pine resin incense, gave the space a sweet scent. A miniature tree *pén jǐng* sat on a wood tray, reminding me of bonsai arrangements.

It was nice to see what Cam was up to during his free time.

Wood-framed, glass-encased panels of two folding screens illustrated fragments of vegetation, such as the Yellow Mountains' pine treetops, bamboo branches, and butterflies and pink flowers.

"Those flowers and butterflies…," I started to say, my voice fading. I wanted Cam to confirm my educated guess.

"Yes, Finn. They are indeed allusions to love." Cameron's voice, soft and smooth as silk, caressed my senses till I sighed, passion simmering in my belly. "I don't use this room much. Mostly I paint by the main balcony that opens to a southern view over the mountains."

I took note of an easel, a simple wooden chair, and a small round table with watercolors on it. I shifted to see what Cam was working on. A Wǔ Xíng painting depicted the peaks, pines, and mists of Huángshān.

"Is there nothing you can't do?" I asked, once again in awe of his skillful gifts.

"I have yet to achieve enlightenment."

My mouth hanging open, I whirled to face him, flabbergasted. His lips twitched with pent-up amusement and mirth danced in his *qīng*-colored eyes. "Shit, I knew it. You're yanking my chain. Jerk."

Cameron laughed, and I chimed in. Then he inclined his head. "I don't have chains here but I will be yanking on something else you'll be attached to."

Stunned, I followed his nod. A four-poster bed, made of dark brown wood and carved with gold-colored dragons, took center stage in the room. Plush was the name of the game, from the plump pillows to the puffy comforter. And the color was fire red. I approved. On one of the side tables grew a deep purple orchid, adding life to the space. A bowl of ripe peaches rested on the other side table. The curtains tied to the posts were sandy yellow and not too bright.

I might have squealed a little. "Now that's a great fucking bed."

Cameron chuckled at my side, and I blushed at the double entendre I hadn't realized I'd made. "Oh, Finn. I do hope so."

UNDRESSING ME, Cameron treated my body like a priceless work of art. His caresses lingered as his fingertips ghosted over my skin, giving me goose bumps. With each strip of skin revealed, he planted a soft kiss there. Every touch awakened my senses and my cravings, the burning within me escalating.

I didn't move. I let him do as he willed. It wasn't me being passive, but me yielding to his delicious mastery of me. He eased my shirt off, letting it slide down my arms to fall and pool on the floor.

He took my hands in his. His gaze locked with mine as he smiled, a sort of hesitation in his gestures and tone. "Does this please you?"

I nodded firmly. "Last time we were together… it was kind of hectic, wasn't it? A bit out of control. The timing, the place, all that. And that hot dirty talking you did? Wow, took me by surprise, in a pleasant way. So I'm not saying the sex was bad. Far, *far* from it. Just that it was… a lot, you know what I mean?"

He bowed his head a tiny increment. "I do, yes. Rest assured, Finn. We will make slow love tonight."

Cam released my hands, shifting his own up my arms to gently grip my shoulders, brushing over my collarbones and my Adam's apple. I swallowed hard at the unhurried touches, so tender and so exciting, filled with promises as sweet and sensuous as his words.

He regarded me with a sweetness I hadn't, quite frankly, expected from him. From the beginning, Cam had been stalwart but distant, kind but serene. A show of erotic tenderness was my wish, but I hadn't fully believed him capable of such a thing. Last time our encounter had been wild and savage and reckless, our captors close-by. I was glad we had this opportunity to be… uninhibited in a different manner.

Centuries separated our levels of knowledge. I didn't think that was an issue, in truth, as he had demonstrated more than once that he appreciated my fresher insight into things.

But it didn't hurt to remind him I wasn't an uneducated dunce.

"Will you share a peach with me?" I asked.

Cam stopped, his hands halting at my chest. He looked up at me, clearly astonished by my remark. Then he chuckled. "I do love you, Finn. While I do have a fondness for the old euphemisms of homosexual love, I don't need to hear them right now. You have nothing to prove to me. You have shown me your worth many times. I already hold you in high regard."

My cheeks flamed, undoubtedly reddened by the mild reproach. "I… I guess I wanted you to believe I could belong here, in the Yellow Mountains, with you, sharing what you like, to show you we have things in common."

Cam planted a kiss on my forehead, then on my closed eyelids, the tip of my nose, and finally on my lips, the pressure barely there, a soft warmth to his touch. "You belong with me. No matter where we are or what we do. Together we share the southern wind."

I quirked an eyebrow at him, grinning at his choice of words. "Oh, so *you* can deliver literary references to gay love but I can't?"

Cam laughed. "We'll read together in bed, side by side. But… after."

He sealed our lips together, and I didn't want to talk either. His tongue tested the seams of my lips, not forcing it. Our tongues rubbed together, and I shivered all the way down to my toes. He tasted of smoke and green tea and peaches. He was becoming my favorite flavor. The kiss was far from tentative, but it proceeded without rushing, savoring each sensation.

I sucked Cam's tongue into my mouth, licking around it, yearning for more. He bit my bottom lip, then kissed away the sting. I think he felt as ravenous as I did. He breathed hotly against me, and I responded in kind, panting from the rising passion.

Cam slid his hand to the back of my neck and pulled me closer. Our bodies touched, head to toe. His other arm wound around the small of my back, his hold on me tightening. His hard cock pressed against my lower abdomen as mine did against his upper thigh. He was taller than me, but I could still shamelessly rub myself on him. I rocked my hips back and forth, seeking friction and fierce contact. He didn't still my motions, for which I was infinitely grateful.

Then again, I didn't want to blow before we'd even begun.

"Too fast," I muttered into the kiss, my orgasm approaching like a hurricane.

Cam pulled back from the kiss and my mouth. I might have whined, but just a little. I anticipated him admonishing me for indecisiveness, but he merely smiled.

Then he rested his hot palms over my hips and pushed me back till my legs hit the bed and I toppled over onto the comforter, sinking into the softness. Being naked under his gaze while he was still dressed turned me on. My cock jumped on my lower belly, and a pearl of precome gathered at the slit.

"Mmm," Cam murmured appreciatively, and I blushed in response.

Then he removed his clothes, and I damn near swallowed my tongue. His sun-kissed skin was hairless, like that of many Asian men was. His long black mane flowed over his shoulders, past his pecs, the tips reaching his abdomen. I longed to card my fingers through the silky strands. His muscles bulged and rippled, not massively buff but steel-like and lean, giving him a streamlined, sleek look. The sight of his six-pack made my mouth water—till the vision of his cock standing at attention practically left me in a pool of my own drool.

I'd had him inside me, so I knew I could take him. But though my eyes ate him up, my mind entertained a host of scenarios where his impressive cock might be too much for me. Since I was a pain slut, most of these fantasies only had my erection straining my already taut skin.

It was funny but I hadn't actually caught even a glimpse of his prick last time we were together. Probably because my face had been buried in pillows for a good bit of the fucking. I had him dead to rights now, though. His cock was uncut, the color of garnet. The silky and spongy head was crimson, a translucent bead of precome clinging to the slit. Pulsing veins adorned the shaft like ornamental vines.

"Did you get a good look?" Cam asked, hands on his hips as he stood there on display, like a statue of an ancient erect sex god.

"Never." I had no other reply. I watched with glee as Cam's eyes darkened to cerulean blue, or midnight green, or a mix of both. I wondered if I'd ever get enough of staring into his eyes.

He bent one knee on the bed as he gently pushed my legs apart, intimately opening me to his gaze. Then he settled between them and braced himself above me with straightened arms framing my shoulders, a beautiful man who desired me as much as I hungered for him.

Then his hands abandoned the comforter—and yet he still floated above me.

"A-are you… f-flying…?" I asked, astonished.

Chapter Thirty-One

CAM SNICKERED. "We can both fly, remember? I'm a fairy dragon, and you're a paradise-crow phoenix. But have no fear. I promise I won't ruffle your feathers."

I rolled my eyes. "Funny ha-ha." I laughed because the sound and emotion bubbled inside me, and I refused to contain it.

Admittedly a big part of me longed to fly. I had wings now, and the daring to test the winds grew every day. I couldn't control the wings very well yet, only on pure instinct. One day in the near future, Cam would teach me to fly *and* how to unfold my wings without burning my clothes off in the process.

I forgot all about my feathery aids when Cam slid his hands down my sides, ghosted over my hipbones, and tickled my inner thighs. He dipped down and took one of my nipples into his mouth, suckled on the jutting teat, licked and nibbled till it hurt in that excruciatingly pleasurable way. I writhed beneath his touches, feeling his lips, tongue, teeth, palms, and fingers everywhere.

"Oh God, yes," I whispered, my body brimming with passion and need.

Cam chuckled against my chest, his hot, moist breath causing me to shiver. "I see the butterflies go deeper and deeper between the flowers, / And dragonflies in leisured flight between drops of water. / As we're told, passing time is always on the move. / So little time to know each other: We should not be apart."

I half laughed, half hiccupped. "Dù Fǔ again?"

"'Winding River,'" Cam answered, licking a line between my pecs and blowing on them till I squirmed. "I prefer the ones from his earlier years. Spring and youth and optimism are there still."

I grinned wickedly up at him. "When I decided I was going to come to you, I recalled another poem of his.

For all this, what is the mountain god like?
An unending green of lands north and south;
From ethereal beauty creation distills there,
Yin and yang split dusk and dawn.
Swelling clouds sweep by.
Returning birds ruin my eyes vanishing.
One day soon, at the summit, the other mountains
will be small enough to hold, all in a single glance."

Cam quirked an eyebrow. "And what meaning did you derive from that?"

"You are my mountain god," I replied as he let his fingertips tease the hardened peaks of my nipples, tweaking them between his thumb and forefinger and sending frissons of pleasure through me. "I gaze upon you, my all."

Cam chuckled, a spark of mischief in his viridian eyes. "Ah. Not to mention all that delicious swelling."

I tittered, flushing with heat. "Yeah, well, that too. Like minds, eh?"

He planted a tender kiss on my cheeks and then on my lips, a mere graze instead of a full touch. "Three things can never be hidden: the sun, the moon, and the truth." I didn't know that one, and my expression told him so, because he explained with a single word. "Buddha."

"You are well read," I commented breathlessly, my brain idling when Cam drew little loopy circles around my bellybutton, tantalizing me with the swirling dance of his fingertips.

"As are you." Pride glowed in his eyes for me. I felt enormously proud as a result.

He reached behind him, under the covers, and whipped out a golden collar with weird inscriptions written on it. He grinned at me, raising the collar for my inspection.

"Like I told you back at our tree prison, I procured myself a negation collar." His taunt made my toes curl. He'd remembered, and now we were reaping the rewards of his discovery. What could be better than that? He nodded toward the object. "What think you of my vow?"

I twisted the collar around in my hands. Like a wedding ring, the collar had an inscription on the inside. It read Property of Finn Grayson. I grinned like a loon. "Oh. Cam, you never cease to amaze me," I gazed up at him, my expression undoubtedly dreamy. My heart definitely floated high as a kite. "You're mine?"

Nodding firmly, Cam fastened the collar around his neck, a snick indicating the lock had closed. The golden letters briefly glowed, attesting to the magical quality of the beautiful artifact. I touched it carefully, feeling the indented letters with my fingertips.

"So... we're never gonna have sex when you're in your dragon form?" I asked. I wasn't sure if I was disappointed or relieved, or a mixture of both.

Cam smiled enigmatically. "Never say never, Finn."

Then he hiked my legs up over his shoulders, crouched down, and sucked my balls into his mouth, shifting them around with his tongue. I moaned in delight. Whether he was licking or sucking, Cam did it with gusto. In a flash, I was five seconds away from busting a nut.

But he appeared to be in tune with my body because he let my sac go, moved up, and took my flared cockhead into his mouth. The tip of his tongue pressed on the sweet spot beneath the crown, and then the flat of his tongue swept over my weeping slit. He lapped up each droplet as they appeared.

When he stopped my hazy brain didn't immediately register it. "Huh?" I muttered.

Cam leaned over me again, holding himself at bay with his powers of flight. God, he was hot.

The daze disappeared in an instant when Cam locked my left wrist to the bedpost with a padded leather cuff. Shocked, I glanced between the restraint and his face.

With flourish, Cam smirked and winked at me. "What? Didn't you expect a dragon to have a dungeon?"

A breath whooshed out of me. Endless possibilities of pleasure and pain blasted my mind wide open. A cavalcade of BDSM fantasies rushed through my mind's eye. "Cops and robbers?" I asked, testing the strength of the cuff he'd attached to my wrist.

"No. I was thinking... dragon and his booty," Cam replied, simpering as he snapped a second cuff to my other wrist, essentially locking me in place. I didn't need to try and wiggle out of them, as I had literal first-hand knowledge of their soft firmness.

In short, I was splayed before him, spread-eagle, like a sensual feast. I fully expected him to devour me whole. *Yum-yum.*

"Do you feel well and truly trussed up, my quaint little bird, my *kaitō*?" he purred in my ear. I blinked and stared up at him. I didn't recognize the word. A term of endearment, perhaps? Cam grinned. "It's Japanese for a gentleman thief, a phantom who comes and goes unseen."

"Oh." Well, it sure sounded better than any other term I'd been called. After all, most of them carried a negative stigma on purpose. "Wow. That's kinda cool." Then I locked gazes with him in earnest, growing serious. "Cam, I know you don't approve of my shadowy profession. I've been thinking about a career change. It's not like I ever planned to continue stealing for the rest of my life." I meant my statement too, as I had a feeling the Fire Shard would frown upon unethical activities. Cam was the second, but the most important, reason.

Cam smiled, not relieved exactly, but content. "As long as your decision is yours and yours alone." I nodded stoutly, determined to make a fresh start. "All I want is for you to be happy, Finn."

"I'm happy with you, Cam," I said, speaking from the heart. Cam inclined his head and kissed me, gently tangling his tongue with mine. I tasted the salty-sweet precome he'd drunk from the fountain of my sex.

Nevertheless, it was kind of a thrill to have a notorious pseudonym in the underworld.

Kaitō Fèng, they would call me, and fear the night. I chuckled inwardly.

Then I no longer thought about my dark reputation when I heard the snick of a bottle cap. Cam popped open the top of a tube of lube. He'd gone back to sucking my cock, which I didn't object to, and he insinuated his wet fingers past my perineum to circle and press against my hole.

"Oh, oh, oh, fuck, yeah," I murmured, my hips bucking at the sensation. Hot flashes stormed me in undulating motions until I felt like I was surfing the crest of the pleasure wave.

As I yanked on the chains binding me to the bedposts, Cam entered me with his fingers. I pushed back against his invading digits, demanding and needing more. One finger turned to two, then three, and I thrashed on the bed, every part of me animated with sensuality.

Then Cam replaced his digits with his hot dick, steadily pressed against my twitching hole until he popped the flared head in. I cringed, the initial sting and burn there as always. But I loved it, had since the first time. I shoved my ass back as best I could.

Cam stopped me outright, his fingers digging into my hips and buttocks. "No, Finn. Did you forget I am the master and you the pupil?"

"Don't you mean slave?" I asked, panting, sweat popping up all over my body as heat rolled through me, inside and out.

"No." Cam advanced an inch. The spikes on his cock sent an electric jolt up and down my spine. Cam chuckled at my reaction. "I am the master of pleasure because of my centuries of in-depth studies. You are my novice for now, but one day you and I will be masters together. Equals, in and out of bed."

"I like that," I said, an emotional lump in my throat making my voice hoarse. I did like the fact that Cam already saw us as equals on the same footing. Sure, I had a ways to go when it came to the art of love, but I had zero doubts that one day I'd be on par with, or even surpass, my master.

Cam slid his hands beneath me to cup my asscheeks while he crammed his cock into me. The knot surely stuffed my channel full, leaving me a panting, sweating mess while I tried to accommodate his girth and length.

"God, you're so fucking big," I groaned, loving the feel of him inside me.

"I have been inside you before, my love, so I know you can take all of me." Cam's soft whisper damn near made me cream myself. As if one step ahead of me again, Cam gripped the base of my prick and squeezed, staving off the imminent explosion. I was grateful because I didn't want to come until I was good and ready. And I wouldn't be until he was fully seated inside me.

With a steady advance, Cam pushed his cock deeper. Moans escaped my throat even as I twisted in his relentless grip. When I felt his balls slam against my ass, I knew he was in to the hilt, and we both sighed in satisfaction.

"I've never wanted anything this badly," I murmured, staring up at him past half-lidded eyes. His sizable cock was buried deep, and I longed for him to move. Even while I couldn't move, not an inch. I tugged at my wrist cuffs. They gave way only enough to keep my circulation going, but not enough to shatter the illusion of captivity.

Cam grinned. "A dragon never surrenders his jewel." Suddenly he leaned to the left of the bed, and I tilted a bit in response.

I watched his hand disappear under the covers, and I couldn't help but imagine what device of torment he would produce next. A flogger? A riding crop? A whip? All of the above?

His closed fist came up, and I couldn't see what he was holding. My curiosity flared despite the fact that we were in the middle of a lovemaking session. "What have you got there?"

Cam's eyes narrowed, as though he didn't appreciate me asking. He leaned over me in a hotly menacing manner and got his point across with a tiny pull out and a hard thrust in. My back arched as pleasure cascaded over my spine. I think I might have howled.

He held my legs and lowered them from his shoulders, yanking me closer. His cock entered me deeper still. I huffed out a bated breath, my heart thudding so hard I could scarcely hear a thing.

"Dragons have a strong sexual drive," Cam said in a low voice, dangerous and sexy. "I will show you soon. However… our mating instinct is stronger when we find the perfect mate."

With his thick dick such a long way inside me, it was difficult to think, let alone form a coherent question. "Say what?"

Cam chuckled, a self-confident, alluring sound that reverberated through my being as a pounding music might beat inside a rib cage and transfer to dancing feet. "When dragons find such a perfectly matched individual, they give them a gift. A betrothal boon."

Startled, I raised my head and shoulders from the comforter, trying to read his mind by examining the depth and breadth of his expression. "A… a what?"

Laughing, Cam extended his arm and opened his fist. On his palm rested a black pearl, shining in dark rainbow colors in the gloom of the lit paper lanterns above. And the grand gem was magnificent, not only because of its perfect spherical shape, but thanks to its magnificent size—it filled Cam's whole palm.

I gulped and tried to speak. My mouth went dry. "B-bah…."

"Do you like it?" Cam asked. He sounded absolutely at ease. Then again, he would, since I was a thief and just as attracted by shiny things as a dragon. Cam chuckled and added, "Will you accept my betrothal boon, Finn?"

I nodded frantically, unable to speak, my jaw trembling and my vision growing misty as a sheen of tears brimmed in my eyes. That precious stone had to be worth millions. I'd never seen a pearl of that size. I couldn't even imagine the proportions of the clam able to produce such a jewel. Must have been a mythical mollusk from beyond the Veil.

Cam smiled. "Good." He placed the black pearl over my chest, where my heart beat a frenzied rhythm, part love, part gratitude, part… well, greed. In the spirit of honesty.

Cam didn't wait for me to awaken from my trance. Instead he hooked his arms under my knees and brought me intimately as close as possible. Then he dropped down onto his braced arms, slid his hands under my shoulders and plastered his bigger frame over me, crashed his mouth over mine, and rammed into me like a feral beast.

I grunted into his mouth, sharing his heated breath, chasing after his playful tongue in my mouth. The black pearl caught between our bodies. I couldn't move my hands but I could wrap my legs around him, crossing my ankles over the small of his back. With the soles of my feet I felt his firm, round cheeks move as his hips snapped. He fucked me good, and I loved every minute of it.

Kissing became arduous as we both grew breathless. But we did our best anyway, the need to be close and inside in every way possible directing our instinctive actions. Cam plunged his cock into my channel, the spikes hardening in congruence with his erection. The closer he got to an orgasm, the sharper the tiny needles became. Sweet endorphins washed over me, an injection from him, born of love and lust.

He kept me tight to his surging body, a stationary object of desire he could fuck to his heart's and cock's content. I wanted to yield to him, to witness his mastery of my sex and over my release. I wanted him to succeed. And he wasn't far off, in every sense, as his dick grazed over my prostate with every glide in and stroke out.

I was suddenly free. Cam growled under his breath, tore the restraints off me with his dragon claws, pulled back to sit on his haunches, and dragged me along to sit across his lap, astride his dick.

The move splayed me open further, and somehow, maybe by magic, he lodged deeper inside me. I groaned, the feel of him rammed to the end of my channel almost unbearable.

"Finn? Are you all right?" Cam sounded concerned.

God, but I loved him more than words could say. I wound my arms around his neck, did what I'd dreamed of since we met, which was thread my fingers through his long silky hair, and kissed him silly. I hoped that would assure him of my well-being. Judging from the way he wrapped his arms tight around my lower back and neck, he got my message.

Now I had control over our lovemaking. I rose upward on my knees, as if prepared for a ride (which wasn't far off), and then dropped down on his cock. The sudden motion shoved all the air out of my lungs, and he moaned into the kiss, as sloppy and unrefined as it was.

I swirled and swiveled my hips, grinding on his dick. He grunted several times until he pushed up, meeting me thrust for thrust. I gyrated and rocked while he pounded into me, our pace quickening, our rhythm at first in sync, then faltering as we neared mutual climax.

"Cam, oh Shòushān," I whispered onto his lips, my own tingling at the rough, luscious smooching. The smells of male musk, precome, and smoke filled the air, creating a cocoon of pure unadulterated intimacy around us. I hugged him tighter, my balls boiling over, and he embraced me equally harshly, his hands hot and sweaty against my back, his nails digging in painfully, his hips pistoning up, and his cock swelling inside me.

My beautiful dragon.

I tossed my head back and cried out as I came, my prick spilling creamy jets onto his chest, between us, smearing us with proof of our shared lust. Cam moaned, stilled like a statue on the precipice of pleasure. Hot liquid filled my channel as he shot his seed inside me, spurts of his spunk continuing to stream. The knot, now tumid, kept us interlocked, unable to move.

"Oh. My. God." Panting, I flew up on a cloud of suspended bliss. My voice was husky, and I realized I'd probably shouted my head off during my orgasm.

Then I noticed Cam and I were actually floating, at least two feet above the mattress.

Behind him glimmered huge, rainbow-colored butterfly wings, spread wide, fluttering a little. A brush of wind over my own back and a glance over my shoulders, and I saw black-as-midnight feathery wings expanding from my back as well.

My body felt overheated, my flesh enflamed, my skin covered in a fine sheen of sweat and spunk, my dick still pulsing with the aftershocks, and my channel constricting around Cam's still notably erect cock since we were literally joined at the hip and would continue to be for a great length of time.

The wings added a curious sensation of lightness to our sexual communion. Eager to delve deeper and do some practical research, I couldn't wait for our next bout of lovemaking. I had a sneaking suspicion that session was not far off.

"H-how…?" I managed to gasp out.

Cam laughed soundlessly into my neck, stirring my hair with puffs of air, the tuft of his little beard tickling me. He pulled back to look into my eyes. The lines I'd thought were born of worry now appeared in their true form as laugh lines. His smile, to my eyes, epitomized beauty. I loved him so much I thought my heart might burst. I felt his heart skip a beat along with mine. We were as one.

He rubbed his nose against mine in a sort of a kiss. Then he whispered in my ear, joy making his voice shake, "How do you think, my silly goose? Magic."

Duh. I giggled in a fit of mirth. With a languid kiss full of exploration and mystique, I was reminded of the words of the grand master of badassery, Harry Houdini. "I am a great admirer of mystery and magic. Look at this life—all mystery and magic."

All I knew was that Cam and I, together we were magic.

Lifting the Veil: Book One

Kris Ellis thought that the time of arranged marriages was long past—but that was before the Great Unveiling revealed creatures of myth living among humans. Now a routine medical test has determined that Kris has a mate, a werewolf named Rafael King.

Kris is fresh out of college and has plans for his life. None of them include being tied forever to someone he's never met. But then Rafe calls him, and Kris starts to reconsider. After all, what must it be like to wait for your soul mate for two hundred years?

Rafe is patient, strong, and kind, not to mention attractive. True to what Kris has heard about mates, sparks fly the second they meet. But Kris and Rafe are very different, and the werewolf way of life is dangerous. Is the fight for love really worth it?

www.dreamspinnerpress.com

Sequel to *The Wolfing Way*
Lifting the Veil: Book Two

Ten years ago, the Great Unveiling revealed the presence of supernatural beings living on Earth. But the residents of the ruined city discovered in Majlis al-Jinn are long dead—or so junior archaeologist Pip Butler thought until he accidentally unleashed a very naked genie named Jinn.

Even though he's been shyly pining for his charismatic supervisor, Val Velde, Pip has a hard time refusing Jinn's flirtatious advances. He barely has time to even consider the fact that he has an all-powerful genie and three glorious wishes at his fingertips when ruthless mercenaries sweep down on the dig to collect the most valuable artifact of all—Jinn's lamp.

So Pip, Val, and Jinn have to work together in a race against the clock to discover the secrets of the ancient city, free their captive colleagues, and keep Jinn from the mercenaries' clutches—all while trying to sort out their romantic tangle.

www.dreamspinnerpress.com

Sequel to *The Wolfing Way*
Lifting the Veil: Book Three

Ten years ago, the Great Unveiling revealed the presence of supernatural beings living on Earth, but not all humans know much about them—or care about them as anything other than a paycheck.

Kieran Knight is a freelance mercenary who hunts mythical beings for money. He abducts a man called Gabriel King, intending to turn him over to his client. But Gabriel isn't any ordinary cowboy. He's a powerful werewolf and the beta of his pack—and as he and Kieran soon discover, he is also Kieran's mate.

Kieran knows next to nothing about how mating works, and he isn't gay—but that doesn't mean he doesn't feel the chemistry heating up between them. To save Gabriel, Kieran orchestrates an escape, but his clients won't give up their werewolf without a fight.

www.dreamspinnerpress.com

Lifting the Veil: Book Four

When PI Sam Garrett is hired by eccentric billionaire toy maker and child genius Mozart "Mo" Chance—*after* his apparent suicide in the hills of San Francisco—Sam takes the case out of sheer curiosity. In a world where the Veil lifted a decade ago and exposed mythical beings living among humans, Sam faces a big challenge as the mystery surrounding the case deepens.

The inheritors of Mo's fortune—the uncle, the butler, the nanny, and the bodyguard—all possess secrets, and some are willing to protect them at any cost. The trouble is that Sam's partner and lover, Rex Ford, is suddenly under suspicion as well.

Clouded by doubt, Sam continues to search for answers as tapestries of crimes begin to unravel and powers beyond his imagination are unleashed. If Mo endured horrific nightmares about monsters under his bed, there's no telling what dangers await a nosy PI. What dangers lurk in this darkness? Sam is about to find out.

www.dreamspinnerpress.com

Lifting the Veil: Book Five

Trying to jumpstart his waning career in travel and nature journalism, Jim Faulkner jumps out of a plane in the middle of the night to get the inside scoop on werewolves in Connor's Crossing, Wyoming. Unfortunately, he lands in a tree and gets stuck. His rescuer is a mysterious and solitary man living in a cabin in the woods. Although Jim feels an odd connection to Dakotah, Dak's silence is all but hostile.

Jim won't give up though—he finds ways to be around Dak, both for the bond and his belief that Dak is a great source for wilderness information. As Dak continues to dismiss him, Jim is suddenly surrounded by progenitors—the most powerful werewolves in existence—who all seem to want Jim as their mate. After one abducts him, Jim has to fight for his freedom and for his one true mate. No matter how reluctant said mate is.

www.dreamspinnerpress.com

Susan Laine, an award-winning, multi-published author of LGBTQ erotic romance and a Finnish native, was raised by the best mother in the world, who told her daughter time and again that she could be whatever she wanted to be. The spark for serious writing and publishing kindled when Susan discovered the gay erotic romance genre. One of her books, *Monsters Under the Bed*, won the 2014 Rainbow Award for Best Gay Paranormal Romance.

Anthropology is Susan's formal education, but she has set her long-term sights on becoming a full-time writer. Susan enjoys hanging out with her sister, two nieces, and friends in movie theaters, bookstores, and parks. Her favorite pastimes include pop music, action flicks, chocolate, and doing the dishes, while a few of her dislikes are sweating hot summer days, tobacco smoke, and purposeful prejudice.

Website: www.susan-laine-author.fi
E-mail: susan.laine@hotmail.com

To prove to his annoying older brother that he's a man, well-to-do sculptor Rupert Pemberton tries to repair his broken toilet. But he has no knack for practical tools and no know-how. After a flood of biblical proportions, he has no choice but to call for help.

A gorgeous hunk of a plumber named Paul Cooper shows up at Rupert's doorstep with a ready toolbox and a sexy smile. With Paul at his side, Rupert realizes he wants more than a quick fix. After a couple of cozy dates and a few bouts of steamy sex, Rupert wonders how he can keep Paul around for good.

www.dreamspinnerpress.com

www.ingramcontent.com/pod-product-compliance
Lightning Source LLC
Chambersburg PA
CBHW070101260626
47160CB00004B/1275